Jennifer Castle

PENS now

HARPER TEEN
An Imprint of HarperCollinsPublishers

HarperTeen is an imprint of HarperCollins Publishers.

What Happens Now
Copyright © 2016 by Jennifer Castle
All rights reserved. Printed in the United States of America.
No part of this book may be used or reproduced in any manner whatsoever without written
permission except in the case of brief quotations embodied in critical articles and reviews. For
information address HarperCollins Children's Books, a division of HarperCollins Publishers, 195
Broadway, New York, NY 10007.
www.epicreads.com

ISBN 978-0-06-225047-6

16 17 18 19 20 CG/RRDH 10 9 8 7 6 5 4 3 2 1

First Edition

FOR JAY AND SUE,
AS TIME GOES BY

PROLOGUE

In the end, there were two Camden Armstrongs. One I watched for a whole summer of relentless craving. The other was the one I fell in love with.

During that first summer with that first Camden, I breathed wonder instead of oxygen. Wonder about what he carried on his broad but skinny shoulders, what made them square off on certain days and what made them sometimes sag. What it might feel like to sweep those nearly black bangs away from his face and get a peek at what was really going on there.

Once you start this type of wondering about someone, they've got you for sure. They own you in a way you can't control. (As if you even wanted to.)

This was also the Camden who, when I closed my eyes alone at night, kissed me against a swing set at the lake playground. He'd hold me in the water while I floated on my back, his palms perfectly spanning the cutout of my bathing suit as if it were made to order for him. Sometimes this Camden-in-my-mind took me on drives to the Lenape Creek so we could dangle our legs off the wooden footbridge. Or he'd do something exquisitely regular, like buying me a road stand ice cream, and we'd eat it sitting on the hood of his car.

Good God. Those imaginary nights. It's kind of amazing, how nostalgic you can feel for memories that never actually happened.

As for the other Camden?

I can tell you this much:

I know what it is to want something so badly, you feel like your cells aren't properly bonded together without it. At any moment you might just crumble apart.

I also know what it's like to get that something.

And honestly, I'm still not sure which is worse.

THE FIRST SUMMER

(OR, THIS THING THAT HAPPENED THAT I
STILL DON'T REALLY UNDERSTAND)

1

My best friend, Kendall Parisi, waved her arms over a patch of rubbly grass near the edge of our town's tiny swimming lake.

"I hereby declare this to be our spot for the summer," she said.

It was Memorial Day weekend, and that meant the lake was finally open for the season. The lake had a *name* name that nobody used, a retired reservoir with a halfhearted beach, the water cloudy but cool. I'd grown up thinking we were lucky and special for having it, and still believed.

"And I declare it to be a *good* spot," I said just as seriously, dropping my bag on it. Staking our claim.

The spot was under a tree, but not one of the more popular trees. Yes, there was actually popularity among the trees here. Some things about the lake were a little ridiculous, but that was part of why we loved it.

"I wish we could mark this with a flag," said Kendall, unpacking a rolled-up towel.

"Or urine," I said.

"You're gross."

I smiled wickedly and spread out my blanket on the spot, now officially *our spot*, and everything could begin.

We were almost done with my horrible sophomore year of high school, and the promise of summer sat on the tips of our tongues. It tasted like mint, and sunscreen, and that pleasantly disgusting sweetener in diet iced tea.

I'd be spending most of the next three months babysitting my six-year-old half sister, Danielle, while my mom finished nursing school. Kendall was going to work at Scoop-N-Putt, the ice cream/mini-golf place on Route 299, but she promised we'd still get to hang out at the lake most days. There was also my newly earned driver's license all weighty in my wallet, a key card to a whole extra level of the world.

The perfection of these plans was something I could lay down and bask in. I pulled off my sandals, stretched out on the blanket, and closed my eyes. I felt the long sleeves of my rashguard top ride up, which meant they were no longer covering the three long, expertly straight lines on my left forearm.

It had been four months since that frigid night I'd cut

myself on purpose. For the record, I hadn't been trying to die but rather, to live; to find a way to breathe again. Four months was enough time to turn the scars brown, but not enough to fully understand them, and definitely not enough for me to let others get a look. I tugged my sleeves back toward my wrists.

Kendall wound up her long auburn hair in a bun and collapsed next to me. I could see-without-seeing that my friend was scanning the beach behind her mirrored sunglasses. "Ari, check it out," she said after a few moments. "Maisie just walked in with Andrew. They must have made up after that fight at the prom."

I lifted my head enough to seem like I was, indeed, checking it out. "Mmm."

It was important to Kendall to know the Five Ws of journalism about people—the who, what, where, when, and why—and whether they applied to her, too. She used to write field guides to native North American wildlife as a hobby. Now she did this.

Kendall had been my best friend since sixth grade. My only close friend, you could say, if you wanted to be mean and specific about it. But she'd been all I needed when it came to the big things. She taught me how to put in a tampon—the normal way, not like the school nurse had shown us in health class, with one leg up like you were tying a shoe (*yuck*). When we started high school, Kendall joined the newspaper and urged me to check out Mock Trial. So, you know, we'd have some kind of life.

After I cut myself, Kendall visited me on every one of the

five days I stayed home from school. I hadn't been able to explain to her why I did what I did, or why I hadn't asked her for help. She pretended she didn't want to know. Things changed between us, after that.

I lay down again and shut my eyes. Secretly, I wanted to be reading my book, a vintage *Silver Arrow* novel I'd just bought online. I'd made the mistake of putting it in my bag and now the thought of it kept tugging at me. But Kendall didn't get *Silver Arrow*—she didn't get any sci-fi, especially not a TV series that aired before we were even born—and I wanted us to have a good time together.

We were both at the lake on opening day, as we'd always been and were supposed to be. As if it were etched on a Dead Sea scroll somewhere.

One type of antidepressants had made me sick but the second was working. I knew it was working because the sun right here on my face felt like every good thing that had happened to me plus all the other good things that hadn't happened yet but would absolutely, definitely happen soon for sure.

Summer.

After a minute, Kendall whispered, "Who the hell is that?"

I sighed, opened one eye, and looked sideways toward the beach. It took me a bit to lock in on who she was talking about, but then I saw the boy.

He was tall, dark-haired. Our age. Stepping gingerly around people while clutching one of those striped Navajo blankets to his chest.

That's all it takes, sometimes. He doesn't have to be saving kittens from a tree or making shirtless jump shots, or dropping some brilliant comment in American History class. But one moment, this person is not in the world for you. The next moment, he is. It's exactly that simple. And also, irreversible.

He was with a blond woman who wore what appeared to be a gigantic scarf tied in eight different places. As we watched, he guided her to a sliver of shade on the opposite edge of the beach, then spread out the blanket and took a tote bag out of her hands without her asking.

"Do you know?" asked Kendall, wrinkling her nose and all her freckles with it.

"Uh-uh," I said casually, then caught my breath and hoped Kendall didn't notice.

He was not from our high school, we were sure of that; there were only sixty-some-odd guys in each grade and most of them we'd known since forever. A summer renter, maybe? Or from another town.

The boy—actually, at this point, I was already thinking of him as The Boy—offered a tube of sunscreen to the woman, who shook her head. We heard him say, "Mom! Cancer!" as he shoved it toward her again. She smiled at him then and plucked the sunscreen out of his hand. He smiled back. Even from where we sat, I could see each one of his carefully carved features participating in that smile. And *dimples*, for God's sake.

Then he turned away and slipped out of his button-down shirt.

His shoulders were wide and solid, but the rest of him was skinny, as if some body parts were losing a contest with others. I couldn't quite identify the color of his skin, but I could tell it was more dark than fair. More night than day.

We watched him, both Kendall and I, alert as cats as he walked across the dock to the rickety diving board at the far end. (If we'd had the right kind of ears, they would have been pricked up.) He stepped slowly to the edge, then turned to do a backward somersault into the lake, lopsided and not very good at all. The splash looked like it hurt.

And I was already halfway gone.

A week later, Kendall and I were sitting low on the beach, our feet in the water, sand seeping into the edges of our bathing suits. I'd found a bumpy rock embedded in the sand and couldn't stop rubbing my big toe back and forth over it. My little sister, Danielle, waded nearby in her mismatched bikini—a top covered in cherries, blue-and-white-striped bottoms. She made it look like a fashion statement rather than what it really was: the result of a messy room where you could never find the proper other half to anything.

"You guys! Watch me!" called Danielle. She started to spin in circles, still holding her plastic bucket. Faster, then faster again. Until she staggered and fell hard into the water.

"Is she okay?" Kendall asked.

"She makes herself dizzy on purpose," I replied with a shrug. "Your question is more complicated than it sounds."

Danielle righted herself and started spinning again.

"Excuse me," said someone nearby.

We turned to see The Boy standing ankle-deep in the water. Looking at us.

He's shorter up close, was the first thing I thought. *But still, wow.*

"Hey," Kendall said to him, Oscar-winning cool and casual.

"That rope out there," he pointed to the line dotted with red-and-white buoys that looked almost exactly like my anti-depressant pills. It marked the far edge of the swimming area. "What happens if you go on the other side of it?"

"The lifeguard yells at you," said Kendall.

"That's all?" asked The Boy, raising his eyebrows.

"He uses a loud, scary voice," I added.

"There's no giant lake squid that comes up from the deep and swallows you whole?"

Kendall and I shook our heads. Dani stepped out of her spin to stop and listen.

"No patrol boat chases you down, scoops you up in a net, throws you in Lake Jail?"

"Not that we've seen," I said, laughing a bit.

"Huh," was all he said, scanning the off-limits area of the lake, something lighting up behind his expression. He then dove into the water and sprinted out to the boundary rope.

Kendall, Dani, and I fell silent, all watching him swim a trail of white froth through the dark water. When he got to the rope, I expected him to dip underneath it into the forbidden zone. But he turned for the raft tied to the corner of the rope and hoisted himself up the ladder.

"I've got to get some intel on Sunscreen Guy," said Kendall after a few moments.

"I've just been calling him The Boy."

"See? We can't go on like this. I'll talk to Mabel."

Mabel had been running the lake's snack shack since the 1980s. Mabel absorbed details about people like osmosis.

As Kendall headed off on her mission, I went waist-deep into the water to meet Danielle. She wrapped her arms and legs around me, buoyant and effortlessly huggable. Her cold wet against my warm dry. That moment of shock, until we became the same temperature.

"Will you throw me out like garbage?" she whispered in my ear.

I lifted Danielle away from my body. "You're no good anymore!" It was part of the game. "I'm chucking you out with the trash!"

Then I tossed her as far as I could into the water. She shrieked with joy.

"Again!" she said when she came back up for air. "This time, let's pretend you're putting me in the recycling bin. It's blue and it's prettier. Now, go!" So I went. Again, and again, and again. Dani was the best distraction ever.

Ten minutes later, Kendall swam out to meet us, and even with her mirrored sunglasses I could tell she had a mischievous glint in her eye.

"Camden," Kendall said simply, paddling a circle around me.

"What?"

"It's weird, but that's his name. Camden."

"All you got was a name?"

"He goes to Dashwood."

"Oh."

Dashwood was a private alternative school on the edge of town, halfway up a mountain, surrounded by forest. Nobody I knew had even seen the place. Most people called it "Crunchwood" because there were few teachers and no classes. Students did what they wanted, when they wanted to do it. The rumor was they didn't even need to wear shoes if they weren't in the mood.

Kendall lowered her sunglasses so she could give me a look. "We think he's cute, right?"

I grimaced. "*Cute's* not the right word." I hated that word and anyway, it didn't belong on the same plane of existence as this boy. *Camden.*

"International Sex God?" Kendall offered with arched eyebrows, pulling out an old phrase from our private best-friend language.

"Perhaps," I said, giving in to the smile.

"I won't tell Lukas," added Kendall.

"Lukas is just a friend."

"Who you made out with."

"That was before." I didn't need to elaborate. *Before* meant, before January. Before my night at home alone with a Lady Bic razor and a bag of frozen peas.

Kendall looked pained, then covered it up and said, "So? He still likes you. He's not scared away."

"He will be, eventually."

She kicked me under the water. I splashed her back.

"Why are you always so hard on yourself?" asked Kendall, but I knew she didn't really want an answer. "I thought we agreed, that's something that would make you happy. To *have* someone. You're close. I wish I were that close."

"I don't need 'someone.' I have my whole family. And lucky for them, they have me."

My mom was working hard to finish nursing school. My stepdad, Richard, was gone most days, running his art supply store. There were meals to prepare and a self-regenerating to-do list stuck to the fridge with alphabet magnets. Also, the small matter of a real live child who needed to be, you know, fed and clothed and supervised. I filled the gaps. Sometimes it felt like there were more gaps than whatever it was that went between the gaps.

Let's keep her busy, I'd heard my mother tell Richard once. She didn't want me to have time to retreat into myself, apparently a place full of dark corners and hazardous material.

Kendall was my friend and wanted to help, too. What was *happy* anyway? A dumb-sounding word, if you really broke it down. *Happy* was something you didn't think too much about because if you did, you knew you weren't.

I turned to look out at the raft where Camden sat by himself, staring off into the sky. I was always confronting the sky with questions, but that didn't seem to be the case with him. It was more like he and the sky were collaborators. Like maybe he had the whole edgeless thing on his side.

How would that even feel? I couldn't imagine. But, oh, to find out.

Soon, summer began in earnest, so hot and green and wet, it was hard to remember what any other season felt like. I saw Camden at the lake a couple of times a week, but it was always from afar and we never spoke. He usually came alone, which totally fascinated me—who had the nerve to come to the lake alone?—but sometimes he did come with friends: a rickety-tall boy and a petite girl with long, straight, jet-black hair. They'd disappear down a trail into the woods for a while before coming back out to strip down to their bathing suits and do yelping cannonballs off the dock.

I knew the lifeguards liked to drink or smoke stuff in those woods after the beach closed at night. Were Camden and his friends bold enough to do it during the day? And if I myself didn't smoke anything and had even washed cars as a fund-raiser for Students Against Drunk Driving, why did the thought of Camden doing these things make my kneecaps feel unattached from my legs?

"We're hardwired for the naughty ones," sighed Kendall once, as we spotted Camden and his compadres come out of the woods. "It really sucks."

Here's one thing I learned watching Camden during those weeks: a person's body can move and not ever touch you, but still have a physical impact on yours. He leaned against the diving board railing as he waited his turn, and it was like *I* was that railing. The motion of his hand as he ran it through his wet hair while talking—long fingers scattering beads of water—or the angles of his elbows as he stretched out on the sand: these things could make the hair on my arms stand up.

I never liked the word *attraction*. It's way too much about magnets, and not enough about why someone's mere presence can make you feel pleasure and pain at the same time.

Crush didn't work either. I wasn't twelve.

What should I have called it? I just called it Camden.

Sometimes, I'd catch him looking my way. A trick of the light, of course. Or the wishiest wishful thinking. Because there was no way I could possibly be worth that.

"Go talk to him," said Kendall the time we caught Camden glancing at us while he stood in line for the snack shack. "*Seize the moment.*"

"I will," I said. "I will."

"I mean, *this* moment. Not some theoretical future moment."

"I have to keep an eye on Dani."

"I have two. I'll keep them both on her."

"Plus, I already have an ice cream. It would be so obvious that I was going over for him."

"So?"

"Then he would know."

"Argh," snarled Kendall. "You're making me crazy with this. What are you so afraid of?"

I looked at Camden again. He was at the window now, joking with Mabel. She was actually laughing. I hadn't even known that she *could* laugh, and that it sounded like a chipmunk on helium.

What was I afraid of? Anything that might tip me off balance and make me fall back into that place I knew was still there, waiting beneath all my newly glossed-over, smoothed-out surfaces. But I couldn't explain it to her, because I couldn't even explain it to myself.

As the summer went on, Kendall gathered more details from one of her three older brothers, who seemed to know everyone with one or two degrees of separation. His mom was named Maeve Armstrong and was a medium-famous artist. They lived in a converted church that was either lavender or turquoise—the reports varied on that. He'd been homeschooled until last fall. The most delicious rumor was that his father was Ed Penniman, the lead singer for the legendary punk band the Stigmaddicts.

All this was unconfirmed, of course. But I knew two things about Camden Armstrong for sure:

1) His eyes were the exact same forest green as the
   diving board.
2) I ached for him in places I never knew could ache,
   like earlobes and collarbones.

At night, I'd lie awake and picture what Camden's life was like. I'd think of him in his turquoise church, painting like his mother. Reading books I'd never heard of. Playing guitar or piano, whichever worked best for the songs he wrote. Because surely he wrote songs, surely it wasn't possible for a boy to look like that and *not* write songs.

I knew a third definite thing about Camden, eventually. I wouldn't have believed it if I hadn't seen it myself.

One day, Camden came to the lake wearing a black baseball cap with a white *X* on it.

It was a specific white *X*. Deeply specific, at least for me, and maybe for him, too: the logo for the short-lived TV reboot of *Silver Arrow* from a few years back.

He knew about my show.

He knew.

About. My. Show.

And so three times. Three times, I started walking over to where he sat by himself on the Navajo blanket. Practicing the line in my head. Laughably simple, really, but then again, all the best beginnings are. *Nice hat. Are you a* Silver Arrow *fan?*

The fourth time was going to be the charm, I swear.

Then Danielle was suddenly at my side, tugging on the hem of my rashguard. "Ari, I got a splinter."

"Again?"

"It's not my fault, it's the freaking dock's fault."

"Don't say 'freaking.'" I took her hand and led her to the lifeguard station, where they probably kept a pair of tweezers with her name on it. And yes, I'll admit I didn't mind the extra time to get my nerve up even higher.

But when we got back, Camden was packing his stuff to leave.

I bit down hard on the tip of my thumb as I watched him walk away.

This is what I remember from the next time I saw Camden. It was late August by then.

Camden and his friends on the dock, waiting in line for the diving board.

The girl—I now knew her name was Eliza, I'd heard the boys yell it enough times—reaching out and taking Camden's hand.

Camden letting her.

Then, Camden leaning in to kiss Eliza.

Eliza letting him.

Their faces breaking apart but their hands staying connected, until it was his turn to dive.

Me not watching that dive. Me not seeing Eliza laugh at whatever he did.

Me, walking up the beach and toward the parking lot and away, away, away from the lake, already closing the book on summer. So mad at myself for being afraid.

And as I drove home, it occurred to me that my thinking about safety could be all wrong. Maybe safety lay in actually pursuing the things you desired. Maybe the real danger was not pursuing them and never knowing what would have happened if you did.

Maybe regret was the thing that really knocks you off balance into whatever's waiting below.

September, then Halloween. November and Christmas.

The dreams would come randomly, when I hadn't even been thinking about him (I swear). Sometimes once a week and sometimes more. Often, they came at the end of a Black Diamond ski slope day, the kind of day where you have to be an expert at life to get to the bottom without breaking a bone.

It was always something simple and pathetically G-rated. We'd be walking. We'd be holding hands. We'd be driving in a car with the windows down. When I woke up, I'd try to go back to sleep and pick it right back up. *More*, I begged the powers of, well, whatever's in charge of this stuff. *Please, please, more.*

"Destructive," was Kendall's comment when I got up the courage to tell her about the dreams. We were back at her house early from the lamest-ever New Year's party, turning on the TV to see the ball drop.

"I have no control over them," I protested.

"Maybe not," she said. "But there are other things you can control. It's not like he moved away or was only visiting town from another country."

"He goes to *Dashwood*. That may as well be another continent."

"Why don't we figure out where he spends time outside of school, and then, you know, go to that place. A radical idea, I know."

"Then I would still need the guts to talk to him."

"Ari," she continued, her patience wearing thin; I could see it. "You either have to find a way to connect with this guy or move on. It's not healthy for you. And it's not healthy for me to watch it be not healthy for you."

I nodded. I knew she was right.

But then a week later, I saw him.

It was the frozen dead of January. On my to-do list that day was a trip to the bookstore to pick out a gift for one of Dani's friends. I rounded a corner toward the kids' section and there was Camden. My mental images of him were so deeply seated in summer that I almost didn't recognize him in his parka, his hair longer as if he'd grown winter fur.

"Check this one out," he said to his friends, the boy and the girl, the *kissing* girl Eliza, as he held open the pages of a graphic novel.

They checked out what he wanted to show them and then they all laughed, hard. Loud. I fought the urge to go peek over their shoulders. Maybe Eliza sensed that, because she started to turn around.

Which is when I fled like I was running for my life. A detour through the cookbooks, through the door empty-handed, the sound of Camden's laughter jingling after me into the cold.

That night was the best and worst dream yet. We were at

the lake, on the raft. He touched my leg.

Just as in a nightmare when you always come out of it right before someone stabs you or the train hits you or the plane crashes, I startled into reality right before we kissed.

That was it. (Pathetic. G-rated. Like I said.) But it felt so intense, I awoke wanting him even more. Like he'd come, then left. Like I'd snatched him away from my own self.

Kendall had been right. There were no answers to be found in the Camden Dreams. I needed reality, and hope, and forward motion. I needed what was actually possible. I was so serious about this, I made it a proper noun. The Possible. *That* was something I could commit to.

Then there was the boy, the real boy. It had been a whole year since that bad, bad night and Lukas was somehow still waiting for me.

So I turned to him.

THE SECOND SUMMER

(OR, EVERYTHING ELSE)

2

This is what bugs me about calendars: all those perfect, emotionless squares. Those squares keep coming, every morning after every night, whether you want them to or not.

When the square of the Saturday of Memorial Day weekend arrived—the end of my junior year—I stayed in bed overthinking exactly all of this.

"The lake! The lake!" yelled Danielle, running into my room and bouncing on the mattress.

"Yes, the lake," I mumbled into the pillow. "But for the love of God, no bouncing."

Mom came in and sat on the bed's opposite edge. Her wet hair hung in tired clumps, fresh from the shower she always took the minute she came home from the hospital night shift. Her eyes hung, too. I was sure they'd somehow moved farther down her face in the last year.

Danielle kept bouncing. Mom did nothing about it, even though when I was her age, I wasn't allowed to bounce. Because of, you know, the inevitable skull-breaking and waist-down paralysis that would result. Maybe bouncing had gotten magically safer in the last few years and I missed the memo.

"That's right," said Mom. "The lake opens today. I'm sorry I can't go with you."

Danielle stopped bouncing and crawled into my mom's lap; my mom wrapped her arms around Danielle and leaned into her. At first glance they didn't appear to be mother and daughter. My mother was a deep brunette, her features severe as if they were drawn with extra-thick Sharpie. Danielle, in her nearly white curls and pale pixie skin, resembled her dad, my stepfather, Richard. I didn't match either of them, with my straight not-brown-not-blond hair you might recognize if you saw the photos I have of my father, who left when I was two. I'd recently cut that hair blissfully short, just below my chin, while Mom's and Danielle's hair was long.

It bothered me that the three of us females in the house didn't look like a family. Maybe if we looked like one, it would be easier to feel like one.

"Let's wait until your next day off," I said to Mom. "Besides, the water will be freezing. I'll do some crafts with Dani downstairs and we'll be quiet while you sleep. And later if you give me a list, I'll take her to the grocery store."

My mother got a faraway look. I knew this was a tempting offer: one less thing to do today. An hour she could have all to herself, sleeping or watching *Millionaire Matchmaker*, which for her was basically like going to the spa.

"Arianna, no," she finally said. "It's going to be a beautiful day. I can't let you hang around the house. You both need to be out, being active. I'll pack up some snacks."

She left the room. Danielle watched her go, then turned to me and bugged out her eyes.

"Maybe your guy will show up!"

"Shhh!" I lowered my voice, hoping Mom hadn't heard her. "What do you mean, my guy?"

"You know. Your summer crush." Now she smiled that evil genius kid smile.

"How do you know about things like 'summer crushes'?"

"Because I *live*. In the *world*. Also I eavesdropped on you and Kendall talking about it once."

"Well, that's over, and you're not allowed to talk about it. Actually, don't even think about it. Don't think about thinking about it."

(That went for me, too.)

"You're no fun," said Danielle. Her expression turned sad and she added, "I wrote a letter to Jasmine about the lake because I wanted to know if any of her friends live there. But she didn't come last night."

Oof. I usually knew when there was a fresh note for

Jasmine, Dani's fairy pen pal. I'd slip into Dani's room once she was asleep and grab it off the windowsill, then write back on special green vellum paper I kept hidden inside an old math textbook.

"You know what happens sometimes," I told her. "Jasmine gets busy working at the fairy vet hospital and can't write back for a while."

Danielle nodded, apparently satisfied with this. I loved that I could make things better for her so easily.

My mother came back in, holding out some cash like it was the most brilliant idea she'd ever had, and said, "Here's something for ice cream. A special treat to celebrate summer." Her face got suddenly serious again. "Promise me you won't get the kind with artificial colors."

Dani rolled her eyes. I sat up, swung my feet to the floor, and took the money from my mother.

The Possible, I chanted to myself.

Everything is Possible.

Maybe I would continue to believe it. Maybe it would even be true.

❊ ❊ ❊

Every summer, Danielle created a rock collection that she arranged in meticulous groups along the edges of our front porch. To most people, they looked random and unremarkable, easy to dismiss as a little kid's Accumulation of Crap. But I'd learned to see what was special about each one.

As soon as Danielle and I stepped from the car across the

lake's parking lot, she bent to pick up the first member of the new crop.

"Look," she said. "It's a perfect oval. And so smooth." She held the rock and stroked it with one finger as if it were alive.

"Mmmm," I said in not-faked admiration. "Good for drawing a face on."

Dani nodded, then clutched it to her chest as we walked over to the admission kiosk. The kiosk was actually a tall, narrow wooden house, and years ago Kendall and I decided it looked like a latrine so we called it the Crapper. A kid from school named Julian was working the Crapper today, perched on the metal folding chair, reading a book.

Kendall. God, I wished she were here and not camping with her older brothers, that she'd chosen me over them this weekend.

"Hi, Julian," I said as we stepped up to the Crapper window. "One adult, one kid, please."

"Hey, Ari," said Julian, taking my money. He swished his eyes toward my arms. It had been over a year, but the buzz about my scars was still humming, because people could see them now. I'd stopped covering them up. I wasn't trying to show them off or anything. At some point, they'd become a part of me. I woke up one day okay with them, the same way you're okay with a birthmark or a white spot on your skin from a long-ago mosquito bite you never stopped picking at.

It was like a physical reminder of my depression, a way for me to accept that even though I had fought and won, it would always be there with me. And also that I had power to fight again.

"Ready for the season?" I asked Julian, who was still fixated on my arms. *What do you think? Were they what you imagined?*

Julian glanced back up. "There's carpeting on the dock this year. Splinter-proof."

"Fancy." I smiled. *No worries, you're not the first person I've caught looking.* The lookers used to bother me until my therapist, Cynthia, suggested that maybe people saw a little of themselves in those lines on my skin.

I'd recently asked Cynthia if I could take a break from our sessions for the summer. I was tired of talking about feeling okay and thinking about feeling okay. I wanted a chance to just, you know, *feel okay.* She'd said yes, but she'd also made me set an appointment for the first week in September to make clear this was a trial run. It felt like a challenge, and one I wanted to win.

It was early, the opening day crowd beginning to trickle in. I led Danielle to a nice spot under a tree far from last year's. As far as I could possibly get from last year's. Then I did a quick casing of the joint to confirm that nobody I knew was here yet, and that nobody else of particular interest—oh, for instance, nobody I'd had boring-devastating dreams about—had shown up either.

I prayed for him to come. I prayed for him not to come.

Danielle was ankle-deep in the water before I could even get the blanket spread out. "It's so freezing ice-cold I'm gonna die!" she yelled. "Come in with me!"

"Wow, you really know how to sell it."

"We'll play whatever you want. Mermaids, dolphins. Sea monkeys!"

"Tempting. But I didn't wear my suit today."

Dani scanned my regulation tank top and black jersey skirt with distaste. Maybe that's really when you become one of the grown-ups. You come to the lake and don't even bring a damn suit.

"You're not leaving *those* on, are you?" Danielle asked, pointing at my feet.

Oh. I'd forgotten about my boots. I'd worn them every day of the two months since I'd bought them and they didn't even feel like footwear anymore. They were just soft purple leather perfectly molded around all the stuff at the bottom of my legs. Like I was a doll and someone had painted them on. Actually, that doll existed. I had two versions of it at home, one of them mint in box.

"They're my Satina Galt boots," I said. "You know I wear them everywhere."

Danielle made a face. Which was really rich, coming from a child who often wore the same outfit three days straight, only taking it off for a mandatory change of underpants.

Satina Galt was the character who made *Silver Arrow* what it was, to me. The boots made me feel strong. They made me feel like something Possible. Maybe if I wore them long enough, I would actually be that something. My mother understood the boots. She never let on, but I could tell by the way she looked at them sometimes, like they were a memory of a memory. Occasionally, she looked at me that way, too.

Something over my shoulder caught Danielle's eye and her face lit up. "Oh! Madison's here!"

I turned to see a girl I recognized from Dani's class, and the kids ran to each other, hugging and squealing like they hadn't spent seven hours at school together the day before.

When does that stop? I thought. When you're not afraid to claim your friends, to clasp them to your chest and shout to the world, *Mine!* When you know for sure, pinkie promise, that the way it is now is the way it will always be.

Kendall and I hadn't hung out in weeks. We'd both been so busy, of course. She had the special year-end edition of the school newspaper and already started work at Scoop-N-Putt. I had Dani and a job at Richard's art supply store and a really packed schedule of hanging out alone in my room, lurking on *Silver Arrow* fansites.

It stung, to watch the little girls now.

I located and approached Madison's mother: huge sunglasses, stylish beach hat, paperback in hand.

"Hi," she said, grinning. "How are you?"

"Good. How are you?"

"I'm fine, thanks. I actually meant, how *are* you? You look like you're doing really well."

I smiled and said, "Thank you."

I said it because I lived in a small town, and people don't want good stories to end, and everyone thinks they know a little bit about depression, and because these were just a few of the terms I unknowingly agreed to that night over a year earlier.

"I have to go to the restroom. Do you mind keeping an eye on Dani for a few minutes?"

"Of course not, sweetie. She's lucky to have you."

Yes, she is, I thought as I walked toward the restroom building, my head swimming. *I miss Kendall. There was still gossip about me.*

Inside, the cool and the dark and the silence and the quick bliss of being unseen.

I went into an empty stall and jiggled the lock shut. *You look like you're doing really well.* What exactly does that look like? What would not-doing-well look like? Because I had once been not-doing-well for a long time and nobody noticed at all.

Turns out, I wasn't completely alone in the bathroom. I could hear someone in the next stall going, too. It was one of those awkward situations where you find yourself in sync with a stranger.

After I was finished (*first!*), I stepped out of the stall to wash my hands. I heard the other stall door open and glanced up into the mirror.

"Am I in the wrong bathroom?" asked Camden Armstrong. Like it was simply an intellectual question.

This is where I wondered if I was having a hallucination.

Then in the mirror, I could see a urinal on the wall behind me.

And this is where I panicked.

"Um, no," I managed to say. "Apparently, *I* am. Sorry!"

I ducked my head and walked quickly past him out the door. I'm not sure what ducking my head was going to accomplish, but as I mentioned: the panic.

No. No, no. *Pleasetellmethatdidnotjusthappen.* I stumbled across the beach, my feet not going where I wanted them to go, trying and failing to get away from my own mortifying self.

Once I got back to my blanket, I waved at Madison's mom and she waved back. The two girls were swimming nearby. I grabbed my phone and texted Kendall with quivering thumbs.

Just saw Camden Armstrong at the lake. Went into the men's restroom by accident. Call me.

Those days, I was always looking for things to connect over with Kendall. Our friendship was like the drawstring in a pair of sweatpants, always slipping out of sight and out of reach. We always knew it was there. One of us merely had to retrieve it with that safety-pin trick until next time.

I waited for a reply, looking out at the lake so I wouldn't have to watch Camden come out of the restroom, so maybe he wouldn't see me back. He was here. I had spoken to him. I wasn't sure what I felt other than an overwhelming urge to dive into the lake, swim past the far boundary rope, then keep going and never come back.

My phone chirped with a message from Kendall.

Bad reception here, can only text. But now very intrigued.

I was in the middle of typing out more details when Dani bolted up the beach from the water, full-body shivering, lips nearly blue.

"Make me a burrito," she demanded, as if she knew I needed something else in my brain that moment. I put my phone down, grabbed her towel and wrapped it tight around her body and arms, tucking in the end corner at her neck so only her head and feet stuck out. Then I pulled her into my lap as she giggled.

"Mmmm. I'm so hungry. And look at this delicious lunch!" I pretended to take a bite of her belly.

My mother never pretended Danielle was a burrito. If she had, it would have had to be a whole-wheat one, with no sour cream because that adds too much fat and dairy. I loved giving Danielle these moments she never got from Mom. That *I* never got from Mom. It was like I was giving them to both of us.

I heard a noise on the diving board, a loud whoop, and looked up to see Camden backflipping into the water.

As if the last year had never happened. As if someone had rewound the tape, and here we were, in the exact places we'd been exactly twelve months before.

But I'd become a different person since last May, and a switch inside me flicked on. There was a blinking YES in neon lights.

Oh God those green eyes and those shoulders and the shaggy straight hair, and oh God.

And that thing that took place in the restroom, that ridiculous and horrifying thing we shall not talk about ever again, did that count as a conversation?

They say, there are no do-overs in life.

I say, anything is Possible.

3

"What are you thinking about, ducky?" asked Richard the next day.

I was kneeling in Aisle 2 of Millie's Art Supply, staring off into space.

"I'm thinking there are way, *way* too many colors of craft sand in the world," I said.

My stepdad didn't bat an eye. "Yes, I agree. War, poverty, climate change, and craft sand. Times are bleak."

I really loved him a lot.

"Look," I said, pointing to the bottom shelf and the bags I'd already arranged in official rainbow order. "I went all ROY G. BIV, and then I opened the last box and found this. *Turquoise!*"

Richard sighed. "I'll help you make a space between the green and the blue," he simply said, and sat down beside me on the linoleum floor.

Working together like that, stacking bags of craft sand in swift, efficient movements, it was easy to feel that what we were doing was important. Like an aesthetically perfect shelf display could change someone's life. (And who says it couldn't? It totally could.) It was these microscopic here-and-now moments that had helped me the most. I had a lot of them in my job at Millie's, which Richard owned. Three afternoons a week and all day on Sundays.

Which of course was going to make it that much harder to quit.

Finally, we got down to the last two bags of turquoise. "If there's a box we don't know about," said Richard as he balanced them on the pile, "and it's filled with, say, *eggplant*-colored sand, I may have to kill someone."

It was almost six o'clock and closing time. He patted my back and stood up slowly, stretched, then walked over to lock the front door. He took a moment to carefully smooth down the lost-dog notice someone had posted inside the vestibule. *FIND VERA!* it shouted at us all day.

"Come on," said Richard. "Mom and Dani are waiting." We were supposed to meet them at the restaurant next door for our regular Sunday session of "all of us sitting down in the same place at the same time," occasionally known as dinner.

"Will you do me a favor in there?" I asked as we headed

out the back. "When the moment's right, can you ask me if I'm excited about summer?"

We all had our things at Moose McIntyre's.

My mother liked to line up the scalloped edge of the paper place mat with the edge of the table, as if she could get this one thing to be perfect, everything else in life would follow.

Richard always studied the menu intently, right thumb stroking his right eyebrow, even though he ordered the same exact thing every time.

Danielle did the maze on the kids' menu, then the word search, then colored the turtle who was named Shelly and wore a sailor suit for reasons nobody ever understood.

I sat next to the window, counting every familiar face that walked by outside. My record for a single meal was forty-eight.

After we got our food, but before everyone was done, Richard gave me a look and I nodded.

"So, Ari," he said. "You've got what, two more weeks of school? Excited about summer?"

He was good. Convincing. We'd done this little show before. It was Mom Management Vaudeville.

"I am. In fact, I have an idea I want to run by you, if you'll promise to keep an open mind."

Mom put down her grilled chicken wrap and rested both hands on her place mat. "We always keep an open mind," she said, in a way that would never convince anyone she had an open mind.

I glanced at Dani, who was snugly in her own little world, focused on her turtle. I took a deep breath, then looked squarely at Mom. The only way out was through.

"There's a morning-shift housekeeper job available at the River's Edge B&B, and I'd like to apply."

Mom and Richard didn't react, like they were waiting for the punch line.

"River's Edge B&B?" I added pointlessly. "Up on 9W?"

Mom frowned. Certain lines on her face appeared only when she frowned this much. "But you already have a job." Mom looked to Richard, but I kept my eyes on her. Seeing Richard's face right now would destroy whatever resolve I had.

"I'd like to do something different this summer," I said.

"But Richard depends on you." Mom touched Richard's arm and I looked at it, her limp hand on his wristwatch.

"I'm replaceable." I'd anticipated exactly this objection from Mom. I'd done some prep. "There must have been four college students who stopped in today, asking about work for the summer. He'll have no trouble finding someone else."

"But why, Ari?" asked Mom. She turned to Richard. "We need to know why. Right, honey?"

I dared look at Richard now. He tilted his head, staring at me. I knew I owed him an explanation.

I thought of Richard's face in the doorway of my room after they found out what I'd done. My mom had gone into nurse mode, checking my cuts to make sure they'd stopped bleeding, getting them properly cleaned. She didn't have the time or luxury to be shocked or hurt or regretful. At least not right away. (Or ever. I still couldn't tell.)

But Richard did. His face. So sad. It was the kind of sadness that shifts a tectonic plate somewhere inside that person.

In some ways, watching Richard realize my truth was harder than watching Mom and Dani do it. Because he was the first person I would have gone to for help, and because I didn't, and also because I had no idea why.

"I've worked hard this year," I finally said, then realized I had to clarify. "Worked hard at feeling better."

"We know you have," Mom said, dipping into a whisper.

"Better feels different. I feel different. I *am* different. So I want to be somewhere different this summer, doing something different."

That word, suddenly stuck on a loop in my head.

"The B&B is all strangers just passing through," I continued. "Nobody knows me, and they don't know about . . . my history. It's kind of a way for me to start fresh."

I forced myself to shut up at that point. I'd already given away all the raw honesty I could spare.

Mom's face softened. Her frown lines seemed uprooted for a moment, not sure where to go.

"Oh, Ari," she said, my name catching on its way out of her mouth.

The change in her tone was enough to make Dani stop coloring and look up, to examine Mom for signs of Mom-ness.

"You don't notice it," I said, "but I do. The way people still look at me, or at these." I offered my forearm.

"I get it." She held up a hand for me to halt. It was almost comical, how squeamish this particular RN was about these particular scars.

"I can make do without her," volunteered Richard. "But it's your call." He always backed away from the tough stuff. He knew where Mom had jurisdiction.

Mom took a deep breath in, then out, as we waited. Finally she said, "I hate the idea of you driving all the way to the River's Edge. That's a busy road, lots of traffic in the summer. What if you can't make it in time to pick up Dani from camp? At least at the store, you know you'll never get stuck there." She paused. "And really, Ari, you can't run away from your problems. There must be other ways to 'start fresh,' as you say."

"There aren't. I've looked."

"Keep looking. You can find them. I know you can."

I felt my throat close up. She did this, my mom. She made assumptions about what I was capable of, what I could handle. I knew she was trying to lift me up, but it only felt like more pressure at a time when I didn't need more pressure.

Suddenly I was climbing over Dani—her black crayon scraped my leg—and rushing out the door to the street. I may have said, "Excuse me," at some point, but I wasn't sure to whom, or why.

I sat down on a bench outside the restaurant, grabbed my head with my hands, looked at the purple of my boots against the pavement. What would Satina do right here? Would she go back in and fight for her cause with a perfectly articulated speech?

The front door swung open, and I saw my mother's sandals appear on the sidewalk. Then Dani's sequined Mary Janes next to them. A cheap shot that Mom would bring Dani, or more likely, let her follow. Like she'd lawyered up. It was always harder for me to lose it around Dani, which was, you know, both good and bad.

"My problems," I said.

"What?" asked Mom.

"You said my *problems*. Call it depression, Mom. It's not like pneumonia or Lyme disease, the stuff you help people with. You don't have a case of it, then get cured."

It haunts you, I wanted to add. *Like a ghost that refuses to move out of the only house it's ever known.*

Silence. Mom sank down onto the bench and said, "I know about depression, Ari." Her voice was heavy and even, laced thick with extra meaning. I knew she knew. I'd been there when she went through it, but we never talked about that.

"I'm sorry," I said to her. Or to myself. Or to the wood on the bench beneath me, where someone had pen-carved *I love u JP u so HOT.*

"I just need things to go smoothly this summer," said Mom. "My job, you know. I love it. But it's tough, Ari. Really tough. What makes it easier is knowing I can count on you."

43

"You can," I said, and meant it. I couldn't not mean it.

"Also, I like the idea of you working with Richard. So he can . . ."

"Keep an eye on me?"

"I was going to say support you. If you need it."

I didn't plan on needing it, but I was glad she was thinking about what I might need.

"So we're okay?" Mom pressed. "The store, like we all planned?"

It wasn't worth it. The fight, the resentment, the lingering anger all summer. I'd been stupid to think there was a flicker of a shadow of hope.

"Yes," I said.

"Here," said Dani, holding up the kids' menu. "I gave Shelly a blue mohawk this time. I want you to have it."

I took the drawing from her and rumpled her hair. "Thanks, baby. He looks badass. I love it."

I stood up and put one boot in front of the other. Mom reached for the door to go back inside and held it open for us.

"Don't say 'badass' around Dani," she whispered to me as I walked by.

On the second floor of Seamus Fitzpatrick Memorial High School, there was an alcove. Unremarkable, to be honest, with its regulation water fountain and bulletin board. Most people walked by it two, three, maybe four times a day. But Kendall and I used it for rushed, heated mini-conferences between classes. We'd trade gossip or the guilty pleasure of a joke at some kid's expense, but only because one of us really, really needed the laugh. Like when Kendall had to regroup after finding out she'd gotten a low grade or didn't understand a class lecture.

It was our place. Even though we hadn't been there for a while, this hadn't changed.

Kendall texted me on the Tuesday after the long weekend.

Meet me at the alcove before English.

I went gladly and arrived first.

"So," she said, walking up to me, hugging her copy of *The Scarlet Letter*. "It's taken you a full year to exchange more sentences with Camden Armstrong in a humiliating restroom mix-up. What's next?"

I bit my lip hard, trying to figure out which of eight different ways to begin. "This sounds crazy, but I think I could actually talk to him now."

"That's how to spin it! See it as an icebreaker, not a tragedy."

"For all I know, he's with someone. Maybe Eliza, still."

Kendall smiled her old smile for me. "Even if he is, that doesn't mean you can't get to know him." Now she grew serious. "Life is short. Summers are even shorter. We're going to be seniors in a couple of weeks. Don't you think it's time to start doing whatever the hell we want to?"

Kendall had earned the right to say that, I knew. My friend was smart and insightful and creative—her newspaper essays and personality pieces were legendary—but distracted and disorganized when it came to actual schoolwork. She was fun and drop-dead witty, a girl who held her own against three older brothers, but for some reason got quiet and awkward around guys. This meant she hadn't yet secured the boyfriend she so desperately wanted. I could tell she was fed up with wanting.

I glanced sideways to the river of students rushing past, glimpsed the top of a dark, shaggy head moving toward us. Something stirred on the back of my neck even though of course, of course, Camden would not be in my school. It was just some kid with a vaguely similar non-haircut, a sophomore who suddenly seemed much more attractive than he used to be.

"It's not that easy for me," I finally said to Kendall, hoping she would get it. I was not going to be making ice-cream cones for everyone in town or collecting multicolored golf balls out of a fake pond. I would have very little time where I wasn't being relied upon by a family member. She could do whatever the hell she wanted to, but I could not.

Kendall spotted something over my shoulder and made a cringe-y face. I turned to see, and there was Lukas coming down the hall, walking with his friend Brady.

"Ugh," muttered Kendall, which really said it all for both of us.

Brady stopped and said, "Hi, guys."

Lukas grabbed him by the shirt and yanked, shaking his head. It didn't seem malicious. It was more like, *I'm not prepared to do this right now.*

Kendall asked, "What's up?"

I stared at a suddenly riveting spot on the wall.

"Too much and not enough," said Brady, grinning with newly braceless teeth. Kendall had always liked Brady. There had been talk of a double date, when Lukas and I were together. They both had last names as first names, so why not give it a try?

It still hurt, with Lukas. To not-quite-see each other this way. He was the third person I ever kissed, and the first who ever wanted to call me his girlfriend. His hands, which had been all over my body. His lower lip, which I'd held lightly between my teeth. How he made me sigh on the plaid couch in his basement, wanting more but not wanting more, desperate to lose control while gripping it as tightly as I could with white knuckles.

I didn't want to think about that other part of him, which I could almost still feel on my fingertips.

"Hey, Lukas," my mouth said without consulting my brain.

He looked straight at me now, and I was reminded of how much we resembled each other. It was one of the things the Mock Trial kids said from the beginning. They called us "the Siblings," but Lukas took it as a sign we were supposed to be a couple. He had the same wavy, dirty blond hair and brown eyes I did. As prosecuting attorneys, we'd seemed united.

"Ari," he said. Simply and flatly, like my name alone told the story of the cruel way I cut myself off from him. Lukas turned and walked away. Brady shrugged at us, then trailed after his friend.

I had made that, what had just happened.

"Do I get points for trying?" I asked Kendall, blinking the sting from my eyes.

"Sure, but I'd say you've got a big deficit to make up. You messed the guy up bad."

"I never meant to do that." I shook my head hard, shook that thought out. "I'll never forgive myself for it."

Kendall must have sensed how serious I was. "Would it have been so hard to simply, you know, break up with him?"

"I thought it would be easier to ignore and avoid him until he finally got the hint," I replied. "Easier for me, I guess. For him, not so much."

I winced at the memory of Lukas's emails, the note he left in my locker.

Please, please tell me what I did. Is this about what happened after the party?

I'm sorry if I pushed you too far, but you never told me to stop. We can dial it back.

Talk to me, Ari.

I don't deserve the silent treatment.

He was right. He didn't. But my fear of confrontation beat out my sense of what was mature and, you know, kind.

Kendall put a hand on my shoulder. "He was your first boyfriend. How the hell were you supposed to know what to do? Now, at least, you know better."

"I know a lot of things better," I added.

"Then take that and do what you need to about Camden Armstrong. Otherwise, you are not allowed to pine for him from a distance and then talk about it all summer. Agreed?"

"Yes, ma'am."

"Okay, then. Let's go figure out what the hell Hester Prynne was thinking with that creepy Arthur Dimmesdale who was *so* not worth the hassle."

I followed her down the hall, happy to have orders.

4

I was loading up the car after a morning at the lake with Dani, and suddenly there he was. Lashing his bike to a rack in the reservoir parking lot. Like a normal human being who, you know, exists. It had been a full week since the Bathroom Incident and I'd replayed the scene so much in my head, it was easy to forget he was three-dimensional and could move of his own accord.

I looked away and wasn't going to glance again but of course I did it anyway, when I was reaching up to pull the hatchback down. Naturally, this was when Camden saw me. My arm caught in midair as if I were waving. He waved back.

My adrenaline level went from Zero to Holy Crap in a millisecond.

Now he was walking toward me. I unfocused my eyes so all I really saw was the bright white of a button-down shirt with the sleeves rolled up, set against the brown skin of his arms and the dark blue of his jeans.

In the middle distance, two other people pulled into the parking lot on bikes. Eliza, and the other boy from last summer, so tall he made his bicycle look like a toy. And Eliza, well. All I noticed at first was that she still had lips. The ones Camden had kissed.

I closed the hatchback and leaned against it for support in case I'd have to see them do whatever they were going to do together, as a couple. Camden kept approaching, and in a moment of terror, I wondered if he was not actually coming over to *me* but headed somewhere else, and this was going to be even worse than the restroom.

"Hey," he said, finally stopping a few yards away.

"Hi." It somehow came out normal. Maybe this would be fine.

"That was you the other day, in the men's room."

"Yes."

"It was funny."

"It was?" Come on, Ari. Say a complex sentence. With clauses and stuff. "I thought it was a little bit devastating."

"Eh. Men, women. Toilets are toilets."

I laughed. He made me laugh. "At least nobody was changing in there."

"True. You got lucky it was just me." He paused. "You're Ari, right?"

He knew my name. His voice saying it made me flush. I could only nod.

"I'm Camden."

"Hi, Camden." I made it sound as if I didn't know, and that felt like a lie.

Now the other guy and Eliza were walking up behind Camden. I'd forgotten how the boy teetered as he moved, with all that height, and how nonchalantly stunning the girl was. Like she glowed and knew it and didn't let it change anything.

"Thanks for totally *ditching us* at the traffic light," she said to Camden.

Camden halfway turned to them. "I told you. I can't ride slower than that, it's physically impossible for me. Sorry."

He didn't go to Eliza.

Instead, he looked at me. "This is Ari. Ari, this is Eliza and Max."

"Hello," I said, with a wave in their direction. Okay, then. So now we'd officially met. It was like characters from a book I'd read over and over, suddenly stepping off the page.

Max said, "Hey," but Eliza simply scanned me from the top down. She stopped dead when she saw my purple boots.

"Satina Galt," she said, pointing with her chin at my feet.

"Totally," said Max, taking off his bike helmet. The previous summer, his hair had had streaks of blue and purple in it, but he'd cut the colors off and now his head was covered in brown duckling fuzz.

Camden rolled his eyes. "I apologize for them. They're a little obsessed."

But there I was, feeling suddenly, thrillingly, seen.

"No apologies necessary," I said, sticking out one foot sideways to better display the boot. "They're comfortable and practical and surprisingly stylish, regardless of where in time or space your hypership lands you."

Camden and Eliza and Max exchanged the same deeply impressed look.

"Season Four? When she had those shiny pants, too?" asked Eliza. It was like we'd all lapsed into our native language. The only other person I'd ever spoken it with before was my mom, multiple lifetimes ago.

"Actually, Season Three," I said. "They changed her boots first, before they sexied up the rest of her uniform."

"Ah, right," said Eliza. "Wherever did you find these beauties? I figured spray paint was the only way I'd make a full Satina uniform happen."

"I got lucky at the thrift store in town."

More impressed looks. The whole story was more complicated than that, but I wasn't going to get into it.

"A perfect thrift store find is the universe wanting you to have something," said Camden, making those scandalous dimples *for me*.

"I like to think so," I said, willing my voice not to shake. Keeping myself together while having this conversation took an amount of strength I could only attribute to the boots. The boots made me able. The boots made things Possible.

Camden was about to say something else when Danielle came running into the parking lot.

"Freeze!" I yelled on instinct.

She froze, but snapped back, "You told me to hurry up, so I'm hurrying!" Then she noticed Camden, Max, and Eliza, and her eyes widened. "I remember you guys . . . ," she said.

"We've got to go," I said quickly, cutting her off. I could already hear Dani's next comment. *You were Ari's summer crush last year!* Or maybe: *I'm pretty sure Ari dreams about having babies with you. What's your name again?*

I grabbed Dani's hand and pulled her close to me. Camden regarded us. I couldn't read his expression. Amused, maybe, fringed with sadness. Wistful. Everyone was silent for a few moments, not sure what was supposed to happen now. A white parking space line divided me from them, and the boundary suddenly seemed important. If Dani hadn't been there, would I have stepped over it to more Satina, more *Silver Arrow*, more everything?

Finally, it was Eliza who ended the awkwardness and said, "Well, hopefully we'll see you around, Specialist Galt." She moved toward the entrance gate, gesturing for Camden and Max to follow.

In the car on the way home, my right foot solid on the gas

pedal, I wiggled my toes in the boot.

"That was him, right?" asked Dani from the backseat.

Him. That *X* on Camden's baseball cap last summer, and how it was like he'd been marked for me. *This is The Boy.*

"Yes," I said.

Already, it hurt extra hard to be driving away from the lake, knowing they were there and I was not.

"Why did that girl call you Something Galt?"

Most of the time, Dani already knew the answers to the questions she asked, but she liked to hear them come from someone else.

"Satina Galt. From *Silver Arrow.*"

"And that's your favorite show, right?"

She knew it was, but I still said, "Yes," then added, "It was Mom's favorite show, too. When she was a teenager."

I wasn't sure if Dani knew that, but had a feeling she didn't. Judging from Dani's surprised expression in the rearview mirror, I was right.

Thing was, "favorite show" did not even scratch the surface of it.

And another thing, a *terrible* thing was, I felt glad Danielle would never know that.

It was me who watched *Silver Arrow* with Mom going as far back as I could remember, in our basement apartment with the once-green-but-now-yellow carpet, where it always smelled of hot dogs even though we never ate them. She'd come home from her job at the bank, change into sweats, make two cups of tea with lots of sugar, then pull out her DVDs of all five seasons that first aired in the 1980s. I'd watch her select a disk and handle it so delicately, with two fingers, that I was afraid to ever touch these glimmering things myself. I believed you could stare into them, like a mirror, and see a different reality staring back.

My mother needed an episode every day. She especially needed Satina Galt, the sole human woman among men and aliens and androids in an interplanetary crew.

As for me? I was five years old. I could recite the alphabet, the Pledge of Allegiance, and this speech from the opening credits of the show (and I could do it in a slow, deep voice that sounded eerily like the one on TV):

Behold the Arrow One, *a twenty-third-century hypership designed for long-range space travel! The shining beacon of an ever-unfolding future!*

But an accident on its maiden voyage has torn a hole in the universal continuum. Now it hurtles randomly through time and space while its crew tries to get back home.

Where, and when, will the Arrow One *hit next?*

Wherever. Whenever. It was always Satina's intelligence, her independence, her toughness, and her sense of humor that made all the difference. At least, that's how Mom and I saw it.

She stopped watching around the time she met Richard. I didn't.

The universe wanting you to have something, Camden had said about my thrift store find.

Some people were fans. Some people wove their fandom into the threadbare places in their lives, to make them stronger. I wondered if Camden Armstrong was one of these people, and where he wove, and why.

The next Monday afternoon, I stepped out of my AP French final and took a deep breath. It was almost worth it to get sick with stress about a test, to have this. One delicious moment of relief that it was over.

I found Kendall by her locker. She'd just come out of her chemistry exam and looked appropriately destroyed.

"A C at best," she said, throwing a stack of study notes in a nearby garbage can. "I am so sick of this shit."

"I'm sorry, Ken," I said.

"Me, too." She didn't meet my glance. I knew from past experience that she was feeling a special combination of embarrassment and anger. Her parents, who were both college history professors, would have to put on their supportive-but-disappointed expressions that even I knew so well.

"What are you doing later?" I asked. "Wanna come over and cram for English?"

"I'm meeting up with Sasha, Caitlin, and those guys to do that," she said, looking truly torn. Sasha, Caitlin, et al., were Kendall's friends from the newspaper. I'd never clicked with them. Still, she asked, "Why don't you join us?"

I hadn't told her about the parking lot and Camden's friends, and how a bona fide conversation had happened. I liked having the memory of it pressed against my palm, facedown, where it could only be felt and not examined to death.

"Sure," I said.

Kendall smiled. I rarely said "Sure" to anything when it came to the newspaper masthead. Suddenly, my phone dinged with a text from my mother:

Coming to pick you up. Can you be at the loop in 5 min?

"My mom," I said, worried.

"Everything okay?"

"I don't know. She's picking me up."

"Call me later." Kendall squeezed my shoulder before I rushed off to gather my stuff and head outside.

"What's wrong?" I shouted when Mom drove up.

She had all the windows open, a news report blasting on the car radio. She pushed her sunglasses to the top of her head and frowned.

"Nothing's wrong. I figured I'd drive you home so you had extra time to study."

"God, Mom. I thought something had happened." I went around to the passenger side and climbed in.

"What would have happened?" Mom asked after I slammed the door.

"You're the nurse. Accidents? Fires? Death and dismemberment?"

"Is it that unusual for me to surprise you at school with a ride home?"

"Uh, *yeah.*"

Mom looked hurt. Oops, she must have wanted me to lie. "I'm trying to help, Ari. I know how important it is that you finish the year with a bang." She clutched the steering wheel tighter and eyed some other students outside, like maybe if she threw one of them in the car for a ride home, she'd get the gratitude she was hoping for.

"It *is* important. Thank you."

As we waited to make the right turn out of the school's main driveway, I studied Mom's face in profile. From this angle, you couldn't really see the dark circles under her eyes. She looked more like the Mom I remembered from when I was little, sitting next to me in the evening light, watching TV.

"Shouldn't you be sleeping?" I asked her.

She shrugged. "I woke up early and have tonight off, so I figured I'd go do stuff." She paused. "Sometimes I forget what it's like to be out in daylight."

"You should be gardening, or taking a walk."

"Shush. Will you please let me do this?" Her voice caught a little at the end. "I feel like I'm never around for you."

Then just talk to me, I wanted to say. *Ask me how my day was. Ask me if I had any good moments and I would tell you that, yes, I did. And I might even share them with you.*

But I knew this simple car ride was all she had to give right now.

At home, Mom shooed me straight to my room to study. She said she'd bring me a snack, get Danielle off the school bus.

So I let her do that. It was all I really had to give back.

I heard Dani's musical voice fill the house when she came home, Mom whispering for her to be quiet and that she couldn't go see me right away. Dani protesting, then some kind of food being unwrapped and the TV turning on, and Dani not protesting anymore. I put on music and reintroduced myself to my history notebook.

Sometime later, I heard Richard come home. Voices, footsteps down the stairs, up the stairs. Raised voices.

Then, crying.

I leapt up, opened the door, and poked my head out of my room. My mom was at the kitchen table with her laptop, her head in her hands. Richard stood above her, holding Dani in his arms, her limbs pretzeled around him.

"You couldn't hear it? Come on, Kate. I caught at least three F-bombs between the front door and the den!"

"I got involved with something online!"

Dani saw me, then scrambled out of Richard's arms and came down the hall. Neither Richard nor Mom seemed to notice. They continued bickering.

I motioned for Dani that it was okay to come into the safe harbor of my room. After she stepped inside, I closed the door and turned to her.

"What was that about?"

"Uh. Nothing."

"*Dani.*"

"I may have started watching an inappropriate movie. I

didn't mean to, I was trying to get to Nickelodeon. But I don't know how to use the remote!"

"How inappropriate are we talking?"

"Boobs."

"Fantastic."

I put the pieces together. Richard was often mad at Mom for not spending time with Danielle. In most houses, it's the mother accusing the father of that. We were Mirror Image Bizarro World Family.

And now here I was, curling up on the bed with Dani instead of reading about the War of 1812, folding her against my body so maybe she wouldn't hear my mother's words as they swirled down the hall.

"I just needed some downtime, Richard," Mom was saying, her voice high and squeaky. "When do I get a break from taking care of people?"

You chose to be a nurse, I thought. *You chose parenthood. How is "taking care of people" a surprise here?*

Okay, so I knew it wasn't that simple. She was tired. She was giving so much, she was losing track of herself. I understood all that; I understood more than I wanted to admit.

"They've been fighting a lot lately," said Danielle. "One of them always goes to the store or takes a walk around the block. Why do they do that?"

"So that person can come back and everything can be okay." I pressed my cheek into the back of her head. Her hair was so damn silky and she never even shampooed it.

"Was it like that with Mom and your dad?" she asked.

"I don't really remember. I was only two." I didn't want to tell her that I imagined it had been like this. The muffled but angry voices down a hallway, and way too long between good memories. "But it must have been worse," I said instead, "because eventually, my dad didn't come back."

I'd gotten none of the real story. Only gift cards on my birthday and Christmas from an address in Oregon that looked like a small rectangle of a house in online satellite photos. Not that I searched for it (that much).

"Do you think that'll happen?" asked Dani. "Would Daddy leave and never come back?"

"Absolutely not," I said, with conviction about the second part of her question. Richard would always come back, to her at least. And if he left, he wouldn't go far. He wouldn't go anywhere, except maybe a really sweet condo in one of those new developments with a pool and workout room. Dani would get passed back and forth like a hot potato, and she'd get used to it. Two birthdays, two Christmases. An extra bedroom to fill with new toys. There were worse things.

Like me, and how much I'd miss Richard.

And also my mom being the way she was in the years before she met him.

"It's just a little fight and it isn't your fault," I said to Dani, turning her face so I could look her in the eye and she'd know I was telling the truth. "All parents have them. It's going to be okay."

Here's what I discovered about talking to my sister: sometimes I said things because she needed to hear them, and sometimes I said things because *I* needed to hear them. It never mattered that I couldn't tell the difference.

5

Finals were over and school was done, and the days now stretched as tall as they could go.

So here was summer, all official. The white noise of cicadas and crickets, rising and falling against the hum of my bedroom fan. The two big trees outside my window sighing with the breeze. Somewhere on the other side of them was Camden Armstrong.

When I got to Millie's for the first day of my new schedule—nine o'clock to two o'clock, five days a week—Richard looked up from the greeting card catalog he was flipping through, putting sticky notes on the ones he wanted to carry in the store. "Hey, ducky," he said. "It won't suck too bad, will it? Working here? I remember what it felt like at your age, to be forced to do something."

I adjusted the stool at the register to my height. "You understand why I wanted a different job, right? It had nothing to do with the store." *Say it, Ari. He deserves it.* "Or you," I added.

Richard's face warmed, even though I hadn't answered his question about the suckiness. "I do understand," he said, "and I also understand that your mom's in a weird place right now. She's worked so hard to get where she is. I think she's afraid it's all going to fall apart any second."

"We make sure it holds together," I said.

"Just until the glue dries."

"I always think of it as Velcro. When things do come undone, we can easily stick them back on."

"See, Ari. If you didn't work here, you wouldn't be allowed to use craft metaphors so freely." Richard scooped up the catalog along with some others and headed toward the back room. "I have some ordering to do," he called over his shoulder. "Holler if you need me."

It was a slow morning. Art students from a summer college program buying jumbo drawing pads. A mother and her son looking for a Batmobile model car kit, their joy at finding the last one as if we'd saved it especially for them. An elderly woman spending over twenty minutes trying to decide between two fancy journals—you know, the kind you can't actually write in because they're too beautiful—then eventually putting them both back on the shelf and walking out.

God, it was going to be a long summer. The next time the door chimed, I really had to force myself to look up and do the HiCanIHelpYou smile.

Camden's friend Max was standing in the vestibule, unstrapping his bicycle helmet.

Something in my throat now. A sandpaper-wrapped grapefruit, perhaps, or aquarium rocks. Whatever it was, I had to swallow it down if I wanted to keep breathing.

This was what always happened the summer before, seeing Max or Eliza. I'd have some kind of physical event, because it meant Camden might be nearby. I grew to know the backs of their heads as well as I knew the back of Camden's. It's an unsettling side effect of being infatuated with someone. The infatuation bleeds into everyone surrounding the person, and the sphere of things that make you feel sick with longing grows dangerously wide.

Max saw me at the register and it took him a moment to figure out why I was familiar.

"Oh, hey!" he said. "The lake, right?"

"Yes." My voice caught.

"Are you . . . Millie?"

"Oh. No. Millie's dead. My stepdad bought the store from her daughter, so I guess he's Millie now." I sounded weird to myself. High-pitched.

"I was kidding."

"I know," I lied. "Can I help you find something?" That was better.

"I. Um. Am supposed to find yarn."

Move, Ari. Act normal. Human, at the very least.

I stepped out from behind the counter and motioned for him to follow me down an aisle.

"We have some, but not very much." I glanced at Max and he smiled at me, and I realized he was only a guy looking for yarn. And that was odd, yes, but not exactly intimidating. "There was a business feud for a while," I added. "Between Millie and the lady who owns the knitting store down the street. They worked it out. We honor the treaty."

Max looked at our selection of yarn, then shook his head. "I need a super-specific color. It needs to match this." He held out a fabric swatch.

"Agnes at Knit Your Bit. She's your woman."

He shook his head again sadly. "I was hoping to avoid that. Let's just say, Millie wasn't the only one she had a feud with. We're sort of banned from shopping there."

I didn't know who "we" referred to, but the more appropriate thing for me to ask was: "What do you need it for?"

"My girlfriend, Eliza . . . she's making me a scarf."

"In the summer?" Also, *Girlfriend + Eliza.* Processing that.

Max gave me a look, and although I didn't know him, I could tell it was supposed to be a meaningful one. He held out the swatch again, so I looked at it again. Really looked at it.

Then I understood. There was a character on *Silver Arrow* named Bram, a tall alien with silver hair. And he always wore a scarf that was this color.

Eliza was making a Bram Scarf (on the fansite message boards, the real Arrowheads referred to it with one word, a Bramscarf).

Girlfriend + *Eliza* + *Bramscarf.* Still more processing needed.

"I can order the yarn for you," I said. "But don't tell anyone. You know, because of Agnes."

"No problem there. Agnes scares the shit out of me," said Max, who then leaned in closer because apparently this had become some shady deal. "How long would it take to come, if you ordered it?"

"Probably two days."

Even though I could pick the color out of a lineup from thirty feet away, I snapped a picture of the fabric swatch and took down Max's phone number.

"I'm really curious about why Agnes banned you from shopping at her store," I said, feeling more confident now.

"That answer would also involve my girlfriend. She has, you know, artistic vision. It's pretty strong. She wants what she wants and sometimes she gets a little crazy—I mean, intense about it. That's why she sent me today. She didn't want to piss anyone else off." He looked at me and smiled. His two front teeth were crooked, parted like a tiny curtain. "If she'd known it was you working here, she would have come, I'm sure."

"I'm here for all your *Silver Arrow* needs."

Max laughed hard, as if I'd said more than I'd thought. "Will you be at the lake today?"

Max asking felt like Camden asking. That mammoth lump in my throat again.

"I might." It came out as a croak. "Will you?"

"Yeah, maybe. See you then. Maybe."

Then he was gone and the door chimed, and the *FIND VERA!* poster fluttered in the sudden gust like the wave I should have made but didn't.

The town day camp was held at the rec center, whose cinder block walls and unfortunate orange-and-green interior design scheme had seen the birth of dozens of pot holders, God's eyes, and sock monkeys for at least a decade, including several I'd made as a kid myself.

When I walked into the gym, I found Danielle's group and spotted my sister standing off to the side, her counselor's hand on her shoulder. Dani was crying. When she saw me, she ran up and wrapped her arms around my waist.

"What happened?" I asked, partly to her and partly to her counselor, a college student with a headband and clipboard.

"She fell."

"Not by accident!" barked Dani, then shot a dirty look at two girls standing nearby.

"Danielle and those girls were on the playground, and they were involved in some kind of game," said the counselor, trying hard to sound calm and professional. Not really succeeding. "I guess there was a disagreement and Danielle got angry and ran away from them."

"To Lava Island," corrected Danielle.

"To Lava Island," said the counselor with emphasis, "but she fell. The nurse checked her out. She's fine. We didn't feel it necessary to call anyone."

"But it still hurts!" cried Danielle, the tears coming again. "And if they hadn't made me run away, I wouldn't have fallen!"

I took my sister's hand and started leading her out. "Thanks," I called back to the counselor. "We'll see you tomorrow."

I marched a weeping Danielle through the parking lot, me not saying a word because what was the point in saying any words, and opened the door for her when we got to the car.

"Get in," I said, rubbing her back. She did.

"We were pretending we all had imaginary ponies and then the other girls changed it to actually *being* ponies, and that wasn't how it was supposed to go!"

"I know." I reached over her to snap her seat belt. When I looked at her face, I saw one stray tear traveling down her left cheek. I pressed my finger to it, then pulled my finger away, and it was like it had never been there.

"I want to go home," said Dani, her voice shaking.

"We can't go home. Mom's sleeping. We're going to the lake."

"I don't want to." Danielle sniffled.

Yes, we could have gone somewhere else. But I'd told Max I'd be at the lake. Max had probably told Camden I'd be at the lake. I was going to the lake, dammit, melty kid sister or not.

"But I want to teach you how to dive this year, and today's

the day we'll start." I pulled that one out of nowhere. I wasn't afraid to admit I was good.

After a few more sniffles, she said, "Okay."

By the time we made the left turn at the sign for the lake, she was humming something to herself. I didn't recognize it, but it was catchy.

First order of business: a couple of warm-up jumps into the water from the side of the dock. Me first, then Danielle. Then together at the same time, both of us holding our noses. Then I showed her how to get down on one knee, point her hands into a jackknife, look at her belly, and trust.

"I'm afraid," Dani said.

"It's only water. I promise it's soft and wet, like always." I sat down a few feet away from her.

She stayed still for a long time, then finally took a deep breath and leaned all the way forward until her head broke the surface of the lake. Her feet barely cleared the dock as she went in, which made me flinch, but I wouldn't tell her that.

"Yee-haw!" she yelled when she popped out of the water. She climbed back up the ladder to the dock, and did it again. And again.

"Whenever you're ready, you can do it from standing," I finally said.

Danielle looked nervous but intrigued. "Will you show me, Ari?"

I couldn't remember the last time I dove. I used to do

it constantly when I was a kid, from the board at the end of this very dock. But the older I got, the higher the board seemed. The harder the surface of the lake looked. One day, I just didn't feel like it anymore, the way I didn't feel like doing a lot of things. Tiny things. Too small to put a name to, especially a giant one like *depression*.

"Okay," I said to Dani now. "Watch."

I stood up. Bent my knees, stretched out my arms. My body remembered.

In that last second before I broke through, the water looked suddenly green instead of brown. The shock of cold, of water in my nose, the dirty-clean and foreign-familiar taste of it. Then, a sensation of being welcomed back to something but only briefly, before the laws of buoyancy lifted me away. My eyes were closed but I could feel the light growing on my face as I floated toward the surface. When I came up, Danielle was cheering.

And Camden Armstrong was standing on the dock.

I blinked away the sting of the water a couple of extra times to make sure.

"Hey," he said, sitting down so his ankles were in the lake. Then he motioned toward Danielle. "I want to see if she does it."

"I will," said Danielle.

"Will you?" asked Camden, narrowing his eyes. I caught a teasing gleam there.

She matched his expression. "*Duh.* But I have to do five more kneeling first. Okay?"

"Okay. Then, go."

As Danielle was setting up for her dive, I climbed the ladder quickly but not too quickly, feeling self-conscious about the ten pounds I'd gained as a side effect of my medication. Then I sat down on the edge of the dock a few feet from Camden and crossed my arms so my scars weren't showing.

"I forgot," I said as the splash from Dani's dive sprayed us both. I was determined to talk to him first, and this was the best start I could come up with.

"Forgot what?"

"What it feels like, to dive."

"Why did you decide to remind yourself just now?"

Because suddenly it felt Possible.

"I wanted to show her," I said. "I can't teach her if I can't do it myself, right?"

Camden looked me in the eye for a gripping second, then glanced away. I was close enough to see his eyelashes for the first time. Thick and long. Almost girlie.

He drew one leg out of the water to scratch his ankle and said, "Forgive me for the cheesy-pick-up-line quality of this question, but do you come here often?" My heart crumpled for a moment, that he didn't remember me from last year. Then he added, "I mean, I know you've come here a lot. In the past. But this summer. Do you plan to come often this summer?"

Danielle splashed down in another dive, and I took advantage of the sudden distraction to swallow hard, breathe normally. What was he really asking?

"It's the lake," I said as calmly as I could. "Everyone comes here often." I paused. "I thought you were going to ask me something like, 'What's your sign?'"

Camden looked straight at me again, almost surprised. Crap. Those eyelashes. "I'm an Aries."

"Oh." *Oooookay.* "I'm a Libra."

"And an Arrowhead, apparently," said Camden.

I smiled. "That, too."

"I don't generally like labels, but every once in a while, it's nice when you can say you definitely *are* something. 'I am male. I am six feet tall.'"

"'I am a fan of a campy sci-fi TV show,'" I added.

Camden laughed and I waited for him to ask me more about *Silver Arrow.* Wanted him to. Badly.

"I go to Dashwood," he said instead, and the way he said it, it didn't seem like a change of subject. "Do you know where that is?" He stared out at the water as he spoke, squinting slightly, as if trying to see the words as he formed them.

"Up by the nature preserve, right? I've never been there, but I've heard of it."

It was hard to keep a straight face here. Hard to pretend this was all news, the details of his life we had so desperately hunted down a year ago.

I turned to see Danielle, who was climbing onto the dock, shaking water out of her ears.

"That was five, right?" I said, glad for a break from this conversation that was thrilling me and stressing me out at the same time. "I think you're ready."

She shook her head. "No, not yet."

"Danielle . . ."

Camden got up. "Look at it this way. You're not standing. You're just . . . not quite kneeling anymore. I'm Camden. Can I show you?"

She nodded.

Then he turned to me. "It's okay?"

"Yes. Thanks for asking." *That made me crush on you 5 percent harder.*

He went over to Danielle and asked her get down on one knee again. Then he gently picked up her bottom leg so her knees were parallel and she was squatting. He held her around the waist.

"I've got you. Try it now."

She took a few moments to psych herself up, and then she did try it. She went into the water clean.

When she surfaced, Camden let out a "Woohoo!"

"I did it!" Danielle screamed, then scrambled up the ladder. "Now I'm going to try it without you!"

"Good," said Camden, and with that, he dove into the water and swam quickly, almost sprinting, out to the raft. I watched him climb onto it and unfold in the sun. He reminded me of a cat that came up to you for petting, then ran away at the moment he seemed to be enjoying it most.

Maybe I'd offended him. Or bored him. Oh, God. Boring would definitely be worse.

I imagined diving in after him—yes, diving again—and swimming to the raft, too. Reaching for his arm and holding on tight as he helped me up. Sitting down next to him so we could continue our conversation, if that's what it had been. Showing him how astonishingly un-boring I really was, and maybe even convincing myself.

Then I heard splashing behind me and turned to see Max and Eliza rushing into the water from the beach. Squealing, because that's how cold the water still was in late June, that's the kind of pleasure-pain-pleasure dance you did with it.

I watched them swim under the rope dividing the shallow end from the deep end, headed to the raft. Doing the exact thing I'd just envisioned, the distance between me and them growing wider with every kick they made.

And in that moment I decided for sure to make that distance go away. It wasn't going to be now, because it couldn't, but it could be—*would be*—soon.

"Come on," I said to Dani. "If you do one more dive on your own from standing, I'll buy you any treat you want from the snack shack and we won't tell Mom."

6

Kendall had finally learned to make the soft serve
end in a perfect point. Last summer, they always flopped over
no matter how hard she tried. Now, when she leaned down
through the order window at Scoop-N-Putt and handed me
my chocolate-vanilla swirl in a sugar cone, I didn't even want
to lick it, it was such a work of art.

"I'm not done until nine," she said.

"That's okay," I said, sliding my money across the counter.
"I'm just happy to hang. Mom's at work and Richard told me to
go out and do 'teenage things.'"

"It's on me." Kendall pushed the money back. "Take advantage of the perks."

I sat down at a picnic table with my copy of *Silver Arrow: Velocity Matters* spread open flat so nobody could see the cover. A moment to appreciate the fact that it was eight thirty, yet the sky was still light enough to read by. The beauty of ice cream that melted exactly as fast as I could lick it. The gnome over there at Hole 1, always with the broken fingers on one hand that made it look like he was flipping you off.

Half an hour later, Kendall was done with her shift. She came out of the building wiping her hands on her shorts.

"I've started dreaming about ice cream," she said. "But not in a good way."

"Like, nightmares?"

"Yeah. Like, *The Blob*." She sat down next to me, but facing the other way, with her legs out. She pulled one knee to her chest in a stretch.

"Do you have to go straight home?" I asked.

"Not really, if I'm with you. What did you have in mind?"

"Remember last summer when we weren't allowed to drive at night yet, and we kept fantasizing about taking a ride somewhere after dark?"

Kendall smiled knowingly. "Your car or mine?"

"I've got Richard's, with the moonroof."

Once we were driving west toward the mountains, our hair whipping and snapping, Kendall kicking off her shoes to press her blue toenails against the windshield, I turned the radio up. Night air, finally dark and thinning out, puffed through the car and we simply lived in it for a few minutes.

This was an okay silence. It was the silence of knowing how to be with someone.

"Tell me some gossip," I finally said. "You must get premium dirt through this job."

"You don't really care about that stuff, do you?"

"But *you* do. This is me making an effort."

Kendall smiled mischievously. "Okay. Well. Chris Cucurullo's brother got arrested for DUI. That's the latest good one."

I hated Chris; he was a walking stereotype with his varsity jacket and excessive use of the word *bro*.

"I have to admit that neither surprises nor upsets me."

"It makes you a little glad, right? I hear the brother's a bigger douche bag than Chris. See, now you're getting the whole point of gossip."

We laughed.

"I talked to Camden yesterday." That just came out. I hadn't even been sure I wanted to tell her yet.

"A conversation?" she asked with a raised eyebrow. "Not like, *I'm sorry I'm in the men's room and we accidentally urinated together*?"

"A real one. Several minutes long. He helped Dani learn to dive off the dock."

"So . . . what? You're obsessed with him again?"

I shrugged. I'd had a Camden Dream the night before. In it, we were sitting side by side, reading the same book. Who has lame-ass dreams like this?

"You don't know anything about that guy," said Kendall.

"I know enough."

"Oh, right. Dashwood and the pink church and his painter mom."

"Lavender. You said it was lavender, or turquoise."

Kendall closed her eyes and held them there. She seemed exasperated.

"And his mom isn't a painter," I added. "She's a fabric artist."

"He told you that?"

"I Googled it." We were quiet for a few moments. Not the good quiet, anymore. "I'm sensing disapproval coming from that side of the car."

"I'm remembering how much it hurt you last summer to see him with that girl, how pissed off at yourself you were for not doing anything when you had the chance. Or in your case, a whole shitload of chances."

That made me wince. "He's not with that girl anymore. He may be with someone else, I have no idea. But I need to at least investigate further. I don't want to have any regrets like last summer."

Kendall stared at me for a moment, then nodded and said, "Fair enough."

Suddenly a song by the Shins came on the radio, a song we both loved. It was one of those moments when radio karma finds you when you need it most. I turned up the volume and Kendall started tapping her feet against the windshield, making her hands dance to the chorus, and just like that we were rescued from the intensity of the conversation.

"So where are we going?" I asked.

"Let's head up to the lookout."

We drove through town and into the cornfields, past the farm market and the orchard nobody liked, toward the place where the road dead-ended into another road that would take us up the mountain. One hairpin turn, and then we were there. A scenic overlook for the tourists that offered only a stone wall separating you from certain death down a vertical rock face.

I parked and we got out, then sat on the wall. The lights of the valley below us, the geometric shapes of crop fields, and the vague suggestion of hills and an unseen river in the distance. It was home.

"Want to share this with me?" Kendall asked as she pulled a beer out of her huge purse.

"You know I don't drink."

"Just checking, in case that's changed."

I gave her a look. "Still on the same medication so no, that hasn't changed. But that's classy, carrying beer around with you."

Kendall shrugged. "This would be part of the 'doing whatever the hell we want to' program. That girl, Claire, from work? Her father has a craft brewery. She gives these to me as a thank-you for covering for her when she's late for her shift."

She opened the bottle and took a sip, made a face, but then took another sip. Kendall had more freedom than anyone else I knew—she was the youngest of four and the only one left living at home, so her parents were pretty much over it—she never seemed compelled to take advantage of this. Until now.

I watched her, wondering how drinking a homemade beer was going to help bring her all the things she felt she'd been missing. Finally I asked, "Do you think it'll be a good summer, Kendall?"

"It might. But there's so much pressure. I mean, what makes something a good summer, anyway? Is there a checklist of things we're supposed to do?"

"It didn't used to be that way. We just had fun."

"Well, now we have other stuff." Kendall paused, took another swig of beer, and then turned to me. "Although I was thinking about how we used to hang out on the raft at the lake and play Truth. We haven't done that in a long time."

"Could that be because we're not thirteen anymore?"

"Aw, come on. You're never too old for Truth."

"Who goes first?" I asked.

"Me."

"Okay. Bring it on."

Kendall shifted on the wall and placed the bottle down beside her, took a deep breath, and then quickly pushed out the words. "When you sliced up your arm. You've always said you weren't trying to kill yourself. Is that really, truly true?"

Now that the question had been asked, she seemed to deflate with relief.

"Yes," I said. "Of course it is. All this time, you never believed me?"

Kendall's face took on extra shadow. In that shadow, I saw

the things that kept changing between us, all the distances and differences we were constantly trying to bridge.

"Can you blame me for not being so sure?" she asked faintly.

I held out my left arm and pushed up the sleeve. "Look how high these cuts are. They're nowhere near my wrists or even a main artery. You think my grasp of anatomy is that bad?"

Kendall looked long and hungry-curious at the scars. I'd never invited her to examine them before.

She swallowed hard. "So then, why?"

I paused and looked up at the sky, which seemed full of extra stars. I couldn't articulate it to myself, let alone Kendall. The pain, and the urge to punish myself for feeling it in the first place, and the need to let it out. The unbearable relief of watching my skin open up. Imagining the gashes were mouths that screamed *Help* into the silence.

"All I can tell you," I finally said, "is that at the time, I couldn't not do it. Does that make some kind of sense?"

Kendall thought about it for a moment, then nodded. "It actually does. But why . . . why . . . the other stuff . . . ?"

"You mean, why was I depressed in the first place?"

"Did something happen or . . ."

She stopped, hoping I would finish the sentence and maybe it would be one shocking revelation that would explain it all. Here came the truth I'd only admitted to my therapist.

"That was the hard part . . . ," I began, forcing the words out quickly. "Nothing happened. There was no reason. I have a mom and a stepdad and a half sister who love me. I didn't get hurt or traumatized. My biological father checking out on me was pretty bad, for sure, but that was so long ago."

I paused, and Kendall stared, and in the darkness I hoped she could see how tough this was for me.

"But still," I continued. "It came. Or maybe I should say, I think it's always been there. I get now that it's part of who I am."

A car pulled into the parking lot just then and we both glanced up to watch it. A young couple climbed out and perched themselves on the hood to light cigarettes.

"Truth," I finally said, smoothing my sleeve back down. I didn't want Kendall to say anything; I wanted it to simply be out there, floating on its own, with no need for a response to make it more true. "So now it's my turn?"

"Yup," said Kendall.

I thought hard about which honesty I wanted, and realized I wanted honesty, period. The specifics didn't matter.

"Tell me something you haven't told anyone else."

"Too vague. Don't wimp out on me here."

I sensed she was inviting me closer, over some extra barrier I didn't know was there.

"Tell me something you've been afraid to tell me," I said. The words felt risky and raw.

Kendall smiled, like I'd asked the right question, then searched my face. For what, I wasn't sure. Then she turned back to the view and finally said, "I'm spending the first semester of next year in Europe."

I laughed hard. But she gave me a look.

"Oh," I said. "You're not kidding."

"It's called the Movable School," added Kendall. "It's just for girls. We're going to England, France, and Italy. I'll get full course credit, but the classes aren't traditional. Everything's a hands-on experience. And I'll get to write. I've already set up a blog where I'm going to post travel pieces and photos."

I examined her face. "You're really not kidding."

She took a sip of beer, swallowed hard. "It's been set for a while, but I didn't know how to tell you. And I couldn't tell anyone else before I told you. So now I'm telling you."

Kendall had never said anything about wanting to spend a semester away. In Europe. I wasn't sure what was worse: the fact of her being gone, or that she'd kept all these plans to herself.

"You know how hard school has been for me," she said, wiping her mouth. Staring out at the lights scattered in front of us like ships in their own ocean. "This is my chance to save this whole four-year sentence and turn it into something meaningful."

"You're going to have a blast," I said. Which was true. We were still playing Truth, right?

"You're not upset?"

"I'm excited for you." Another truth.

I asked Kendall more about the Movable School. How many students would be in the program, where exactly they were going, and all the other things I knew I was supposed to ask. Things I really, honestly, did want to know. (*Truth*.)

She'd be leaving at the end of August.

"Some seriously exciting stuff might happen to you with this," I said in response to all the details. "New people, new experiences. You can even be a new you, if you want, because you won't be here."

"That's the idea," she mused, staring off so far, it could have been halfway to London already. "Jealous?"

"Green-eyed raging monster."

She nodded. We were quiet for a long time. Was this still the silence of knowing how to be with each other?

"Truth," said Kendall finally.

"It's a bitch," I said.

On the way back into town, I stopped to get gas. I couldn't afford to fill up Richard's car completely, but I thought half a tank would matter. Kendall waited in the car, air drumming to the radio as I operated the pump. My hand was starting to ache from squeezing the nozzle when I noticed two people rummaging in the dumpster nearby. One was so tall, he could just bend over at the waist and his head disappeared into the dumpster. He pulled out a big cardboard box.

"Nice," said the girl he was with, and this is when I realized these people were Max and Eliza. Eliza already had some stuff at her feet: Styrofoam, two or three boxes. A white vintage SUV sat nearby with the back open.

When I was done with the pump, I leaned into Kendall's window.

"Those are Camden Armstrong's friends over there. Should I go say hi?"

"Duh," she said.

So I walked over. Max was now loading the boxes and Styrofoam into the back of the car. It was Eliza who saw me first.

"Satina Galt!" she said.

"Hi."

"We go to this gas station for dumpster hauls because nobody ever comes here. What's your excuse?"

"Joyride up to the overlook."

"Ah. Nice night for it."

"What's the haul for?"

"Arts and crafts," she said. She was wearing a black skirt, a white T-shirt with the collar hacked off, and silver gladiator-style sandals. Her hair hung straight, partially in her face, and it seemed intentional. She stepped closer to look at me, at my standard-issue cutoff jean shorts and T-shirt, my purple boots. "Max tells me you're hooking him up with some yarn. Does Camden know you have that capability?"

She made it sound like I ran some kind of underworld knitting circle.

"I don't really know Camden. Just from the lake."

"Are you coming to his party?"

I stared at her blankly.

"You should come," said Eliza. "It's the first party he's ever thrown. He's worried nobody will show up."

I'd never been to a party at an unfamiliar house before. But, hell. If Kendall could go to Europe, I could go to a party full of Dashwood kids.

"I'll show up," I heard myself saying.

"Good! It's on Saturday. Do you know where the barn is?" She said it like a proper noun. The Barn.

"I thought he lived in a church."

Eliza shook her head and rolled her eyes, as if she'd heard this before. "Nope. It's a barn." She walked back to the truck and I heard a ripping noise. She came back with a trapezoid of cardboard and a highlighter pen, writing an address on it as she walked.

"Here," she said, pushing it at me. "Bring friends."

Max was getting in the SUV now so she climbed in on the passenger side. I felt hopelessly inarticulate around Eliza. I wanted to change that.

"Why are you making a Bramscarf?" I found myself shouting up to her through the window.

Eliza gave a crooked grin that somehow made her even more striking. "Saturday night. You'll see."

They both waved as they drove by, and I waved back. When they were gone, Kendall, who had heard it all, stepped out of the car.

"Did that happen?" she asked. I held up the cardboard as proof. "You're going, right?"

"If you're coming with me."

Kendall whipped out her phone. "I'm lining up a shift

switch for Saturday," she said as she started typing on it. Then she paused and looked me right in the eye. "We're going to have a lot of fun before I leave, Ari, and it's going to start with this party. I can feel it."

"No regrets, and all that?" I asked, running my finger along the edge of the cardboard.

"All that," said Kendall, "and more."

On Saturday morning, Mom dragged Dani and me to Target, intent on being there the minute it opened. The previous night had been her night off and her opportunity to sleep when most other humans do, so now she had the energy for her favorite hobby: shopping.

My mother loved to buy stuff, pure and simple. The things she put in our cart weren't fancy. They were items that felt useful but weren't really, if you thought about it for more than three seconds. Multipacks of shampoo and packages of thank-you cards, new sheets for the sofa bed even though we hadn't had anyone stay over in years.

As Mom decided between two portable car vacuums, I thought of the first time she and I went to the supermarket after we moved in with Richard. He'd given her some extra money and told her to pick up some "treats." Things had been so lean for us since my father left, when she was barely making enough as a bank teller to cover the basics. "Treats" were not in the budget. But that day, she let me choose a package of cookies. I went right for the Chips Ahoy!, because that was what Cadence Lowery from my class always had in her lunch box, and Cadence Lowery was everything.

Now, finally, Mom earned her own money, and it was pretty good money, too. I understood the mini-shopping sprees, I really did. She worked hard for the pleasure she got out of them. And Danielle? Let's just say, she'd never known how a package of Chips Ahoy! could feel like Christmas. Which was great, and also not-so-great.

As we passed the toy section, Dani asked, "Can I get a Littlest Pet Shop blue monkey? It's new. Madison has one."

"God, no; those things are so ugly," said Mom.

"And you have a hundred of them," I added.

But Dani raced down the aisle before we could stop her. She had the thing in her hand so fast, I couldn't help appreciate her talents in that area. "They have it! They have it!" she squealed.

"We're not buying any toys today," said Mom. "We talked about this. Why don't you do some chores at home, save up, and we'll come back next time."

"Ugh!" grunted Danielle, then accented it with a foot stomp. "That is the totally boring way to do it!"

Mom took a deep breath and turned to me. "Ari, I have to buy a gift for one of the nurses on maternity leave. I will meet you and *this child* in the baby department."

She made a frustrated waving gesture toward my sister as she walked away. I was the Finisher.

I stepped up to Dani, took the monkey gently out of her hand, and placed it on the shelf. Then I grabbed that hand and led her out of the aisle.

"Come on, kiddo," I said softly. "Like Mom said. Save up, and you'll get it next time."

Dani began to cry. "I know. But I really wanted it today."

"Anything worth having is worth waiting for."

"But I really wanted it *today*."

I knew how it would go. She would not be able to break out of this thought cycle. I could use a thousand rational arguments. I could hire a celebrity lawyer to explain it to her. Nothing would work. All I could do was get her out of there and stop talking about it.

We found Mom in the baby department, holding up a pair of minuscule jeans.

"What do you think?" she asked, as if nothing had happened and Dani did not still have tears pooled in her eyes. "Aren't these the most ridiculously cute pants you've ever seen?"

At home, when Mom and I were unloading the bags and Dani was in her room, I thought about all the stories from the last few days—Camden and Kendall and Max—and whether or not I wanted to share them with her.

Even after going down, down, down to *that place* then scrambling up, up, up to the Possible. The strength I'd fought to gain ounce by ounce, then using that strength to gain more. All that, and it was still so hard to talk to my mother about anything. Easy, though, not to think about why, or try (even begin to try) to fix it.

"Hey, Mom?" I asked, yanking the tag off a garlic press. "Can I sleep over at Kendall's tonight? She said she can pick me up here and drop me at the store in the morning."

Mom put down the new over-the-door towel hook she was holding. "I don't see why not," she said, squinting out the window as if she were, in fact, attempting to see why not.

"Thanks."

Tell her that you're also going to a party. Tell her about Camden.

I was about to do that, really I was, but then suddenly Mom said, "Are you sure you can trust your sister alone with me for the night?" She was peeling the price sticker off a toothbrush holder, not meeting my glance.

I dropped the garlic press and looked at her. "What?"

"I mean, clearly you're the only one who can handle Danielle." Mom's voice was cool and flat, almost robotic. It scared the crap out of me.

"Mom . . ."

"The last time you were out, she didn't even want me to read to her." Still looking at the damn toothbrush holder.

"Mom."

Then she did it. Glanced up. Saw me. *Saw* me. And the glossy topcoat of tears in my eyes. In an instant, hers welled up, too. One of those moments with someone where you know everything and also nothing at all.

"I . . . I'm sorry. Arianna . . ." She shook her head and stood up, spun away from me. "Tell Kendall I said hello," she choked out, then walked quickly down the hallway to the bathroom, toothbrush holder gripped in one fist, and closed the door.

In an alternate timeline, I might have gone to her.

In this one, I didn't.

7

We called the GPS Lady in Kendall's station wagon "Gwendolyn" because she sounded judgy and fake-British. When she took us some way that didn't feel right, Kendall would often snap something like, "Where the hell are you taking us, bitch?"

Tonight, though, we needed to trust Gwendolyn. The address from Eliza's cardboard looked completely unfamiliar. It was possibly something made up. Who lives on Chokecherry Road? And what kind of person names a place Chokecherry Road?

We drove in silence, no radio, for a while. That comfortable quiet again. The windows down and the air streaking past as if we were the ones staying in place. I ran my fingers along the embroidered red tree that stretched down the side of my brown long-sleeved shirt. With the shirt, my most-faded jeans, and a hopeful amount of eyeliner, I felt like myself but also a little bit *not*, which was a good night-out combo for me.

"We're going to a Dashwood party at some barn," said Kendall finally, as if saying it out loud made it officially happening.

"Remind me to take a photo of something at some point, so we have proof."

"I'm proud of you. A year ago, you never would have."

It was true. Sometimes you need a visible marker to remind yourself how far you've come.

"So if it's horrible," I said, "we leave, right? Should we have a secret signal if one of us wants to bail?"

"We say, 'I need to grab my copy of George W. Bush's autobiography from the car,'" proposed Kendall. "And then they'll be glad to get rid of us."

Gwendolyn led us down several winding roads and eventually told us to turn onto a dirt path with no sign. Kendall flashed me a face like, *Shit's getting real.* We passed a field of grazing horses. Then a small white outbuilding that had likely been a storage barn but now gleamed with skylights and sliding glass doors. A few hundred feet past that was an enormous barn.

"It's just red," said Kendall as she slowed the car. "I thought it was lavender."

"Or turquoise."

"How terribly disappointing."

I laughed. "Should we turn around?"

"Well," said Kendall, "this does change *everything*, but I think we should forge on."

We heard voices and music now. Kendall parked the car on the edge of a gravel driveway behind a Prius covered with bumper stickers. One said: *Do not meddle in the affairs of Dragons, for you are crunchy and taste good with ketchup!*

Kendall read it and asked, "Who the hell are these people?"

"I'm nervous," I said.

"Don't be," she said, but then undid and redid her ponytail for no reason.

"On three?" I suggested.

Kendall counted, and together we opened our doors and climbed out of the car, walking toward the lights and the sounds.

A covered porch stretched along one side of the Barn. On the porch steps, two pretty girls sat smoking. They wore gauzy sundresses and reminded me of fairies without wings.

"Hi," said one when she saw us.

"Hi," said Kendall. "This is Camden's house, right?"

"Welcome," said the other, and for some reason this made me even more nervous. She waved us inside.

We went. Forward motion, not thinking about the alternative. Through the door and into a space that was a little bit of everything and also a lot of everything.

The floor, the walls, and the ceiling were all exposed wood, weathered yet shiny. A set of evenly spaced beams tracked up both sides of the cavernous room and met in a point at the top, making it look like the house had ribs. A spiral staircase led to a second floor, which took up about half the space as the first. There was a kitchen area with a huge island, a dining area with an outrageously long farmhouse table. Beyond that, a living room zone and a set of sliding doors, open to a patio with couches and an outdoor fireplace.

The house was filled with unfamiliar faces. Some looked seventeen. Some looked twenty-seven. Some looked older and younger and in between. Out on the patio, I spotted Camden's mom sitting with a few other adults.

I wasn't even sure where to start. Kendall looked just as baffled. What had we done?

Then I heard a voice behind me.

"Satina!"

I turned to see someone in a pixie-cut brown wig, gray tank top, gray cargo pants, and a black armband on her left arm. It took me a few seconds to figure out who it was. And then I laughed, and it was a real laugh.

"Satina!" I said back.

When Eliza hugged me, I could smell the chemical scent of the wig. She wore fake silver eyelashes that felt like butterfly kisses against my cheek. The surprise of her being dressed like this, the way this recognition washed over me. I laughed again, then caught Kendall's confused expression.

"Reboot Satina meets Original Satina," said Eliza. "This is why I was hoping you'd show up."

Eliza was dressed as Satina Galt from the short-lived revival of *Silver Arrow* that aired five years earlier. They'd made the character younger, brooding and rebellious. Everything about that version of the show had been darker and more gritty, a palette of tarnished metal, social commentary, and graphic violence. Most old-school Arrowheads hated it, including my mom, but I thought it was great and never dared tell her. I watched it online in my room, at night, wearing headphones.

"This is my friend Kendall," I finally said. Eliza offered her hand and they shook.

Max walked up behind Eliza, and thanks to his silver wig and the whole yarn thing, I instantly knew which character from the *Arrow* universe he was supposed to be.

"Bram," I said. "Sir."

Max smiled, then slipped on a pair of dark sunglasses—Bramglasses—and half-bowed to me before moving on to another part of the party. Bram didn't talk much. I was impressed with Max's commitment to the character.

I scanned the room again and noticed some other people wearing costumes, or parts of costumes. A girl with a bright orange wig and skintight silver dress who looked vaguely familiar—maybe something from one of Lukas's video games? There were two other girls dressed in slutty Hogwarts uniforms, and a guy channeling Loki from *Thor*.

"Is this a costume party?" asked Kendall.

Eliza shrugged. "It didn't start out that way, but then it sort of morphed into a cosplay meetup. Here, let me show you where the drinks are." She said it in a way that prevented further questions.

Where was Camden? I couldn't wait to see him. I was terrified of seeing him.

The kitchen island had been turned into a bar. There was wine and beer, and a pitcher filled with what looked like brown sludge. But there was also seltzer and lemonade and something labeled "homemade organic herbal iced tea with rosemary" that offered way more details than necessary.

"Try this," said Eliza, pouring a glass from the pitcher. "I made it with frozen bananas, peanut butter, and two kinds of chocolate liqueur."

She handed me the glass and I took the tiniest, it-doesn't-count-as-drinking sip. It was possibly the worst thing I'd ever tasted.

Then I looked up, my mouth still trying to twist around the drink. Standing in front of me, as if he'd been there the whole time but I was only seeing him now, was Captain Atticus Marr.

Well. It was Camden.

But he was dressed like Atticus Marr. The younger, brash rookie version from the reboot rather than the seasoned and contemplative Original Marr my mom had admired so much. (Or was superhot for. I finally got that a few years back.) Like Eliza, he wore a gray T-shirt and gray cargo pants, but his uniform included a silver collarless flight jacket. He'd even swept his hair, with the help of gel or something else that looked shellacked and impenetrable, into the exact right cowlick.

It was a faithful, eerie re-creation. No question about that. Both incarnations of Atticus Marr made fangirls light-headed. I would have needed to step outside for some fresh air, if Atticus Marr were my thing.

Except he wasn't. Marr was sometimes arrogant and obvious. I liked the repressed, suffering, telepathic Dr. Azor Ray. I liked him more than a lot.

"Ari!" said Atticus/Camden. He smiled like he was glad to see me. Like that could be a real thing. "Eliza said you might be coming."

"Hey," I said, scanning the outfit. "Or do I need to call you Captain?"

"I knew you'd appreciate it. You like? It's a test run for the SuperCon later this summer. Oh, good, I see you have a drink already." He turned to Kendall, who was looking at him in a way that I didn't even want to interpret. "I'm Camden," he said. "I've seen you before."

"Ditto," said Kendall. "Your house is amazing."

"Thanks. I'll give you a tour later, if you want. Not that there's much else to see—it is a barn, after all. But I'm happy to show you the bedrooms." There was an awkward pause. "Wow, that came out wrong. I so didn't mean it like that."

Kendall laughed, then Camden did, too, when he saw he'd made it okay.

"I want to talk to you guys, but I have to give my mom

something." He grabbed a glass and poured some wine into it. "I'll be right back."

He moved away from us toward the outdoor patio, and Kendall leaned in close. "Do you think Ed Penniman bought this house for them? I wonder if he comes and visits, and where he sits."

"You didn't see the Ed Penniman Chair over there? It's got a plaque and a velvet pillow."

Kendall slapped my arm playfully. Then we were quiet again, watching Camden hand his mother the wineglass, bending down to say something in her ear, his arm protectively sweeping her shoulder.

"That must be one of her pieces," I said, directing Kendall to a large felt disk hanging on the wall, a swirl of colors like a sun from the next galaxy over.

"It is," said Eliza, reappearing and stepping between us. "I have a smaller version hanging in my room. She made it for my birthday because she knew I loved this one so much." Her eyes misted up.

It was a son's girlfriend gift, and it was also really hard not to wonder what Camden and Eliza's relationship was like now that Eliza was with Max. How long had they gone out? Was it a dumping or a mutual split? And why would Camden ever let her go because look at her, she was a freaking superstar even as Reboot Satina.

"How long have you known Camden?" asked Kendall, as if reading my mind.

"Since he started at Dashwood two years ago."

"We've never met anyone from Dashwood," said Kendall. "Isn't that weird?"

"I have a couple of friends at Fitzpatrick," said Eliza, not answering the question. "What do you do there?"

"What do you mean? We go to school."

"What are your *interests*? Activities?"

"I'm on the newspaper staff," offered Kendall.

"Perfect. Then I know exactly who to introduce you to." She grabbed Kendall's elbow and guided her away. I started to follow them, but then caught sight of Camden moving back toward me. So I stayed, and turned to him, and tried to keep breathing.

He looked down at my drink. "How is that?"

"Um . . ."

"I assumed as much." He took it out of my hand and placed it on a nearby counter, and there was something simple and chivalrous about the gesture that made that floating thing happen to my kneecaps. "Your friend seems to be gone. Do you want the tour anyway?"

I nodded, and he nodded back, then indicated that I should follow him. A simple tilt of his head, with his eyes on me. My God. Did he know that's all it would take for me to go with him anywhere?

He led me out of the kitchen area and through the living room zone, then up the spiral stairs, past some guy sitting on a single step playing the mandolin as if that weren't completely random. The stairs were narrow and steep, which made me focus on putting one foot in front of the other. I gripped the railing hard.

On the second level, there was a small landing with a couch and wood-burning stove. Three closed doors led off of it. A floor-to-ceiling window overlooked some hills to the west, where the sun had just set and the sky was an abstract quilt of reds and blues about to fade forever.

Without a word, Camden slid one panel of the window open, then the other, and stepped up to it so the tips of his boots were practically on the ledge. There was no screen. He took a deep breath and closed his eyes.

I hung back, but he turned to me and tilted his head again. *Come try.*

One foot in front of the other, again and again. If only all clichés could be so true and useful.

Eventually, my purple feet lined up next to his glossy black combat ones, the toes slightly over the ledge.

Air. Light. Smells. Sounds. I felt the overwhelming temptation to take a step forward out the window, but also the self-control to not do it. The thrill of that. The power of choosing one over the other.

The power of knowing my choice might have been different eighteen months ago, but that was not now.

"My mom put in this window so we could do exactly this. I mean, she practices yoga and meditation here. But I like to just . . . be exposed." He shook his head. "Camden, why do you keep saying creepy shit? I meant, not in a naked way but in a—"

"I know what you meant," I said.

He sighed with relief and turned back to stare out the window. Or rather, the absence of a window.

"What's it like, going to Fitzpatrick?" he asked. "I've never been to public school. I'd never been to school at all, before Dashwood."

"You were homeschooled?"

"Yup."

"I could ask you what *that's* like. Because *that* seems much more interesting."

"But I went first."

I shrugged. "It's high school. There are a lot of rules. Some of them are official, and some aren't."

"And you have to follow them all?"

"If you want the whole experience to be tolerable, then pretty much yes."

Camden nodded, but still looked wistful, as if I'd made it sound like a place worth being. "But don't you go to football games and everyone cheers for the team?"

"I've never been to a football game."

"Oh," he said softly. "If I went to Fitzpatrick, I'd go to the football games. So I could be part of something."

He grew suddenly quiet. I felt like I'd let him down somehow.

"But I do Mock Trial," I offered. "Or I did. That's also a

team. An incredibly nerdy one, but still a team."

"I would cheer for that. For you."

We were silent for a moment. His eyes met mine. The *for you* seemed visible in the air after he said it, like breath on a cold day.

"We get to wear costumes," I said, trying to keep the conversation going, keep myself from freezing up. "Sort of. Lawyer-type suits and whatever clothes your character would wear. Not like actual cosplay. Pretty impressive, by the way."

I motioned to his silver jacket. He looked down at my boots.

"I know, I know," he said sheepishly. "You're a fan of the *Arrow* Original, right? You think the *Arrow* Reboot was lame and ill-conceived. Something they did to capitalize on the fandom."

"I didn't like what they did to Satina, and the relationship between her and Marr, but some of it was really intelligent."

"But you prefer the original."

"Do I have to choose one or the other? Can't I love them both in a complicated way that doesn't involve nicknames and acronyms?"

He smiled, and I caught a glimpse of something that looked like respect in his eyes. "Of course. Of course you can."

"What about you? Do you have a preference, or is that a stupid question given your choice of outfit?"

Camden thought about it for a while, blinking those long lashes at the sunset.

"Sometimes you think you like something because your

friends like it," he finally said. "Because you want to join. You go along. And then, by going along . . . that's your way in. You discover it for yourself. You own it in a way that's different from how anyone else owns it. Is that a backward way to fall in love with a thing?"

He looked expectantly at me, into me, as if my opinion actually mattered.

The word *no* had possibly never been so hard or taken me so long to form on my lips. It was almost out, and many more words after that, when a loud cheer came from downstairs. Then a wave of clapping. I heard someone banging on a drum set, rapid and sudden like gunfire.

"Sounds like the band is about to start," said Camden. "You don't want to miss it." He closed the window and took a few steps away, then stopped and turned back to me.

"You're staying the night, right?"

"Pardon?"

"The campout. When my mom has a party, it tends not to end. People sleep over, on couches or the floor or they pitch tents in the back. And we don't have to worry about everyone getting home safely."

"Eliza didn't tell me that. I didn't bring anything . . ."

He reached out and took my hand. His skin on mine. Warmer than I ever imagined. In all my fantasizing, I never took body temperature into consideration.

"Good, because you don't need anything. You just need to not leave."

We looked at each other for two full seconds before his gaze fell to the ground and away. He let my hand go and I let it drop, as if stunned and rendered useless.

I thought of Mom and Dani and Richard, each in their pajamas and frustration. I thought of the small, small windows of my house and the to-do list on the fridge. Kendall downstairs somewhere; she would not be able to stay, too, but would definitely lie for me.

And there it was again, no longer a whisper in my ear but now a *whoosh*.

The Possible.

I followed Camden Armstrong close down the spiral stairs and into the rest of his world.

The house was mostly empty now, and the music from outside was louder. Camden and I stepped through the door to the patio, where most of the party guests had gathered in a dance cluster. Off to one side, there was a band set up. Not some crappy high school band but a real one. With adults. Who I recognized.

"You hired the Plastic Masks to play at your party?" I yelled to Camden over the bass line.

"Not hired. They're friends with my mom." We watched and listened for a few moments, then Camden added, "Speaking of which, I want you to meet her."

He took my hand again—*zing!*—and led me to where Maeve Armstrong stood near the side of the barn. I didn't have time to protest, to feel weird about it, to get nervous. Suddenly we were there, in front of this woman who managed to appear removed from the action, but also at the heart of it, simply in the way she leaned against a wall.

"Mom," he said, letting go of my hand but putting his fingertips gently on my back (*zing!* again). "This is Ari. She's a new friend."

Camden's mother lit up when she saw him, then stayed lit up when her gaze traveled to me. At close range, she looked much more weathered, with streaks of gray in her auburn hair, deep lines around the freckles. She reminded me of what Kendall might look like in twenty-five years. There was even less resemblance between her and her son than between my mom and me, except Maeve and Camden had the same green eyes.

"Ari," said Maeve carefully, as if she was tasting my name on her tongue. "I saw you once at the lake with that adorable little girl. You were so good with her."

"My sister," I said, and fought the urge to bow my head or drop to one knee. Why did it feel like I was meeting royalty? "You have a good memory."

"For things that strike me as beautiful, yes."

Those green eyes searched into me exactly the way her son's did. I felt revealed.

"Ari goes to Fitzpatrick," said Camden after a pause, making it sound like an interesting fact.

"Fitzpatrick," Maeve repeated, unsure.

"The public high school you wouldn't let me go to?" Camden

turned to me then. "I wanted to. She was against school for me, period. Dashwood was a compromise."

"Dashwood was the right choice," said Maeve, reaching out and tucking some of Camden's hair behind one ear. It seemed like he wanted to shrink away, but forced himself not to. "Not Fitzpatrick. Classes where you have to sit at a desk? Tests? Homework? I couldn't do that to you." She turned to me. "I'm sorry, I don't mean to be insulting to your school."

"You can be as insulting as you want," I said. "It's nothing special."

"See?" said Maeve to her son. "*You're* special, Camden March Armstrong. You don't belong somewhere that's not special."

Maeve was a parent who was against her kid having homework. Maeve casually said things to her son like *You're special.* Maeve helped her son throw a party with the Plastic Masks.

"Are you real?" I blurted out.

Maeve looked confused for a moment, then threw her head back and laughed. "Yes," she said. "We do exist, the cool parents." She glanced at Camden, who was examining his fingernails. "As do the children of the cool parents."

Camden raised his head to glare at her for a second, then touched my shoulder and motioned with his head toward the dancing. There was something pleading in his eyes, like *Get me away from this.* I nodded yes.

We wove ourselves into the knot of people until we found a little loop of space. He spun toward me and smiled, all dimples and dazzle. As if everything was a private joke between us—the party, the music, the thousand stars in the purple sky. He struck a *Saturday Night Fever* disco pose, and I laughed, and then it was happening. We were dancing. Together.

And he was dressed like Atticus Marr.

I got that feeling you get when you want to enjoy every second of an amazing situation, and you totally would, if the amazingness weren't completely freaking you out.

I felt a tap on my shoulder. There was Kendall, smiling her old smile for me. It took me a few seconds to realize there was a boy dancing *with* her. Blond curls, thick glasses. Dorky adorable.

Kendall leaned in close and said, "James."

I just said, "Nice."

The four of us danced in a square, and I could feel the awkwardness falling away until we were practically trampling it.

Suddenly, Eliza appeared between Camden and me, pulling Max along behind her. She turned and wrapped her arms around Max's—well, not his neck because she couldn't reach that, but his chest and back—and kept them moving all over. She pressed her body into his and they both had their eyes closed. Satina Galt dancing with Bram, breaking all the rules of the *Silver Arrow* universe. Not even caring.

Camden pushed them aside.

"Get a room, you guys!" he yelled as he moved closer to me. Eliza flashed him a devious glance, and I wondered why she'd done it, placed her bump-and-grind couplehood in between us like that. Was it for Camden's benefit? Or mine? There was no trace of jealousy on Camden's face. Only annoyance.

Camden took my hand and raised it high so I could twirl all the way in one direction, then all the way back. When I was done, I found myself releasing his hand and taking a step back. James had pulled Kendall into a close dance hold, like they were about to do a waltz, and she laughed loud above the music.

Atticus Marr and Bram and Satina Galt.

Around us, almost everyone in pairs, most of them close or touching. The air thick with anticipation and meaning. The intensity of it, and the effort it took to pretend I didn't notice the intensity of it.

So much like another night, at another party, at another boy's house. Lukas and I had been dating for three months, and there had been expectation that night, too. When the party started to disperse and I let him lead me down to his basement family room, I'd felt like I was keeping an appointment it would be rude to cancel at the last minute. There was pressure to be part of the program, to go along with the plan.

So I'd done things I didn't want to do. They made me feel meek and malleable, a feeling that threatened to knock me off the delicate balance I'd gained at the time. After that night, everything was different between Lukas and me. After that night, I began to push him away.

This is different, I said to myself. *And also, Camden. Camden, Camden.*

Eliza pulled Max's head down so she could lasso her arms around his neck, then jumped onto him so her legs were wrapped around his waist. They were kissing madly.

Camden stopped dancing so he could watch them.

Was this giving him ideas? Was there some drama unfolding here that I was about to get sucked into?

Before I understood why, before I could overthink it, I leaned into him and said, "I have to run inside for a minute." He nodded and I pushed my way out of the crowd.

Back in the kitchen, I was drinking a glass of the long-named iced tea when Kendall appeared.

"Ari?"

I slammed the iced tea down on the counter. "Yes. That's me. The person who was just dancing with Camden Armstrong to the Plastic Masks. At least, I think it was."

"I saw you run inside. You okay?"

"Me? I'm having the time of my life."

"And . . . ?"

I paused, thinking of how it felt to stand with Camden in that open window. Like he was telling me he understood about the Possible, although we had never discussed it.

"And it's scaring the crap out of me. You know, Camden asked me to stay over."

"*What?*"

"I mean, along with a whole bunch of other people. I guess it's something they do. For safety? So people don't drive home drunk?"

"Oh. Well. Still. That's a little much." She looked at me more thoroughly. "Are you feeling weird that he asked?"

"I'm feeling weird about everything," I said. "A good weird. A great weird. But . . ."

"A scary weird. I get it." Kendall paused, glancing out to the patio. "Do you want to leave?"

"No," I answered quickly. "Actually, yes. Well . . . no . . ."

Kendall gave me a look. "If you're going to make me leave this party, you'd better be sure."

"Okay. I want to leave."

She nodded grimly. "Then let's go."

"What about James?"

Kendall smiled at the sound of his name. "We already exchanged email addresses."

"Kendall!"

"He's into photography and he's traveled all over England and Ireland." She turned to stare wistfully outside again.

"You met a guy and now I'm ruining—"

"I came for you, Ari," interrupted Kendall. "I'll leave for you, too."

I hugged her. My friend. My best friend. Maybe not forever, but here and now.

After a moment, she pulled away and said, "I'll wait in the car. Why don't you go say good-bye to your boy, and for God's sake, give him your number."

Back on the patio, the band was still loud and people were still moving frenetically, but I didn't see Camden. I climbed

113

onto a wooden chair so I could get a better look at the crowd, but that head, that hair, was nowhere. I circled the outside of the barn once, scanning the darkness for shapes and voices, and found nothing.

I looped back inside. Maeve Armstrong was sitting on some older guy's lap in the living room, deep in conversation, and didn't notice me. I went halfway up the spiral stairs but the landing was empty.

When I came down, I spotted a notepad and pen stuck to the fridge. It was not how I wanted the night to end, but it was better than nothing.

Camden,

Wanted to stay, but something came up. I wouldn't mind more travels with Atticus Mann. Call when you can.

Ari

I left the note on the pad, my number scrawled at the bottom. Every step I took toward the door, part of me wanted to turn back. What good is *no regrets* when there's an equal chance of regretting it either way?

"Am I an idiot for leaving?" I asked as I slid into the passenger seat of Kendall's car.

"I guess you'll find out," said Kendall with a shrug. She paused, examining my face. "This was about that night at Lukas's, wasn't it?"

Couldn't speak. Could only nod.

"I knew it," said Kendall. "I remember how that threw you."

Threw you was a new and interesting way to describe how much I hated myself for letting things go so far, and for realizing I didn't love Lukas. Kendall didn't know about the other parts because I didn't tell her. The pristine white skin of my right arm, daring me to let out some of this fresh pain. The shoe box with the razors and the cotton balls, hidden at the back of my closet. The urge to see it. Open it. The strength it took to resist.

Instead, I'd told my therapist about these feelings (but not about the box, because that was one secret I needed to hold on to). My therapist told my doctor, and my doctor tinkered with my dosage.

"Yes," I finally said. "It threw me good."

We drove home with all four windows down, the breeze deep in my lungs.

I looked at my hand and wondered where the creases on Camden's palm had lined up with the ones on mine.

I'd left my number. It would have felt worse if I hadn't, but I was sort of at his mercy now.

Wait, who was I kidding? I'd been at his mercy all along.

8

I opened my eyes in the half-light of Kendall's bedroom, not sure what time it was or whether I had actually slept at all.

This room was so familiar from our years of sleepovers. The blue shag area rug on the floor next to me, the pile of dirty clothing that was always different but also, somehow, the same. Kendall's ceiling with the hot-air balloon mobile hanging in the corner, the window with the cracked pane, that poster of the kittens eating cake. Even the air mattress under my sleeping bag was a type of home.

In this moment, it was easy to feel like the night before had never happened, that none of its strange magic or glorious surprises had, in fact, been real. Maybe we were still twelve, fourteen, sixteen, and we'd made it all up in a story we'd told each other in the dark.

"Will you help me write an email to James?" said Kendall's voice suddenly from the bed.

"You're awake?"

"Duh."

I laughed with relief.

"Did you sleep at all?" I asked.

"I'm not sure."

I laughed again, then got up, retrieved Kendall's laptop from her desk, and fell onto the foot of her bed.

"Move over," I said.

She scooched close to her pillows and hugged her knees close.

"Do you think he liked me?" she asked.

"Uh, yeah."

"Because they always seem like they like me, at first. But then something changes. I can't figure out what."

"It's not you," I said, not sure if that were completely true. Kendall usually clammed up and got so shy, so nervous. The more she liked someone and the closer they got to something sparking, the weirder she started acting. I could easily see how a guy could misinterpret that as her pushing him away. But I'd never been able to tell her this. Especially after Lady Bic Night, and after Lukas. Our lives had diverged too much in this department.

But right now, we were at the same point, hovering on the edge of something with someone. This changed everything.

"I guess we'll see," said Kendall.

"You've been lying here, writing a rough draft in your head, yes?"

"Oh, yes."

I passed her the laptop. "Okay, show me."

Kendall pulled up to the curb in front of Millie's. We'd pressed Send on her email to James and jumped on the air mattress for a few minutes. I was convinced that light rays of nervous energy were about to shoot out of our fingers.

"You'll keep me posted?" I asked.

"You'll turn on your goddamn phone at some point?" she shot back, pointing with her chin at my bag. I hadn't yet dared switch it on. If it wasn't on, I couldn't *not* get a call.

"Yes, yes."

"Do it now. I want to watch you do it."

I gave her a dirty look. "Fine. But there won't be anything. It's too early."

I fished out my phone, held down the Power button, and the screen lit up. We waited for a few seconds for it to tell me I had a voice mail.

It didn't tell me I had a voice mail.

"Too early, like you said," said Kendall.

We both stared at the phone as if it might offer a more expert opinion. *According to my data, the average turnaround*

*time for a "call me" request to a potential love interest is 18.5
hours. If at all.*

After Kendall drove away, I turned to see Richard standing
in the window of the store, holding up two coffees.

"Fun night?" he asked as I came inside and took one of the
coffees from him.

"Amazing," I said, realizing it was true regardless of what
happened next.

What happened next was that I made myself busy for an
hour. Max's yarn had come in the previous afternoon, and I
packed it up in a crisp brown paper bag with handles.

Two people came into the store during that time, and neither of them bought anything. I watched Richard watch the
FIND VERA! flyer as the door closed behind each one, until it
stopped fluttering and finally became still.

"Aren't Sunday mornings always slow?" I asked, waving my
hand in front of his face.

"Yes, yes," he said, snapping out of it.

"It'll be okay," I offered, even though I wasn't sure what *it*
was. Maybe that didn't matter. It was a fill-in-the-blanks thing
to say.

My phone buzzed in my pocket. My breath caught. My
adrenaline surged.

It was not a number I recognized.

"Hello?" I said, my voice shaking.

"Ari?" asked Camden. He sounded far away. Fainter, and
quieter. Tired, or nervous.

I swallowed hard, to make sure my throat was even working.

"You found my note." I'd discussed this with Kendall, and we'd decided this was the best opening line. It came out okay. Almost regular.

"Eliza found it and stuffed it in my pants while I was sleeping."

"Oh. That's . . . sweet?"

"The Eliza version, yes."

We both laughed, then fell quiet. I felt like we'd traveled successfully up the ramp to this conversation and were now cleared for takeoff. Richard looked up at me from where he sat at the counter.

"Can I have a few minutes?" I whispered to Richard, dropping the phone to my side. Richard smiled and nodded. "Hang on," I then told Camden.

I went through the storeroom and then out the back door, where I sat down on one of the three wooden steps that led into the alley. It was the most privacy I was going to get anytime soon.

"Where did you take me?" asked Camden.

"To the alley behind Millie's Art Supply."

"What are you looking at?"

His voice now. Throaty and curious. The soft curve of interest in it, painfully lovely.

I paused. "Two dumpsters. A blue Ford pickup truck that's been parked here since last winter. A pair of sneakers hanging from the telephone lines."

"What color are the dumpsters?" he asked.

"Black," I said.

"Ah, okay. Got it. I can see you."

Can you, Camden? And what do you see in me that I can't see in myself?

"What about you?" I asked.

"I'm in my room," he said. "I'm looking up at my skylight. It's a perfect rectangle of blue. Kind of looks like someone painted the color right onto my ceiling."

We were silent again. Awkward. But also, not. I wondered where he was in his room. I wondered if he were lying on his bed, but didn't want to ask him any questions that had the word *bed* in them. I wondered if he was in pajamas or had slept in his clothes, the Atticus Marr costume's T-shirt and pants. I pictured the combat boots sitting on the floor, the flight jacket hanging over the back of a chair.

"I'm sorry I had to leave last night," I said, hoping he wouldn't ask for more explanation.

"I am, too."

Silence again. I heard him take a deep breath, and it sent a flush of heat down the side of my neck, how loud and close it was in my ear. How person-like it made him. "I can't talk long," he said after a few moments. "I'm leaving in a bit for Vermont."

I felt something inside me lurch to a stop.

"Oh," I said. "How long are you staying?"

"I'm not," he said, and the lurching sensation dissolved into relief. "I'm just driving my mom up there and dropping her off. She's spending the summer at an artists' colony outside Burlington."

"The word *colony* always makes me think of the Revolutionary War," I said, "but I'm guessing it has nothing to do with that."

Camden snorted. "Think more *leper* colony. They give her a studio and she makes her art, and then hangs out with other artists. I'm not sure how that's different from what she does here, but whatever." He paused. "No, I know what the difference is. The difference is that I'm not there. You know, to distract her. Or judge her."

"Is someone staying at the Barn with you while she's gone?"

"Just Max and Eliza, when they can. Some other friends will probably drop in and out. But if you mean a legal adult there every night, then no."

"Wow."

"It wouldn't be the first time."

I thought for a second about what that might be like, to be left to live alone for an entire summer. A slice of heaven, is what it might be like.

But I didn't tell him I was thinking that. Instead I asked, "How do you manage to NOT turn that situation into a bad eighties movie?"

Camden laughed. Hard. It made every hair on my arm stand on end to hear it.

"Well, we did have the wild party *before* my mom even left," he said.

"That's true. You know how to buck the clichés."

There was a pause on the other end of the line. A car raced down the alley, too fast, the roar of it filling the pause and making it feel like something planned. I tried to picture Camden again, tried to imagine what he was looking at on his end. How tightly he was holding his phone, what he was doing with his other hand. Whether he was still trying to picture me.

"So do you," said Camden.

"So do I what?"

"Know how to buck the clichés."

"I'm not sure what you mean," I said, keeping my voice light and teasing. Giving him no inkling that inside I was pleading *Tell me! Tell me more about what I know!*

"I guess you seem . . . not like the other Fitzpatrick kids I've seen around. Maybe more serious. More mature. Like you've been through something and changed." He paused. "I'm sorry, I don't want to be making assumptions about you. It's those damn Satina Galt boots."

I had no response, stunned that he'd glimpsed me so clearly in such a short time. Camden must have taken my silence for being insulted.

"Anyway," he said quickly, nervously. "Speaking of Satina Galt. Can you meet me at the lake tomorrow? I want to show you something."

I thought about my calendar. My mom was working, which meant I'd have Danielle with me. But Tuesday . . . Tuesday I'd have to myself.

"I can meet you the day after," I said. "I work at the store until two o'clock, but then I'm free." The thought of having to wait two whole days to see him . . . well, that sucked.

"The day after," said Camden. "We'll say two thirty."

It felt like the conversation was over. I knew it had to be. I had to go inside. He had to drive to Vermont. I was torn between not wanting to hang up, ever, and desperate to do so while it still felt perfect. You know, before I said something stupid.

"See you then," I said.

"Okay, bye, Ari."

"Bye," I said, but he was already gone. The phone felt warmer than usual in my hand, the screen glowing a little brighter, I was sure.

One of the sneakers hanging from the telephone line was slowly turning in the breeze. I waited for it to do two complete circles before standing up and going back into the store.

9

It had been a long two days, but now I was leaning against a tree at the reservoir parking lot, watching Camden glide toward me on his bicycle.

Seeing his face in person again and not pressed into the blackness behind my eyelids, I couldn't decide if it looked the same. Was it going to be this way from now on? Every time I saw him, would I have to reconcile the Camden I was looking at with the Camden I'd been thinking about?

He was wearing a cranberry-colored button-down shirt and navy blue swim trunks, sneakers with no laces or socks. I saw the skin of his right ankle as he pedaled and had a sudden urge to lick it.

"Hey," he said, braking to a halt in front of me. "You came."

"Why wouldn't I come?"

Camden stared blankly for a second, then laughed. "I don't know why I just said that."

Before I could respond, Max's SUV pulled up. Eliza waved from the passenger window, then jumped down from the car.

"You came," she said.

"Why wouldn't she come?" asked Camden.

When Max appeared from his side of the SUV, I held out the paper bag with the yarn in it. "I come bearing the makings of a Bramscarf."

Eliza squealed and snatched the bag from me, peeked inside. "Perfection!" she proclaimed.

"It's not quite the color of the swatch you gave me. It's actually a little darker, but more accurate."

She looked up at me, her eyes wide and serious. "You're good. You're good at this."

"I'm good at *Silver Arrow*."

Max turned to Camden and said, "She's going to guess it right away."

"Shhh," snapped Camden. "I want it to be a surprise."

"You want what to be a surprise?" I asked.

"The *surprise*," he said, smiling with delicious mischief. I could taste it even from where I stood.

He gestured for us to walk toward the Crapper, where he paid for my admission. Julian was there again, and it was fun to watch the slow dawning of his expression as he realized I was with Those Dashwood Kids. I followed them toward the beach, but before they got to the spot where the trees stopped and the sand started, they suddenly veered to the left, toward the entrance to that trail I knew led into the woods.

"We're not going to the lake," I said stupidly.

"No," said Camden, hanging back so Eliza and Max could walk in front of us. "We're going to the surprise."

Camden let me go first as I stepped onto the trail, almost a tunnel with its canopy of branches arced above our heads. We walked for a minute in silence, and I thought of all the times I'd watched him and Eliza and Max disappear into these woods. How I'd wondered what they did there, and how the wondering itself burned up inside me. Was this going to be about drinking or smoking something? Whatever they offered me, I wouldn't take it. Was there a way to explain why, without ruining everything?

Ahead of us, Max slid his hand into Eliza's.

"There's dog hair on your sleeve," he said to her.

She reached down and pulled something off herself, flicked it away. "Sorry. I thought I'd thoroughly de-furred." Then she glanced over her shoulder at me and said, "My pet-sitting business and Max's allergies make us a little like Romeo and Juliet, don't you think? But I can't give it up. Cosplay is not a cheap hobby, and you can only get so much raw material from dumpsters."

"You're star-crossed," I said.

She smiled a smile that showed her teeth before turning

back around. Did that mean she liked me? Did that mean it mattered?

"What about you, Max?" I asked, suddenly wanting more of all of them and not just Camden. "Are you working this summer?"

"I'm helping my dad at his computer programming firm. I'd explain exactly what I do there, but it's so boring, you might nod off and fall and injure yourself."

"Thanks for the safety considerations," I said with a laugh.

"You wouldn't know it to look at him," said Camden, "but Max is a coding genius."

Eliza glanced back proudly at Camden. "And Camden's volunteering with the youth hotline at Family Services. He wants to save the world."

"I don't need to save the world . . . ," said Camden softly, shyly. "But maybe one or two people would be cool."

I'd never experienced this before, friends talking as if they were a collective.

"What do kids call the hotline about?" I asked, trying to hide how Camden's job impressed me. Was it wrong that this made him extra attractive?

"All the fun stuff," said Camden sarcastically. "They're being abused, or they want to run away. They realize they're addicted to drugs or alcohol and they don't know how to get help. They're depressed or even suicidal, and they want to hurt themselves but also they don't."

I paused for a second, missing a half step, before continuing.

Back when I couldn't stop thinking about opening up my skin, it had never occurred to me to call a youth hotline. What if it had? What if I'd called and talked to someone like Camden? I felt oddly happy for the kids who did.

Eliza and Max suddenly stopped walking. The trail had opened up, running parallel to a rocky creek about thirty feet wide.

"Wait. Where are we?" I asked.

"I think it has a name," said Max. "Something Falls. But we call it . . ."

"Hush!" said Camden with a meaningful look at Max.

"I've been coming to the lake my whole life," I said, watching the water travel busily downhill, oblivious to us. "I had no idea this was here."

"We only found it by happy accident," said Max. He stepped into the water and held out a hand for Eliza. Together they made their way through the ankle-deep creek and across some smaller rocks to a large one, flat and wide, lit by the sun. There, they crumpled together and started to kiss. Not kiss, really. More like, try to crawl inside each other's faces.

"Come this way," said Camden, touching my elbow as he stepped past me on the trail. "We have to go a little farther down."

After we fell into step together, curiosity overpowered me and I asked, "Does it bother you? That Eliza and Max are so . . . PDA-oriented?"

Camden frowned. "Why would it bother me?"

"Because you and Eliza used to go out, right?"

He paused for a second, then started walking again. "How did you know that?"

"I saw you together last summer. At the lake." I said it as casually as I could, as if I were just remembering it now.

"We only went out for a few weeks, and I was the one who broke up with her. I actually encouraged things to happen with Max. I'm happy they're happy. I'm happy we found a way to still all be together, because I would have hated to lose that." He suddenly sped ahead. "We're almost there," he called over his shoulder.

I followed Camden another few yards and around a bend, until he stopped. The creek ran over a rock face here. It was steep, and I could see the rock was covered in green moss. The movement of the water made the moss appear as if it were moving on its own, a bubbling entity under the surface.

Camden pulled his shirt over his head and hung it on the branch of a nearby bush. Even though I'd seen him shirtless before, I found myself glancing away. He didn't speak, but simply made his way from the trail and down the bank. It wasn't until he stepped into the water that he turned, finally, to face me.

"Does this remind you of anything?" he asked, spreading his arms wide and fanning his fingers.

We had so little shared experience. I knew he must be talking about *Silver Arrow*, and then it suddenly seemed so clear.

"'Do No Good,' Season Four."

Camden threw his head back and practically crowed, Peter Pan–style.

"Do No Good" was an episode set on a planet populated by sentient rocks. (Yes, it was one of the sillier ones. Which probably explained why I loved it so much when I was seven years old.) Azor Ray communicated telepathically with the rocks while Satina and Marr set out to find the largest rock on the planet, known as the Great Mass (the silliness, remember?), for help getting the *Arrow One* back in action. They had to cross a river filled with guardian rocks to reach this big one.

The creek, the rocks, even the way the trees on the bank bent and bowed toward the water—it all looked eerily like that scene.

"This is freaking me out a little," I said.

Camden grinned and held out his hand to me. "Come down here."

"It looks really slippery."

"It is. But I know the good footholds."

I took off my boots and slipped my dress over my head, thinking of how carefully I'd chosen my bathing suit that morning, and draped it on the branch next to Camden's shirt.

I took a step down from the bank and into the water, which gathered so cold and frenetically around my ankles. Then I reached and on the other side of that reach was Camden's waiting hand. I grabbed it, felt a jolt of warmth. Then I stepped up close to him.

"I knew you'd get it," he said. "I love that episode."

"For years, I talked to rocks," I admitted. "Until my mother made me stop."

"I was thinking we could do a cosplay photo shoot here someday."

"But you guys only have the reboot costumes."

"Maybe we'll make new ones," he said, something suddenly ablaze in his eyes. "I have one more thing to show you, but we have to get over there to be able to see it." Then he pointed downhill, toward a pool of water where the creek flattened out about thirty feet away.

"And we do that how?"

"We slide. I'll show you."

He took one careful step, then another, then lowered himself so he was sitting on the rock. He flashed me a devastating smile, then pushed off with both hands. The flow of water caught him and pulled him down the creek, away from me, faster and faster. He let out a whoop as he landed in the pool.

"So easy!" he shouted as he climbed up onto a rock. "So fun!"

"You've never gotten, like, a concussion doing that?" I shouted back.

"No." He scratched his head. "Well, not a bad one. You gonna try it?"

I didn't really want to try it. But also, I did. Badly.

"If you feel like you're going to tip backward and crack open your skull, clasp your hands behind your head. That's what Eliza does."

"Thanks for the tip."

I stood there. Afraid to take even a step, because it didn't seem possible that my foot could find steady purchase on the rock face.

"I'll catch you when you get here," yelled Camden.

I flashed him a thumbs-up, then took a step onto the spot Camden had pushed off from. Sat down on the rock, the moss soft as fuzz. Why was I doing this? To save face, to look like a good sport, to please a boy? Because I'd probably regret it if I didn't? That was all part of it. But I thought of Satina and how this kind of thing was nothing to her. She felt present here.

I pushed, and started moving, and continued moving. It was like the water was playing with me, tugging and nudging, tipping me off balance. I kept my hands firmly planted on the rock, felt its bumps and ridges painfully under my palms as I slid. Before I knew it, I was going feetfirst into the pool, closing my eyes just before I went under. When I came back up, the first thing I saw was Camden's face.

"That was spectacular," he said.

I swam to where he sat on the rock and he helped me up. The rock was barely big enough for him to leave a sliver of space between his body and mine.

We were silent as I took a few seconds to catch my breath. I remembered a scene with Atticus and Satina in the "Do No Good" episode. How Atticus had stumbled on his way across the river, and how Satina had caught him (and how my mother used to shout at the TV, "You go, Satina! Sometimes the men need saving, too!"). How, after Satina had grabbed his arm and pulled him close, they'd had one of those Almost-Something Moments.

Were Camden and I having this kind of moment? I felt like if I turned to look at him, I'd know.

Go ahead, you idiot. Turn to him. Know.

But then Camden pointed with his chin and said, "Look over there."

We were sitting where the creek was about to make a hairpin turn to the right, and beyond that curve was an open expanse of water.

It was a lake.

Oh. Our lake.

In the distance, I could see the dock and the diving board, the red-and-white dots of the buoys. The beach and the colorful smudges of people on it.

We were looking at it all from the far side of the lake. I felt a strange rush of intimacy with it, a new understanding of its many dimensions.

"You're in that forbidden zone beyond the rope," said Camden.

I dared to turn to him now. "You remember that?"

"Yes."

His eyes searched my face and there was no denying it. The Moment-ness of this moment.

I turned away quickly, all instinct, stared out at the scene before us, and asked, "What do you love about *Silver Arrow*?"

Camden took in a long, slow breath. "I like the idea of being on a ship, part of a crew. Part of a whole. Belonging to something." He stopped abruptly and shook his head, as if trying to reset whatever his next thought was. "What about you, Ari? Why are you such a fan?"

He said my name. His mouth wrapped around the same vowel-consonant-vowel progression I'd heard ten thousand times before, but it had never shaken me like this.

"I've never really thought about it."

"Think about it now."

I glanced at him, his expression all serious and earnest. He made everything sound so simple.

"It's the thing I shared with my mom," I finally said.

Camden looked surprised. "You're using the past tense. Why?"

It unhinged me a bit, that he wanted to hear the story. Where would I even start with the telling?

"We don't share it anymore."

"I'm sorry to hear that." He paused. "You can share it with me, now. I mean. All of us."

Now I imagined Camden reaching out to put his hand on the back of my head and drawing my face to his. I even strategized how that would work, without one or both of us falling off the rock and hitting our head. Why was I so obsessed with the thought of somebody hitting their head?

I remembered how scared I'd been at his party. I didn't feel any of that now. Even when thunder suddenly cracked above us.

The sky had quickly darkened in the way that only happens in summer.

"We should probably go," he said. From where we were at the edge of the pool, it was only three big steps across three large rocks to the bank. I stood up and went first. It seemed important that I go first.

When my feet landed on solid ground again, I turned and waited for Camden. He launched himself off the last rock but his foot hit a root half-hidden in the dirt, and he lost his balance. I reached out on instinct and steadied him.

"Thanks," he said, embarrassed.

"Anytime."

He stood up straight now and looked hard at me.

"Shit," he said.

I frowned. "Why *shit*?"

Camden shook his head. "I really wanted to kiss you."

I drew a breath, but only a tiny one. "You can still do that."

Camden shook his head. "I wanted to do it there, on the rock. So, so bad. But I chickened out."

"*You can still do that*," I said again, and swallowed hard.

Camden smiled and took my hand, moving quickly in the direction of the place we had just been. Then somehow we were back on that first rock.

And then, lips.

I wasn't sure who touched the other person's first. It honestly could have been me.

The taste of new and different, but not completely unfamiliar. Like something I'd known a long time ago but had forgotten and now it was here again.

It was only two seconds of *warm soft wet*, maybe three, when we heard Max's voice calling. Camden broke away first.

"Cam? Ari? You guys out on the rocks?"

"Yes, over here!" yelled Camden.

Max appeared on the trail and pointed up. "We should go. Sky's looking mean."

"You guys start," said Camden. "We'll catch you."

Max smiled a smile that seemed to have extra meaning, then turned and disappeared.

Silently Camden led me back across the rocks, his hand gripping mine extra tight, like they were having their own conversation.

When we got back to our clothes, Camden tugged his shirt back on and I pulled my dress over my head, feeling it stick to the back of my legs where I'd gotten wet. I was glad for those two seconds when my face was covered, and I didn't have to worry about looking at him or not looking at him.

When I finally did meet his glance again he asked, "Ready?" with that mouth I'd just kissed. Holy crap.

I nodded. We walked with the drops hitting us *plink plunk*

through the lattice of tree branches. We walked without talking or touching, everything between us quietly and monumentally changed.

In the parking lot, Max already had his car running, the wipers swishing.

Camden turned to me. "Can you come to the Barn tomorrow night?"

"Yes," I said, not sure that was true. I would make it true.

"Good. Great. I'll see you then."

He climbed into the backseat of Max's car and I thought for a second about climbing in after him, about slamming the door and saying *Wherever you guys are going, I want to come, too.*

It would have been an epically Satina Galt thing to do. I could have made it an Ari Logan thing to do, claimed it with a single step forward from the spot where I stood getting drenched.

But before I had a chance to make that happen, thunder rumbled again, and the car started driving away.

"Ah," said Mom when I walked in the door. "I had a feeling you'd be home earlier than planned, with the rain and all. You were at the lake?"

"Yes," I said. The house was cool and dark, the shades drawn. I could hear the TV in the family room. I slipped off my wet boots, noticed a single green leaf stuck to one of them and didn't take it off. Thought maybe I would never, ever, ever take it off.

"Don't worry," added Mom without even looking up from her computer, pointing a thumb toward the family room. "I'm listening to what she's watching."

"Okay," I said, when I really meant *Good for you, but that still doesn't count as spending time with her.*

I walked to the fridge, opened the door. "What are we doing about dinner?"

"Richard's bringing home a pizza. Who were you at the lake with?"

"Some friends," I said. "I can cut up some carrots."

"No, I'll make a salad. With actual green things in it." Mom turned from her computer to look at me now. "Which friends?"

I closed the fridge quickly, as if everything I wanted to tell my mother about Camden and Eliza and Max and the creek were about to burst out of it before I was ready.

"Some friends from school," I lied. Then, without really thinking about what it might lead to, I asked, "Hey, Mom, do you remember the *Silver Arrow* episode called 'Do No Good'?"

Mom's expression changed. Something sparked in her eyes and a few of her lines disappeared for a second.

"Of course," she said softly. "Why do you ask?"

Dani rushed into the kitchen just then. "Ari!" she cried, and wrapped her arms around my waist as if I'd been gone a week. It sort of felt like I'd been gone a week.

Mom stared at us for a moment, then shut her laptop like she was slamming a door. "I'm going to go fold some laundry," she said, then went downstairs.

"Did you have fun with Mom?" I asked Dani.

"I had to go with her to her stupid gy-con-ologist appointment. I have more fun with you."

"Gynecologist," I corrected her.

I watched TV with Dani while the rain beat down against the windows, playing the half kiss over and over in my head. Looking at it from every possible angle, revisiting myself the moment we put our lips on each other. Wondering how something can be so wanted, then take you by dazzling surprise.

Later, when Richard came home with the pizza, Mom chirped, "Let's all eat together at the table!"

Mom rarely chirped. We rarely ate together at the table. Which meant something bad was about to happen; I could feel it.

If Richard sensed it, too, he didn't let on. I watched him and Mom, maneuvering around each other in the kitchen, grabbing forks and plates and cans of club soda. At one point, they bumped into each other and Richard said, "Oops! Excuse me," as if they were two strangers at a buffet.

I couldn't remember the last time I'd seen them touch. How pathetic was that?

Once we were all sitting down and eating, Mom said, "I have some news."

"Good or bad?" asked Dani.

"All good. Really good."

"I could use some really good today," said Richard.

Mom took a deep breath and beamed at us. "I got offered

a new job. I didn't plan to apply for anything, but this opportunity came up. It's a day shift and it pays more, and I start in two weeks."

"Honey!" exclaimed Richard. "That's fantastic!"

"And it's in White Plains," added Mom.

"*What?*" he said, dropping his pizza slice so it landed half on, half off the plate.

It was quiet for a moment. Dani looked back and forth between all of us, trying to figure out why this was a pizza-dropping detail.

"Mom," I said, "that's like, ninety minutes away."

"I know."

"How can you—"

She held out her hand in that way I hated, hated, hated. "It's not ideal. But it's a better job and a promotion, and we need the money."

"Not *ideal?*" spit Richard. "You'd be spending three hours in the car every day!"

"It's a better job, and we need the money," Mom repeated like a mantra. Then she leveled her gaze at Richard. "It's really slow at Millie's. We can't ignore that fact."

Richard looked up and away, at something on the wall maybe. His jaw squared, which meant he was gritting his teeth. It was so obvious because he did it so seldomly.

"I'm not trying to hurt your feelings, honey," said Mom. "I'm just laying it straight out."

"That's straight all right," he said.

Mom looked at him guiltily. "I can't work the night shift anymore," she said, more softly now. "It's killing me."

Richard met her glance and something in him softened, too, but also guiltily. Sometimes it seemed like guilt was the only thread that connected them anymore. Guilt, and its incredibly unromantic relatives: obligation, habit, and regret.

"I understand that, Kate, but honestly. Is this better?"

My mother shrugged. "It has to be," she said.

"You'll barely be around. At least now, you're here in the afternoons. For Dani." Richard caught my glance. "And Ari, too. This is the last year she'll be home."

"Exactly," said Mom. "There's a college fund to worry about."

Ouch. I hadn't realized how angry this news was making me until that second.

"Great," I said. "Make up your mind, Mom. Whose fault is it that you have to work so hard? Mine, or Richard's? Or do we share the blame?"

"I didn't mean it like that," offered Mom, putting her hand on my arm. "I'm not blaming you for planning to go to college. God, Ari. It's the opposite! I want you to have your time for new ventures." She looked at Richard now, her eyes pleading. "But this, right now? This year? Can't this be *my* time? It's not about the money . . ."

Richard gave her a look.

"Okay," she said. "It's a little bit about the money. But you know I've wanted to work in medicine my whole life. It took me so long to get back on track after things derailed." *Derailed.*

I knew that meant my father, and me. Maybe Richard and Danielle, too.

"Please, honey," she continued. "You have the store, and I helped you have that. Now, help me have this."

None of us spoke. The refrigerator hummed. The sound of cicadas and crickets swelled through the screen door to the back deck. Dani worked a hangnail off her thumb, sucking the blood, her eyes traveling from me to Mom to Richard and back again in the same way they did when she was zoned out in front of a cartoon.

Finally Richard said, "We'll need more time from Ari."

Mom looked at me and nodded, genuinely pained. "Just temporarily, until school starts again. You can handle that, can't you, Ari? You're already doing such a great job."

She was worried about me, I could tell, but maybe her own need was stronger than the worry.

"It's okay," I heard myself saying. Not sure what *it* was.

Richard sighed and put both hands firmly on the table. I thought maybe he was about to try to push the whole thing through the floor and into the basement. Then he took a deep breath and said in a resigned way, "All right, then. We'll make this work."

"Thank you, my love!" Mom said with a catch in her voice, then gestured to the whole table. "*All* my loves." I wondered if that included the pizza.

Richard smiled weakly, then got up and went down the hall to the bedroom.

Mom watched him. "There's more laundry . . . ," she said, and went almost eagerly downstairs. I couldn't blame her. Laundry didn't judge.

Dani freed her hangnail at last, peeling with it a long strip of thumb skin that she flicked under her chair.

I sat still, and instead of dealing with the reality of what had happened, what would now continue to happen, I found myself suddenly consumed with a painfully vivid memory of the two seconds my lips spent on Camden's. I wanted to be back there. I wanted the thunderstorm to have passed us by, the afternoon to have unspooled differently. I wanted, period.

10

The next afternoon, I was out grocery shopping with Dani when my cell phone rang, the words *Camden Armstrong* lighting up the screen. When I'd saved his number in my phone, I didn't feel right only entering "Camden." I couldn't yet claim him that way.

"Hello?" I answered.

"It's me," he said. These words, in his voice. In the frozen foods aisle. Worlds colliding.

"It's also me," I said in a way that would never reveal the mostly sleepless night I'd spent thinking about him.

Dani tugged on the back of my T-shirt. "Who is that?"

"Shhh," I said.

"Why shhh?" asked Camden.

"Not you. I was talking to my sister. *You* can talk all you want."

His laugh was like bells ringing.

"You sound busy. I'll talk quickly. James wanted me to ask you if you could bring your friend when you come over later. He'll be here. He was too shy to ask himself."

I smiled. "I'll let her know that her presence has been requested."

We said good-bye and hung up. Dani narrowed her eyes at me.

"*Who was that?*" she pressed.

"Just Kendall," I lied, then looked up at the gleaming case of frozen dinners my mom always forbade us to buy. *If it has an ingredient you can't pronounce, don't get it.* To hell with that. I wasn't going to have time to cook. "Pick out something for tonight," I said, pointing to the packages designed with begging seven-year-olds in mind.

"Daddy likes chicken nuggets," said Dani. "He brings them home from McDonald's sometimes, when he knows Mommy's not going to be there."

"Chicken nuggets it is," I said, opening the case. "Want the ones shaped like dinosaurs or the little smiley faces?"

That evening, I read a long chapter of *The Lion, the Witch and the Wardrobe* to Dani, then sang her a lullaby. Her glossy blond head in the crook of my arm, her fingernails digging into my side. I loved the pressure of her need and want, its lack of shame. She was mostly asleep when I kissed her good night and left the room. On my way out of the house, I rapped on the door of the bathroom, into which I'd recently seen Richard disappear with the new issue of *National Geographic*.

"You should check on her in a bit," I said. "I'm taking off. Thanks for the car."

"You're going out with Kendall?"

"Yeah. To another friend's house."

He paused. "I'm supposed to ask you if there will be parents there, right?"

"Yes, you're supposed to ask."

There was another pause. *Leave it at that, leave it at that.*

"Have fun," said Richard's knowing voice through the door. "Back by eleven."

"Of course. See you then."

I was glad to be the one driving tonight. It was Kendall's night off from Scoop-N-Putt and that felt like kismet, that we could go back to the Barn together under completely new circumstances. It didn't seem possible that Camden's party had been only four days ago.

"How many emails have you and James sent back and forth since Sunday?" I asked Kendall after I picked her up.

"Four. No, five. He signs off as 'Jamie.' Should I call him that now?"

"Yeah, I think you could live on the edge and start calling him Jamie." Kendall punched me in the shoulder. "So, is this, like, a romantic thing? Or a friend thing?"

"I can't tell," said Kendall.

"What do you want it to be? Considering you're leaving for Europe in two months."

"Well, duh, of course I'm taking the *romantic* option. I don't need a *boyfriend* per se. I just need something to happen to me for once, and a freaking lot can happen in two months." Kendall paused, and her demeanor changed. "What about Camden?"

"What about him?"

"What do you like about him, now that you actually know him a little? Now that you semi-kissed."

I pictured Camden. Lying in his room, his arms behind his head, staring at his skylight. He looked small in my mind, like something I could pick up and hold.

"He's different from anyone I've ever met," I said.

"Well, that much is obvious. But in a good way?"

"It feels like a good way. I mean, aren't you tired of meeting basically the same person over and over again? We've been talking forever about finding something new and fresh. And now, here it is."

I could feel Kendall examining my face as I drove. I didn't turn to look at her.

"I'm happy for you, Ari," she said after a while. But I sensed it was something she felt she was supposed to say. It had been hard for her, when I got together with Lukas. That I was inching ahead in some imaginary race. I knew it was one of the reasons why she'd drifted away toward her newspaper friends.

"You're next," I said. That was the thing *I* was supposed to say.

"Hope so," sighed Kendall. "I'm not going to hang out with these weirdos if you're wrong."

"In here," called a voice I recognized as Eliza's.

We walked into the Barn to find her sitting at the farmhouse table in front of a sewing machine. James was sitting across from her with his laptop open.

"Hey," Kendall said to him.

"Hey," he said, and pulled out a chair for her. "I'm editing some photographs I took yesterday. Come see."

She did.

I sat down next to Eliza to watch her work. She was sewing feathers onto something that looked like it was going to be a wing.

"Is this for a cosplay outfit?" I asked.

"Mmm-hmm."

"What else do you cosplay, besides *Silver Arrow*?"

"I have some favorite characters from a graphic novel series. Three completed. Another in progress. Another two sketched out for the future."

Eliza opened a notebook and slid it toward me. I flipped through the pages, which were full of well-drawn figures with no hair or faces, just clothing. I didn't recognize the characters until I got to several different versions of Satina Galt. One was from the infamous episode where Satina got trapped in an ancient Greek brothel and had to wear a sheer white, flowing gown.

"'Temple of Love, Temple of Death,'" I said to Eliza.

She smiled. "In the cosplay world, this here is known as 'See-Thru Satina.' No convention is complete without at least one of them."

"Blech."

"Most guys who attend these things feel differently."

"I hated that they made her so sexy in that season." My mother had felt this way, too. She was a purist.

"I guess that was 'character development' back then," said Eliza.

"Are you going to dress up like that?" I asked.

"I was thinking about it. But then I got a better idea, from the creek yesterday." She looked down at my feet and indicated my boots. "And from *those*." Eliza then grabbed her notebook and flipped through the pages until she found the sketch she was looking for.

It was a drawing of the Season Three Original Satina. The Satina who had finally come into her own, powerful and quick and courageously honest, always. She wore light brown shimmery leggings and a white shirt under a purple tunic-length vest that tied together with a belt. And the boots, of course.

"The Ulster County Fair's coming up," said Eliza.

"Next week, yeah."

"Remember the carnival episode?"

"'Ferris Wheel.'" God, I was such a nerd.

"Wouldn't that be a perfect opportunity for a photo shoot? You, me, Camden, and Max could cosplay the crew, and we could re-create a few of the best scenes. Jamie would work his photographic magic. I'll post the pictures on my AlternateArt page and watch it light up with comments!"

I looked at James/Jamie, who saluted me. I noticed Kendall's raised eyebrows.

"You want *me* to be part of it?" I asked. "Who would I be?"

"Take a flying guess, Boot Girl," said Eliza.

"What? No. That's not . . . really my thing."

"You don't think so, but it seems to me very much your thing."

"I just have a good memory for the details."

"Exactly! That's what would set us apart, as a cosplay group. How we'd make a real name for ourselves. Accuracy is currency with this stuff."

"I'm happy to help you get the costumes right, if that's what you need. And I could probably get you some discounted supplies through Millie's."

"We need a great Satina. I'm a lot of things, but I'm not her." Eliza scanned me up and down, much like the first time we met, but this time with something that felt like respect. "Promise me you'll think about it," she said.

The door opened. Max and Camden came in from outside, each holding a bottle of wine.

"Hi," said Camden, hanging his head so his bangs fell across his eyes, then looking at me shyly through those thick eye-lashes. I wasn't sure which of these things wrecked me more.

"Hi," I croaked.

"Sorry, Max and I went out to the garage to get something to drink with dinner." He held up his bottle. "He's making linguini with clam sauce. Did you eat?"

I thought of the dinosaur nuggets I'd inhaled before leaving, the ketchup and canned peas. "No."

The sewing machine suddenly made a grinding noise. "Fuck!" shouted Eliza. "Sorry. It's this thread, it keeps breaking." She turned to Camden and batted her eyelashes. "Cam, do you know where I might find some *good* thread?"

Camden sighed. "You'll buy her a replacement, right?"

"Sometime before she comes back, absolutely."

He turned to me. "Want to see my mom's studio?"

I nodded. He put the wine bottle on the table and motioned for me to follow him.

We left the house and walked across the lawn to the out-building. He opened a sliding screen door, then made an *after you* motion with his arm. I stepped inside and he closed the screen behind me, then turned on the lights.

I'd expected to see a chaotic space, free-flowing and abstract like Maeve's art. But everything in the room had sharp corners and clean lines: a large storage unit with carefully folded textiles of a hundred different hues and patterns, a bookcase filled not with books but large spools of yarn arranged by shade. Stacked plastic bins held tufts of dyed something—maybe cotton or wool—in another tumble of color. One large table held a sewing machine; another was empty with a black surface so clean and shiny, it reflected light from the moon outside.

"It's the only part of our lives she's able to keep clean and organized," said Camden. "When my thoughts get tangled up, I come here to think. I look at all the colors and pretend it's the thing I'm worried about. Anything makes more sense when you look at it sorted like this."

Camden slid a large plastic case from underneath the sewing machine, opened it, and pulled out a spool of thread. He held it daintily with two fingers, slid it into the pocket of his jeans.

"So," he said, turning back to me. "Did Eliza do the cosplay ambush on you yet?"

I laughed. "*Ambush* is a good word for it."

"Don't do anything you don't want to do."

I couldn't read his expression. "Do *you* want me to do it?"

"Uh, *yeah*. But that shouldn't matter."

He said that like it was the most obvious, most simple thing in the world. Then he drew a deep breath, took a step closer, and leaned toward me.

Yes. This. Please.

His expression, I could read now. *Is this where we left off? Okay to pick up from right here?*

Then there was a new sound in the room, and it took me a second to realize it was my cell phone buzzing in my pocket. I turned from Camden to check it. This was habit: if I wasn't with Dani, I always checked it. "Sorry," I said.

It was a text from Richard.

I'm feeling guilty. Just tell me there's an adult there and I'll leave you alone.

"Everything okay?" asked Camden.

I stared at the text and what it implied, the different levels of trust between Richard and me and Mom and me. The shifting loyalties and alliances. Sometimes I wondered if Richard bending the rules for me was his way of sticking it to Mom. Which, for the record, was totally fine by me.

"Would any of you be eighteen years old, by chance?"

Camden looked puzzled for a moment, then seemed to get it. "Actually, yes. Max turned eighteen last month. He took a year off to live with some relatives in California; that's why he's still in school."

"Excellent," I said. Then I answered Richard's text.

Yes, there is one adult here. All good.

Camden watched me put my phone back in my pocket, bemused.

"My stepdad," I said by way of explanation.

"Is he a good one?"

"Top of the line."

Camden leaned against the worktable. "Two times, my mom came close to getting married. To guys who just plain sucked. Then there were the boyfriends, of course, and the not-even boyfriends. Who I won't even honor with a mention."

My mother had had a few dates before she met Richard on

a matchmaking website. Each one seemed to destroy her in tiny ways. I remember her telling a friend she wasn't cut out for *that stuff.*

"What happened to keep your mom from getting married those two times?" I asked, starting to move around the room, taking in every color and texture.

"I talked her out of it. They weren't right for her."

"She trusts you," I said.

"When she's thinking clearly, yes. When she has her priorities in the right order."

"And what about your dad? Is he remarried?"

Camden's face flickered with something dark and complicated.

"I don't know who my dad is," he said after a few moments.

I stopped and turned to face him. "You mean, like, in a metaphysical sense? Or you literally don't know his identity?"

"That second thing," said Camden. "My mom got knocked up during some music festival in New Mexico. She hung out with a few different guys that weekend, but never got their last names. So she had no way of determining who made, you know, *the donation.* And no way of contacting them."

"Wow," I said, and instinctively moved closer to him. "That's really . . ."

"Crazy? Slutty?"

"I was going to say . . . actually, I have no idea what I was going to say."

Camden laughed, but it was a sad laugh.

"I thought maybe I'd try to track him down, but that's impossible," he said. "It's weird, not knowing where half of you came from. I've always read a lot about other cultures, thinking maybe something would click. I mean, look at me. Odds are, my dad was not white. But so far, I've felt nothing." He dropped his head back and took a deep breath.

I wanted to bring him out of this sadness. "You know, there's a rumor that your father is really Ed Penniman."

Camden was silent for a moment, then raised his head. I watched a smile grow across his face.

"Excellent," he said. "I started that rumor."

"You did?"

"What can I say? I was twelve and really tired of people asking me about my father. My mom and Eddie are friends from way back. He stops by for dinner whenever he's in the area. So, you know, there's some believability there."

"Well, I have to hand it to you. Good choice with the fake father."

"What about yours? Your real dad?"

My real dad. Who felt less real and more imaginary every year. Like a cardboard cutout fraying at the edges, starting to droop.

"He and my mom split up when I was two. I haven't talked to him in years."

"Wow. That sucks almost as much as my story." He reached out and tucked some of my hair behind my left ear. I felt an electric current going down that side of my body.

As much as I wanted to kiss him again, I wanted this more. Him looking squarely at me, me looking back at him without any fear or shame or awkwardness. Both of us understanding that we shared something besides *Arrow* fandom, and it was a big something.

Kendall must have been outside waiting to hear voices because suddenly we heard her shout, "Is it safe to come in there?"

"Board the bridge!" answered Camden, and we both grinned at the *Arrow* reference—it was one of Atticus Marr's trademark lines.

She poked her head in the studio, looked around. "Whoa. Nice."

"Dinner?"

"Yup. And Eliza wants her thread."

Camden ushered us out of the studio, turned off the lights, and gingerly slid the door shut. As we walked back up the hill to the Barn, I reached out for Kendall's hand. She grasped it back.

Inside, we sat down at the farmhouse table, where James had poured wine for us all. There was a giant bowl of pasta and another giant bowl of salad. Garlic bread on a wooden cutting board, steam rising off of it.

"This looks amazing," I said, then turned to Eliza. "Max did this? You're lucky."

"We're all lucky," she said. "It's summer. Anything can happen."

"To summer," said Camden, raising his glass.

"To anything," added Max.

We clinked glasses, then I watched everyone else take a sip of their wine while I put mine back on the table. The food, the drinks, the rising swell of chatter among the six of us made us all appear to be, you know, *people* in the world who *led lives*. Every fantasy I'd ever had about being grown-up and independent and real—it looked a lot like this. But this was happening now, and it didn't even feel like cheating.

Camden took my empty bowl and filled it to the top. I didn't ever want to leave.

After dinner, we ate mini Hershey bars out of the bag and talked until it was time for Kendall and me to get home by curfew. Camden and James walked us to the car.

James opened the passenger door for Kendall and she paused for a second before climbing in. He leaned into the open window and said, "Thanks for coming. I'll send you those links tomorrow," before turning to walk back to the house.

I hovered by the driver's side. Camden took my hand and I realized it was the first time all night he'd really touched me.

"Can I kiss you good night?" he asked confidently. So sure I'd say yes.

I simply nodded. Once again, those familiar lips, which now tasted like garlic and wine. With Kendall in the car, the others probably watching from the house, it didn't feel like we should kiss for longer than a few moments. Each millisecond of it was precious.

I got in the car and turned to Kendall, expecting her to give me some kind of look, but she was staring out the window at the moon.

Neither of us said a word on the way home.

In my half sleep, I thought about the "Ferris Wheel" episode of *Silver Arrow*. It was my favorite of the whole third season, where the *Arrow One* explores a portal that sends them to 1950s Earth. It lands in a cornfield outside a fair somewhere in the Midwest. The ship creates a temporal anomaly where people get on the Ferris wheel, and by the time they get off, they are much younger. Satina and Azor have to figure out how to fix it before word gets out among the locals.

I loved this episode because of what it said about aging and lost youth, and because it was one of the few where Satina and Azor have a lot of screen time without Atticus Marr around.

Eliza thought I could pull off Satina. Camden did, too. If I didn't believe them, what did it say about me?

I grabbed my phone and pulled up Camden's name in my contacts. Letter by letter, I deleted the "Armstrong," and with each backward stroke it was like I was claiming a little more of him.

Then I called.

"Ari?" he said, sounding very much awake. I wondered if I was just "Ari" on his phone.

"I'm saying yes to the cosplay," I announced. "Tell Eliza before I chicken out."

11

The plan fell into place pretty quickly.

We picked three scenes from the "Ferris Wheel" episode to cosplay at the county fair. Accuracy was everything. My job was to look at Eliza's sketches for all the characters—Satina, Atticus, Azor, and Bram—and make sure they were as spot-on as possible. Over the next two days, Eliza texted me constantly with photos of items or fabric she'd found, asking for my thumbs-up. Every time she shared a new element of Satina's costume, I couldn't help but feel like I was being rebuilt piece by piece.

At the end of the second day, Camden called me while Danielle and I were doing the dinner dishes.

"Hang on," I said as soon as I picked up. I went into my room and locked the door before Dani could follow me in. "Okay. I'm alone."

"I can say hi now?"

"Yes."

"Hi," he whispered, and in the fleeting solitude of my room I crawled inside his voice.

"Hi," I practically sighed back.

"What did people buy at the store today?"

"Origami paper. Blank canvases. Fancy pens." I paused. "Did you get any calls at the hotline?"

"A few. I was on the phone with one kid for an hour."

"And you helped him?" I knew Camden wasn't allowed to talk about the details.

"I think so. God, I hope so. He promised he'd come to the teen support group this weekend, so we'll see."

"He'll come," I assured him. "You seem like the kind of person whose advice is worth taking."

He laughed a bit, surprised. "I do?"

"Yeah. I mean, your friends all look up to you. That's obvious."

"It *is*?"

Was it? I flushed with panic that maybe I'd gotten it wrong. Why was I telling this boy about his life, instead of shutting up and listening to that voice talk about . . . well, anything it wanted to.

But then Camden added, "Maybe you're right. Maybe they

do." He cracked up again.

"What's so funny?" I asked.

"I'm remembering this thing that happened last winter."

"Tell me."

"Well, Eliza, Max, and James decided they were going to put on a production of *A Midsummer Night's Dream* at Dashwood. Eliza was doing the costumes, of course. Max and James thought they could direct it together, but that was a total disaster. Max wanted to make the play shorter by rewriting some of Shakespeare's lines, and James was like, completely outraged by that."

"Um, as he should be," I said.

"I know. But then James kept changing his mind about where one particular tree on the set was supposed to go, which drove Max crazy. I'd never seen him that annoyed. Seriously, I thought the whole show was going to implode. I had to step in and tell them how to fix it."

"And they listened to you?"

"I was Oberon. Who's going to mess with a badass Fairie King?"

I laughed, sensing myself falling toward two things at the same time: Camden, of course, and also this group of people who were so important to him becoming part of my life, too.

I'd started telling Camden about a big Mock Trial team fight we had during our biggest competition when Richard rapped on the door and told me that Dani was ready for me to kiss her good night.

"I have to sign off now," I said.

"Want to go swimming tomorrow?"

"I'm with Danielle all afternoon."

"Here's a shocking concept: you can swim with both of us at the same time. I think I can coexist with your sister and not rip a hole in the space-time continuum."

"She'll blab to my parents."

"Let her blab."

"Easy for you to say."

"You, too, Ari."

We were quiet, listening to each other breathe.

Finally I said, "Okay."

I hung up and left my room, and everything looked different. The hallway a slightly deeper color beige, the light fixture refracting tiny diamond shapes I'd never noticed on the ceiling. It was as if every conversation with Camden was taking me another few inches farther from the person I'd been.

I was in the water with Dani when Camden appeared on the beach. The faraway Camden from last summer: the hair and the shoulders, the heartbreaking tilt of his head.

Then he came closer and became the new Camden. My Camden. The one whose stories I'd been learning, who I'd kissed twice so painfully briefly, I almost wished I hadn't at all. Because it was torture, the *more more more* and the *when when when* and also the *if if if.*

This Camden walked onto the dock and smiled at me. I

smiled back, unafraid to offer up how happy I was to see him, that phone conversation still echoing between us. Then he suddenly dove into the lake, coming up a foot from Danielle.

"Squash!" he yelled as he broke through the surface.

Danielle laughed hysterically. "Why did you say that?"

"I don't know, I felt like I should shout something when I came up. That's the first thing that popped into my head."

"You're weird," said Danielle.

"I try," said Camden, and they beamed at each other. He'd already won her over. She'd been almost as easy as I was.

We swam together for a while, and I was glad to have Danielle there between us. Without Dani to distract me, I would have drowned in the *more when if.* Instead, my sister and I showed him the Garbage game and he threw her, higher and farther than I ever could. When we finally stumbled out of the water and I wrapped Danielle up like a burrito, Camden watched us, then asked, "Who does you?"

"What do you mean?"

"Who wraps *you* up like a burrito?"

I shrugged. "Nobody. I don't really need to be a burrito."

Camden flashed a devilish smile. "Don't be silly. Of course you do." He turned to Dani. "Am I right?"

Dani nodded energetically, eyes wide, eager to please him.

He picked up my towel and shook out the sand, then stretched it wide and flat across his long, beautiful arms. We locked eyes. I stepped into it and he wrapped me tight, one side of the towel and then the other. I felt his chest against mine, the quickest sensation of a heartbeat thudding, a precious squeeze as he tucked one corner of the towel at the back of my neck. Then he stepped away.

"What do you think, Ari?" said Dani. "Isn't it the best?"

"Yes," I agreed, feeling my own pulse speed up as my eyes and Camden's found each other again. "There is nothing better."

"Does your mom know?" asked Kendall from behind her window at Scoop-N-Putt. It framed her perfectly, like she was a talking portrait.

I'd brought Dani straight here from the lake. I told Kendall about the swimming but not about the burritos.

"No," I said, turning to check on Dani, who was talking to the rabbit on Hole 3, a cherry-dip cone already melting down the back of her hand.

It was 98 degrees and too hot even for ice cream, so we were the only customers. Kendall's boss was taking a nap in his air-conditioned office upstairs.

Kendall took two sugar cones from the sugar cone tower. She took a bite out of one, handed the other to me. "Why not? She would be jazzed that you're hanging out with other Arrowheads."

"Do you think so?" I asked, and bit into my cone.

"Don't you?"

"Haven't decided," I said, chewing. Which was the truth.

Part of me thought, yes, *jazzed* is the right word. Maybe

she'd embrace it as something that proved yes, we were connected in ways that can never be broken. Especially now, when her presence in our house was about to become even more shadow-like.

Another part of me thought: mine. All of this—Camden, Eliza, Max, *Silver Arrow*, and Satina Galt—belonged to me.

I couldn't think of anything else that did.

"This is nervous eating," said Kendall, crunching another bite. "I'm seeing James—Jamie—tonight."

"What? You wait until now to tell me this? Where are you guys going?"

"Movies. Maybe the diner after."

"That sounds like a date. Kendall, your first date!"

She shrugged, but I could tell she was trying to contain her excitement. "It sounds like a date. Looks like a date, smells like a date. But it might not, in fact, be a date."

"But you like him."

Kendall bit her lip and nodded. "A lot."

"Then you'll have fun, whatever it is."

Kendall nodded again, as if I'd given her instructions. Maybe she'd needed them.

"Are you coming with us to the fair?" I asked.

"You're definitely doing that?"

I gave her a look.

"It's going to be weird, Ari," said Kendall. "I mean, *really* weird. We're going to see people from school there. They might laugh or give you a hard time."

"I've thought about that." I had. In my mind, all I had to do was grab Camden's hand and then everything at the fair would be okay. "But the less I worry about what they're going to think, the happier I am."

Also, the more I'd learned about Camden's friends, the more everyone else faded into the background. Lukas, Brady, the girls at the school newspaper. They were like movie extras who didn't need names or even identities. They had no bearing on me.

"If I go with you, what will I do?" asked Kendall. "I don't want to be some tagalong who's just there for you, and for Jamie." She paused, then seemed to brighten with a brainstorm. "Can I bring my camera?"

"Oh, good idea! You can be the second photographer. I'm sure Eliza would be okay with that."

Kendall gave me the raised-eyebrows look. "You sure? Don't we have to submit some kind of proposal to her first?" Her voice dripped with sarcasm.

"I know. She's bossy. But a cool bossy, don't you think? And she does have mad costuming skills."

"If you say so," said Kendall. "Okay, count me in."

Richard never asked who I was talking to on the phone each night. He knew he should. He also knew he shouldn't.

This little problem got solved one day at the store.

I was ringing up a woman and her kids buying coloring books. It had been a slow morning. They stepped away and

I looked down for a moment, then up again, and there was Camden. He planted his hands on the counter and leaned forward with a smile. Like he was glad to see me. Like that could be a thing. (When would I stop thinking this way?)

"Hey, Ari," he said, his eyes twinkling.

"What are you doing here?" I asked, glancing at Richard, who was now coming down an aisle to see who'd said my name.

"Hi," said Richard to Camden. "Are you the guy?"

"Oh, for Christ's sake." I picked up a paper bag and held it in front of my face.

"Yup, I'm him," I heard Camden say. "Are you the awesome stepdad?"

"I hope so," said Richard. He pulled the paper bag out of my hand. "It's okay, Ari. I don't think I'm required to ask you any embarrassing questions. At least, not here."

The door chimed and we all looked up to see Eliza and Max come in.

"We have some work to do," said Eliza, holding up a laptop computer case, "but you said you couldn't get away today. So we came to you."

She pulled out her laptop and Richard looked at me quizzically.

"It's sort of an art project we're doing together," I told him.

"And this will all make sense in the end?"

"Absolutely."

He jerked his head toward the office. "Go in there. If it gets busy and I need you, I'll holler."

I kissed him on the cheek and led Camden, Eliza, and Max into the back room, where there was a cracked leather sofa and a desk before you got to the shelves of boxes.

"Oooh," sighed Eliza when she saw some of the supplies in storage.

"So what do we need to do?" I asked.

"We need to watch the episode," she said.

In all of our talk about *Silver Arrow*, we'd never actually watched the damn thing together. It was like we were retracing the separate paths of our fandom, and now we'd finally reached a point where they all started. The actual, you know, show itself.

Max put the laptop on the desk and fed it a DVD. It caught the light from the anemic overhead bulb and I thought of my mom. How she was the only other person I'd ever watched it with.

Mom was always very serious about the viewing experience. If I was confused about the plot, I could ask her questions (after we paused the episode), but otherwise she asked for silence until it was over. Then we could talk about it.

Mom, why does Captain Marr do things he knows are wrong? This was my introduction to ethics and morals, and also how people can be assholes sometimes but still mostly good.

Mom, Bram drives me crazy. He just doesn't get it! That was how I first learned about being tolerant of those who were different from myself.

I grew to love the silence of our watching. I knew she was beaten up from her day and this was her downtime. I knew it doubled as *our time,* too, that I never felt closer to her than when we were sitting next to each other on our Salvation Army couch, sharing this thing.

So it unmoored me now, to watch it with Camden, Eliza, and Max. To hear them make jokes and snarky comments. For Eliza to say, "I love this part. Notice how Satina moves around the room while the men stay still? It's her way of checking her power over them."

It wasn't better or worse than watching it with Mom; it was simply a different *Silver Arrow.* A joyful thing, worth celebrating. Worth having your fandom out loud.

We'd reached the scene where Satina and Azor were trying to find their way out of the carnival fun house when I finally had the nerve to turn to Eliza and ask, "So if Camden will be Marr and Max is Bram, who are you dressing up as?"

Eliza paused the DVD. "I'll be Azor."

"*You'll* be Azor."

"I'm actually really excited about it. I've never crossplayed before."

The hardcore Arrowhead in me bristled. Eliza was short. Way too short to be Azor. Azor was quiet and mysterious and repressed, and even though I didn't know Eliza well, I did know she was none of those things. But her dark, hint-of-exotic features were right, from a purely physical standpoint.

And I knew she had plenty of confidence and creativity to pull it off.

"I know," she said, breaking into my silence. "You've been hot for Azor for years. It'll be a little weird for us."

"Is that true?" asked Camden, shifting his position on the sofa so he could face me.

I looked at him, then back at Eliza, then up at the highest shelf of the tallest bookcase.

"No," I lied.

"Why are you embarrassed?" teased Eliza. "Sure, the guy is trained as a Zendian Nocturne monk and all that. But there's that episode where Satina learns about the rumors."

"Okay, stop," I said, still unable to look at them.

"What rumors?" asked Camden, his voice electric with curiosity.

"That the Nocturnes have amazing sexual abilities, and take the vow of celibacy in order to protect others from a pleasure so pure, it leads to addiction . . . *and death.*" Eliza echoed the memorable, overdramatic way that line had been delivered on the show.

"Oh," said Camden. "Yeah. That's pretty hot."

I felt my face flush.

"*A pleasure so pure.* Guys never remember that line," said Eliza. "But trust me, the girls do."

"There is definitely some tension between Satina and Azor in this episode," said Camden. "I always thought it was there for comic relief."

"Can we please watch the rest of the episode now?" I asked, finally looking at them. I didn't want Camden to know how hard I crushed on Azor. It felt like I was cheating on him.

Eliza studied me for a moment, her finger hovering over the Play button on the keyboard. "It'll be okay, Ari. We're going to have an epic time with this."

We finished watching in silence, but even our silence was different from the Mom silence. When it was over, Eliza and I made some notes about the costumes, then I let them out through the back door.

Camden lingered on the step for a moment, his face searching mine. Was he going to kiss me? Were things forever awkward now that I'd been outed as an Azor girl?

"Call me tonight?" he whispered, although I wasn't sure why.

My hand reached out of its own volition and touched his shoulder. "Can't wait," I said. He smiled and jumped down the steps to the alley. It took all my self-control not to follow him.

When I came back into the store, Richard raised one eyebrow at me.

"All will be revealed?" he asked.

"In time, my friend. In time."

On my next afternoon off two days later, when I knew Camden was working at the hotline, Eliza summoned me to the Barn. I drove there through a thunderstorm, wondering what could be so important.

Inside, she had all the elements of my costume laid out on the couch.

"It's done," she said. "All that's missing is you."

I took the costume into the downstairs bathroom and began putting it on. First the brown leggings we'd bought online, which nearly sparkled in the bright lights above the bathroom mirror and instantly itched. Next, the white shirt Eliza had gone to four different area thrift stores to find; it had a slight ruffle underneath the V-neckline. Then, the purple tunic and brown belt, both of which Eliza had designed and made herself. I'd helped by sewing on the belt buckle and three brown triangular buttons—miraculously, we had them in stock at Millie's—down the front of the tunic. Eliza had ordered handmade replica flight pins from some woman in North Dakota, and had already stuck mine on the collar.

Finally, I slipped my feet into my boots.

Silly stupid silly. You're going to look like an idiot.

I turned away from that voice. It was too late to listen. I put on the wig cap and called to Eliza.

"I need some help with her hair!" We were always referring to Satina as "her," the silent third wheel in our new friendship.

Eliza came into the bathroom and smiled when she saw me, but didn't say anything. She picked up the wig, a long cascade of hair the color of cherrywood, and shook it out, held it delicately. I turned toward her and she slipped it on, taking a few moments to adjust it. She bit her lip and then said, "Check it out."

I turned back to the mirror.

I was not me. I was not really Satina, either. I was someone beyond both those people, too shocked to try and figure out who.

"I like," said Eliza. "Do you?"

"It looks . . . fantastic."

"Not *it*. *You. You* look fantastic."

"Yes, ma'am."

"Is there anything that feels uncomfortable? *Physically* uncomfortable. Anything we need to fix before the fair?"

I took stock for a moment, then shook my head. No. The costume fit. The pieces worked. The rest was up to me.

"Okay, then let's move on to the shirt."

Satina changed clothes halfway through the "Ferris Wheel" episode, stealing a plaid shirt from a hook in the stables so she'd be less conspicuous among the 1950s fairgoers. Eliza wanted to do one set of shots where I was wearing that, so she'd found some fabric that was almost the exact same pattern and sewn a shirt from scratch.

I tried it on. She'd gotten this one exactly right, too. We carefully put the clothes back on their hangers and into garment bags, ready and waiting for fair night.

"You're done," she said. "Now, onto Bram." She busied herself with another garment bag and I took that as my cue to leave, muttering a *Byeseeyoulater* as I went.

When I stepped outside, the rain had let up but was still falling in an even rhythm. The air felt newly created, light and unencumbered, as if the storm had washed all seriousness right out of it.

Max had just arrived and was walking toward me with an open umbrella.

"Successful fitting?" he asked.

"She's happy," I replied.

"Well, thank God for that. It's the only reason I'm doing the cosplay. Here, let me be chivalrous." He held the umbrella over me and escorted me to my car. When we got there, Max paused, staring at me.

"What is it?" I asked.

"I'm not going to give you the standard 'Don't break Camden's heart' speech."

"You would never need to."

"But I want to ask, how does it feel? Is he what you imagined?"

I felt heat rush through me. "What do you mean?"

"I remember you. From last summer. I remember how you looked at him."

"Oh," I said, trying to hide the full-body cringe. "Was it that obvious?"

"Only to me. I think I noticed it because I've been there. Not with Eliza. Another girl from school, two years ago."

"You never said anything to him about me?"

Max paused, shrugged. "I knew Eliza wanted him. I didn't want to make extra drama."

"Don't say anything now."

"I would never. But would you?"

I shrugged. "I don't know. Does it matter? I've changed a lot since then. I want him to only know about the me right now."

Max smiled as he opened my driver's side door for me, then put one hand gently on my shoulder.

"People think they change, but they don't so much. They just unlock doors inside them that were always there."

I laughed, then realized he wasn't joking. "That's deep."

"Yeah, well. That's me." He scanned me up and down. "But it's a theory I came up with when I was living in California. It helped me understand some stuff. The you right now? That's the only you who's ever been."

I fought the sting in my eyes, even though Max seemed like the kind of guy you could cry in front of. He might even be disappointed if you didn't.

He closed the door for me after I got in and held up his hand in a wave.

I'd spent the last few weeks so focused on Camden and then on Eliza, but right there I realized Max had his own quiet awesomeness.

I really was falling for them all.

12

On our planned fair night, I watched through the front window as Kendall's car pulled into the driveway. My heart wobbling, nervous as all hell.

"She's here," I said to Richard, and picked up my backpack. The parent-approved plan was that I'd go to the fair with Kendall and some of her friends, then sleep over at her house. That was all a version of the truth.

Danielle rushed down the hall and threw her arms around me as I opened the door. "You'll bring me back something from the fair, right?"

"You're going tomorrow with the day camp," I reminded her. "But nice try."

"You'll call when you're at Kendall's?" Richard asked as he stepped up behind Dani.

"Yes, yes. Don't I always do what I say I'm going to do? Sheesh. See you guys tomorrow."

I blew Dani a kiss and slipped out, closed the door tight. Rushed toward Kendall's passenger side.

"Clean getaway?" she asked.

"Squeaky."

I was surprised to see Max and James in the backseat as Kendall pulled away from my house. Away, away. Toward everything else.

"Hey," I said to the guys.

"Eliza and Camden had some last-minute costume snafus," explained Max, "so they're taking my car and meeting us there. But your stuff and my stuff is in the trunk."

"When you say it like that, it sounds so shady."

"Fun, right?"

James cradled his camera bag on his lap like it was a cat. He was even petting it a little.

"Did your camera meet Kendall's camera?" I asked him.

He laughed. "Yup. They're warming up to each other."

Kendall met Jamie's eyes in the rearview mirror. God, I was so grateful she was here.

After we parked at the fairgrounds and Kendall popped the trunk, Max went to the back of the car and took out the garment bags, then handed me mine. A steady stream of people were filing past the car, and this didn't feel as safe and reassuring as Camden's bathroom. I froze, trying to figure out how I was going to do it. If I was going to do it.

"Come over here," said Kendall, pulling me by the hem of my shirt to the Christ the King Church van parked head-to-head with us. There was an RV parked next to it, and that created a tall alley in between. The closest thing to privacy I was going to find.

Kendall helped me put on Satina's uniform, then the wig. We checked it in the gigantic side view mirror of the RV.

"I thought you thought this was silly," I said to her in the reflection, where she was still Kendall and I was definitely not still Ari.

Kendall paused, and one side of her mouth really wanted to smile. "I'm on the fence," she said.

Someone knocked on the side of the RV. Max, in all his Bram glory except for the silver wig, which he held in his hand. He looked perfect.

"Let's do this," said Max.

Those first rickety steps away from the cars felt like I was trying out stiff new skin. As we joined the flow of people walking toward the fairground gates, we passed a group of kids from my French class who didn't even recognize me. Maybe this would be all right.

The county fair always seemed so magical to me. The fact that a small, snow-covered field in winter could transform into a planet unto itself for seven glorious days in the middle of summer. Every inch of grass packed with booths and rides.

The livestock buildings that sit empty most of the year densely alive with animals and noises and smells. The lights and colors, which somehow look artificial and natural at the same time. When I was younger, I would imagine that the fair was always happening in some alternate dimension, but we could only see it for that one special week.

Once inside the gates, we huddled in front of a cotton candy booth so Max could check his phone.

"They're here," he said. "We're supposed to meet them at the Ferris wheel."

The Ferris wheel was in its customary corner of the fairgrounds, set against an iconic mix of sky and clouds as if it had brought its own backdrop. We walked over to it, but saw no Camden or Eliza. Max checked his phone again.

"She says they're on the other side where the exit is. She says you should go look, Ari."

"Me?"

Max shrugged. I exchanged a confused glance with Kendall and walked around the base of the Ferris wheel, past people who had just gotten off. A small patch of grass and then a chain-link fence separated the fair from the sad yet alluring shantytown of carny workers' RVs.

But then, there was also this:

Azor Ray, coming toward me.

Azor Ray, in his familiar collarless maroon tunic with the buttons down one side, the black pants and the shiny black boots. His eyes full of purpose.

I caught my breath because Azor often made me catch my breath. Something about him had a direct line to the center of me.

Then I caught my breath again. Because this was not Eliza. Too tall to be Eliza. Too *Azor* to be Eliza.

It was Camden.

In Azor's clothes. In Azor's hair, which was barely a shade darker than Camden's but shorter and neat and parted hard on one side. A wig. It was so obvious, suddenly, how much they naturally resembled each other.

Camden, Azor. Azor, Camden. *Camdenazorcamden.*

He stepped toward me and smiled.

"What?" I said, feeling like I'd suddenly changed from a solid to a liquid. Where had my bones gone? What was holding me up?

"Hey, Satina," said Camden. "Wait, sorry. That was stupid." He cleared his throat and made a serious Azor face. "Hello, Specialist Galt. I am getting a highly excited pathos wave from you."

"I don't understand," I said, taking one step toward him. "When did this happen?"

"A few days ago," replied Camden, as Camden again. "I thought it would be a great surprise for you and see, I'm totally right." His eyes traveled all over my costume and he appeared stricken. "You look amazing, by the way."

I took another step. My left hand brushed his right one, and our fingers intertwined.

"You did this for *me*?" I asked.

"Yes."

I knew we'd barely kissed a couple of times. I knew we were in a public place, surrounded by people, and our friends were waiting for us. I knew I was not a bold girl, a brash girl, a girl who took what she wanted when she wanted it. All these things I knew tumbled away.

"Come here," I said, yanking him toward me.

For the record, our mouths met halfway. It wasn't like I attacked him. We attacked each other.

We kissed hard. Our two unfinished kisses plus a hundred more, to make up for lost time. We kissed desperately, voraciously, the way you think you only can in your mind until you do it for real. This was so completely for real. I wrapped my arms under his armpits and up his back, the fabric of his uniform as soft as I always imagined it might be. Camden put both hands on my face, anchoring me to the spot I belonged in.

Azor. Mine. Azor. Mine, mine, mine. Lips, wet, taste. Skin, heat, pressure. Give, take, fall, climb.

Had I always been this greedy?

After a time, Camden drew away. Somewhere in the kissing, he'd threaded his fingers through the hair of my wig. I'd clutched parts of his uniform that I quickly smoothed down, hoping I hadn't ruined them.

"Okay," he simply said, trying to recover his breath. He glanced over my shoulder, then leaned in to whisper. "They're coming."

We broke apart to see the others gathering around us in a circle. Eliza was wearing Camden's Marr costume, but it had been altered to fit her. Her natural bravado and swagger went a long way toward filling an *Arrow One* command uniform.

"Oh please, you two," said Eliza, surveying us, our hands still intertwined. "Don't get all county-fair cute on me. Remember, we're subverting."

"You can be cute and subvert at the same time," said Camden casually, like we had not just done this gorgeous damage to each other, our lips moist and swollen. "You can't tell me you don't want to kiss Max on top of the Ferris wheel or have a bumper-car war."

"I don't want to kiss Max on top of the Ferris wheel," she said firmly. "Although *other* things would be acceptable."

"You guys," said James. "Don't be gross tonight."

"Don't listen to him," said Max to Eliza. "Be gross. Please, please, *please* be gross."

Eliza and Max held each other's glance. Then Eliza looked at me and Camden with pride, and I realized how she'd set it all up. Them coming separately, Camden waiting behind the Ferris wheel so we'd be alone in the moments we first saw each other.

Kendall and James stood side by side with a comfortable gap between them, both clutching their cameras around their necks.

"Okay, here's my plan," said Eliza. "We head straight over to the fun house, because those shots may take us the longest and I want to get them out of the way while there's still natural light."

James nodded. "Golden time, as they say."

"So where's the fun house?" asked Camden.

"It's in the same place every year," I said. "Follow me."

As we walked, I let go of Camden's hand to fall into step next to Kendall, then lean in to whisper in her ear.

"When we're done with the shoot, you and Jamie should go do your own thing. Something's bound to happen at the fair, right?"

Kendall shrugged. "You'd think so."

Fortunately, there was no line for the fun house, which was decorated, as always, with gigantic, distorted portraits of music icons. The leather-skinned carny guy at the entrance looked at us for only two seconds longer than he looked at everyone else.

"They must see it all," said Camden as we walked over the rickety bridge.

"I wonder what it would take to really ruffle them," I said.

Camden shuddered. "I actually don't want to wonder that."

We climbed to the second level where the maze of mirrors started. "Okay!" said Eliza. "This is it. Right here. Things are starting to feel awesome."

She directed me to stand by one mirror, opened her purse, and handed me Satina's trademark measuring-everything device. It was light as Styrofoam, and I remembered that night they were dumpster diving. I laughed, then held it skyward like Satina often did.

"You feel stupid, right?" asked Eliza. I nodded. "It's okay. Embrace that. But in your mind, try to turn the *stupid* into *fun*. And *free*."

I said the word *Satina* in my head. *Do it, Ari. Shake off your skin and feel hers.*

With silence and great seriousness, Camden crouched in front of me, his bare palm spread out on the floor like Azor did when he was telepathically reading a time and place.

"Look at that messed-up picture of Britney Spears," said Eliza, directing us to look at the wall mural. "Keep your eyes on that." She backed up to where James stood with his camera. "Yes! That is so perfect. Hold it there!"

James and Kendall stood on opposite sides of us, moving around a bit to get different angles. We got really into character now. Camden drew his gun and aimed it off camera, and I held out my device to test the atmosphere. After a few minutes, we had to pause to let a group of kids go through. They scanned us up and down, then giggled and kept going.

"Maybe they think we're part of the fun house," I said to Camden.

"I'm sad nobody's recognizing us," he said.

"I'm glad they're not. I'm glad this just belongs to us."

He leaned down and quickly kissed me, then grinned.

"Hey, 'Lize," called Camden. "What about all that sexual tension between Azor and Satina?"

"They never hooked up," said Eliza.

"But everyone imagined it," I said.

We watched her smile. "They sure as hell did. Okay, let's do a little fanfic version."

Camden leaned in close to me, and in this space that was tiny but also infinite because of the reflections, I could truly imagine he was Azor and I was Satina. I had always, always wanted him and now he was renouncing his vow of celibacy. For me. Decades of fans had fantasized about being the one he did it for, but here, now, it was *me*.

Did we kiss for a minute? Five? An hour? I wanted to catapult out of myself again, the way I had for those few forever-moments behind the Ferris wheel, but we were on display now. We were putting on a show.

After we made our way through the rest of the fun house and stepped back onto the midway, Eliza said, "Let's take our time getting over to the dairy pavilion. Just walk. Be *them*."

So we did. I tried to look at the world of the fair through Satina's eyes. This travel-weary woman who had seen so much, but nothing like this. She was trying to get her bearings as to where and when she was, and what was important to the people here. It must have been hard for her every time, despite her strength and independence. And of course, she was secretly, desperately in love with Azor, the man who could not give her what she needed most because he did not understand what it was.

James and Kendall together took about five hundred pictures as we walked. Heads turned, but it was the fair, after all. Everyone seemed to accept us as part of the absurdity they were there for in the first place. When we reached the dairy pavilion, Eliza handed me the plaid shirt and gave Camden Azor's stolen 1950s leather bomber jacket—another thrift store find that Eliza had tweaked.

Max slipped on Bram's silver wig, which really was the attention-getter. I could tell he was trying hard not to feel uncomfortable, and I thought of his comment at the Barn about how he was only doing this for Eliza.

"The cows?" asked Camden.

"Yes, the cows," replied Eliza.

The second scene we re-created was where Satina—who had never tasted real cheese before, what with cows being extinct in the *Silver Arrow* universe—was loading up on free samples while Azor begged them to move on to the Ferris wheel so they could investigate the anomaly. In another part of the sprawling pavilion, Atticus Marr and Bram were trying to find them.

The third series of photos were over by the Ferris wheel itself, and included all four of us—a scene after everyone had been reunited. Eliza wanted the ride in the background as we pretended to be running from angry fifties-era locals.

When we were done, we crowded around James and Kendall as they scrolled through the shots they'd taken. They looked better than I thought they would. I was not convinced that Satina was me.

"I cannot *wait* to post these," said Eliza. "I'm not sure I can even stay at the fair."

"You're staying," said Max. "We're having some fair fun whether you like it or not."

She smiled at him mischievously. "Only if you keep your costume on."

Max's expression flickered with doubt. "You're kidding, right?"

"Not kidding. I'll stay in mine." Eliza stepped up to Max and put one arm around his waist, the other on his chest, her fingers spread. "It'll be memorable."

Max laughed, grabbed the hand that was on his chest, and kissed it. "Fine. But you're buying me a bag of deep-fried Oreos."

They took off. I raised my eyebrows at Kendall.

"I like to see the animals," she said to James. "Some interesting photo ops there. Wanna come?"

"Sure," he said with a smile that could have meant anything. *Sure, let's do that and then finally go hook up somewhere.* Or, *Sure, that sounds safely unromantic, I'm in.*

Kendall led James away toward the rabbit pavilion.

Camden turned to me. "What about me? Should I change or not?"

Our costumes were barely costumes, out of context. My oversized plaid shirt and Camden's leather jacket with our leggings and boots just looked sort of arty. You couldn't even tell we were wearing wigs.

"I'd like to stay at the fair with Azor," I said.

I took his hand and held my breath, until he tugged me

closer to him and rewrapped our hands so our whole arms were intertwined. The leather jacket, heavy and unfamiliar against me, something I knew instinctively that Camden would never wear. We walked away from the pavilion and back toward the midway. The sun had halfway set behind the mountains and the changing colors in the sky made the electric lights of the fair glow even more brilliantly.

Now I could take it all in. The predatory leer of game runners as we walked by and tried not to make eye contact. The little shacks that sold deep-fried everything or food on sticks that really shouldn't be on sticks. The energy between Camden and me felt thick and awkward with questions. I didn't expect it to be so suddenly weird, to be on our own but still in costume. Were we done being Satina and Azor? Were we just Ari and Camden now, but with accessories?

I thought back to last summer. When I came here with Dani and we went on all the kiddie rides together. When I was looking for Camden, because I was always looking for Camden. Thinking once that I saw him walk onto a ride, and waiting until it was over, and then realizing it was not him at all. How stupid I felt.

We stopped when we got to the Scrambler.

"I've only been on this kind of ride once, when I was a kid," said Camden. "Some girl threw up and the barf went flying and hit me in the face."

"That's everyone's worst fair fear! We should go on it and replace that memory with a better one."

"I don't know. It was pretty traumatic."

"Come on," I said. "Otherwise the ride will always taunt you."

He shook his head, but let me drag him toward the entrance.

Once we were on the ride with the bar clicked into place, he pulled me across the red vinyl seat toward him and put his arm around my shoulder. I took a little mental picture of us. *This is what it looks like when you have the thing you've dreamed about.* I wondered if anyone watching had any idea of the path we took to get here. How amazing it was. Or if we were simply another anonymous couple in a sea of anonymous couples, which to me was its own kind of amazing.

As the ride started moving, I turned to Camden and kissed him. I was worried about losing our wigs, and that felt strangely thrilling along with the rush of spins and twirls. He slipped his hand between the plaid shirt and Satina's uniform top. Nobody would be able to see that—we were moving too fast. After a while, it seemed like we were the ones staying still.

I was a little uneven when my feet hit the ground after the ride was over. Camden steadied me and I steadied him back. The crowd was getting thicker now, jostling us as we tried to have a moment of stillness.

"This is a lot of people," said Camden, looking uncomfortable for the first time all night.

"I know somewhere private." And I did. On the far side of the kiddie ride area, between the haunted house ride that was not at all scary and the back of a goldfish-toss game, there was a patch of grass where I once changed Danielle out of wet underwear and into fresh ones. I led Camden there.

"Do crowds make you nervous?" I asked when we rounded the corner. He answered by putting his hand on the waistband of my leggings and pulling me toward him against a telephone pole. Then he put both palms on either side of my face and stared at me, something strong and determined in his eyes.

"Do you know that I haven't been to a fair since I was ten?"

"Because of the puke?"

He laughed, then his features settled into something more serious. "My mother thinks the fair is too commercial and exploits the animals. She's always said it was something people went to because they thought they were supposed to. That it was expected of them. And we were beyond that."

"Did you feel like you were missing out?"

"Yes."

"Well, if it helps, I've gone every year. And I still felt like I was missing out."

"You didn't feel like you were, you know, part of something bigger?"

"Not really. I felt like that something bigger evaluated me, then decided it didn't want me." I paused. "I know what your mom is talking about. There's an expectation here to have a certain kind of experience. No matter how much fun I had, it never felt like the right kind. Until tonight."

Camden looked at me sadly now. He took his thumb and ran it along one side of my face, right where my hairline started.

"I guess we're the same that way." And he kissed me, almost urgently this time. I felt the kiss shoot into the back of my neck and then travel down the center of my body, into my limbs. It filled me with sudden understanding about Camden. He wanted to *belong*. He craved the exact rituals and traditions his mother wanted them to live above.

I felt closer to him now than ever before, right there against the telephone pole. Where all we could hear were the sounds of little kids screaming and three different pop music songs blaring from three different rides.

Finally, he pulled away.

"I want to win you something," he said with a grin. "Something big and cheaply made and ugly."

I wanted that. I wanted what it would mean.

"Come," I said.

Fifteen minutes and thirty dollars later, Camden handed me a large stuffed penguin with dreadlocks and a Rastafarian hat.

"He's hideous," I proclaimed. "I love him."

"And now you have to carry it around for the rest of the night, right? As a trophy to show you're with a guy who's really good at throwing things at other things?"

"I don't mind," I said, not wanting to tell him the full truth. That at least three good fantasies I once had about him involved exactly this kind of thing.

I texted Kendall.

Everything OK?

She answered back:

Yup.

Not *great* or any other adjective that might indicate they were doing more than taking pictures of sheep.

I started to type, asking her if she wanted to meet up with us.

But then I stopped after the *want*. What did *I* want? I did not want her to meet up with us, yet.

Instead I wrote:

Text me later.

Much later, I hoped.

"Let's ride the Ferris wheel," I said to Camden.

"Now that the temporal anomaly has been fixed, I'd love to."

"You're a geek." Then I kissed him.

It wasn't as romantic as I thought it might be, since it stopped and started so much. But for those thirty seconds when it was our turn to hover at the very top of the wheel, I rested my head on Camden's shoulder and hugged my penguin. The breeze there felt like no breeze I'd ever felt before, and from up high the entire fair looked like something we could simply scoop up and tuck inside our jackets. Freeze it, frame it, call it perfect.

When we got off, we spotted Max and Eliza waiting in line for the swinging pirate ship. People were staring at them in their costumes, but they didn't seem to notice.

"Oh, good!" said Eliza. "I really don't want to go on this. Max doesn't understand what a pukefest it can be. Also, I think his wig will fly off."

"But it's a pirate ship!" Max said, jokingly pushing out his lower lip. "I love pirate ships!"

"It looks innocuous," I told Max, "but I've seen it make grown men cry."

"We're going to get something to eat," said Camden. "Come with us instead."

Eliza patted Max on the back. "Sorry, kid. After dinner we can go on the helicopter ride, and you can make whirring noises while you make it go up and down."

Max stepped out of the line and gave Eliza a dirty look. She didn't see it, but I did.

The fair had gotten really crazy now; it always ended up stupid-packed after work hours. I'd seen a few people from school so far, but they hadn't recognized me. I hoped more would show up. I wanted them to see me, and to see me with Camden and Eliza and Max. I loved the thought of them gossiping tomorrow. *Did you see that guy Ari was with? And she was wearing a wig!*

We were waiting at the Greek gyros stand—the one my mother always said was surprisingly authentic—when I heard someone call my name.

"Ari?"

I turned to see Brady. And Lukas. And a bunch of other people from school.

"Hey, Brady."

"Why are you guys dressed like that?"

"It's a long story," I said.

"It's really not," said Eliza, stepping up next to me. "It's a cosplay thing. We were here taking some photographs." She turned to me. "See? Short story. Not even. Just facts."

I looked at Lukas, who quickly shifted his glance from me and examined Max. He laughed. "Dude. *Silver Arrow*, right?"

Max smiled hesitantly. "Yes."

What Lukas knew about *Silver Arrow*, he knew from me. It felt wrong, stolen, hearing him say the name. His eyes slid over to Camden and me again, then quickly back to Max, not sure what to do with the situation.

Without Kendall here, I wasn't sure either.

Then suddenly, from somewhere, somebody shrieked. We all turned to see a ripple in the crowd surrounding the next booth.

There was a guy doubled over, vomiting.

"Classy," said Eliza.

A woman came up to the guy and grabbed his shoulders, but he sank onto his hands and knees and kept retching.

We all looked at one another. Even Brady and Lukas. Lukas and I exchanged a glance and I shrugged. It seemed rude to act as if this wasn't happening, but it also seemed rude not to.

Camden was the only person not ignoring it. He was staring.

"Camden," I said, nudging his hand. "Don't."

But Camden froze, his eyes locked on to the situation like he was seeing something we weren't. I turned to look at the guy again.

Now the guy was convulsing.

"Oh my God," I said. "He's having some kind of seizure."

"Camden!" shouted Eliza. "Go help him!"

Max gave Camden a gentle shove on his back. "You're the hotline guy. You go talk to him, keep him calm. I'll get help."

Max took off running toward the first aid tent, but Camden didn't move forward.

Now the guy was flat on the ground, his body doing things he had no control over. The woman sank down on her knees next to him, holding out her hands like she knew she wanted to put them on him, but wasn't sure where. She didn't seem all there.

"What do you do in these situations?" I asked Camden. But Camden stood frozen, watching. His mouth a flat line, his eyes dull and stony.

The crowd, which had now formed a circle around the area, parted to let a pair of paramedics through. A security guard trailed behind them.

"Clear the area, folks. Let them do their work."

Max reappeared, out of breath, and took Eliza and me gently by the arms.

"Come on," he said.

We took a few steps away and I turned to make sure Camden was following us. But he wasn't there.

"Where's . . . ?" I started to ask.

But they kept walking, so I kept following, not wanting to lose them in the crowd, too. I death-gripped my penguin and followed them past all the other food booths, into the tent with all the hot tubs on display, then finally a booth selling wooden chairs and porch swings.

Eliza sat down in a swing and took a deep breath, patted the spot next to her. I sat. She began to push us gently back and forth with her feet.

"That was a drug thing," said Eliza.

It took me a few seconds to figure out what she was talking about. "Oh. The guy?"

"Yeah." She looked up at Max now, and smiled. "Hey. You're good in a crisis."

"Thanks," he said, and sat down in an Adirondack recliner across from us.

"You may have saved his life. The rest of us were all standing around like idiots."

Max shrugged. "See. You may treat me like a child, but I don't always act like one."

Eliza's expression shifted from smug to stung. Dressed as she was like Atticus Marr, it seemed even more out of place.

"If you have something to say, Max, say it. Passive-aggressive doesn't work on me."

They stared at each other. I stood up. "I'm . . . uh . . . going to see if I can find the others."

Then I walked as fast as I could without actually running. I checked my phone and saw that two messages had come in.

Camden's said, *Meet me at that fence place.*

Kendall wanted to know where we were. I told her to meet

me behind the kiddie haunted house in ten minutes.

At the place which was now *our* place, Camden sat on the grass hugging his knees to his chest. His wig gone, his hair rumpled and misshapen. The first thing I wanted to do was put my hand in it and rumple it myself.

Instead, I kept my distance and asked, "Are you okay?"

He looked up at me. There were giant tears trailing down his cheeks.

"Camden? What's going on?" I crouched down and put the penguin on the ground, but was still hesitant to reach out for him. "Did you know that guy?"

Camden wiped his nose with the sleeve of Azor's uniform. "No. But I . . . I've seen that before."

"Eliza said it was probably an OD situation."

Camden closed his eyes tight and nodded.

I thought of the guy's body convulsing, the woman too checked out to know what to do.

"Tell me," I said.

"Here?" he asked, his eyes still shut.

"Why not?"

"Because I wanted to be Azor for you."

"You were. You are."

"Not *now*. Not *this*."

"Then be Camden for me."

Camden laughed and opened his eyes, his eyelashes glistening. In those eyes, I saw something I hadn't yet glimpsed in him. Something wounded and secret and ashamed.

"I was twelve," said Camden, taking a deep breath. "We were living in Florida with my mom's boyfriend."

I shifted my position so I was sitting cross-legged on the gravel. "Go on."

"He and Mom had friends over; they were partying hard while I was trying to sleep. He came into my room thinking it was the bathroom, and then he just . . . he was on the floor . . ." Camden shook his head as he often did, like he was rattling something free. "I had the phone in my hand like this, on the line with 911." He curled one hand into a tight claw that held an imaginary receiver. "But he died right in front of me."

We were silent for a moment. I had no idea what to say.

"Is the guy okay?" asked Camden. "The one we saw?"

"I don't know. Should we go find out?"

Camden shook his head. "That was mortifying over there, that I choked under pressure. I could have comforted the woman, at least. I have the training. I mean . . . the whole experience in Florida was one of the reasons why I wanted to volunteer at the hotline to begin with. I want to help people, not be a bystander my whole life."

"You will," I said.

"This is a goddamn upstate New York county fair! Not some crappy apartment in Gainesville! This kind of thing should not be happening at a wholesome family event." He stood up and shouted at the sky. "We came here to get away from all that shit. I was supposed to be done with it. Done!"

I stood up, too. He turned to me.

"I have to go home. I have Max's keys. The others can ride home with Kendall, right?"

"The others?"

He caught my arm and grasped it. "Will you come with me?"

I wasn't sure what that meant. What would happen once we reached the Barn.

I didn't care.

"Of course," I said. "Let me call Kendall and let her know what's happening."

"Are you sure?" Kendall asked when I told her.

"He shouldn't be alone."

"So what does that mean, you're going to stay over?"

"I have no idea. But if Mom or Richard call your house, can you cover for me?"

A pause. "Okay." Her voice sounded flat and tight.

"I'll check in with you later."

I hung up and scooped the penguin from the ground.

"Let's get out of here," I said, and took Camden's hand with my free one. He looked at me and the pain on his face, it was so Azor. The memory of our kiss at the Ferris wheel flushed through me. All my unleashed, bold Satina-ness. "The ending sucked," I added, "but until then I had the best night of my life."

Camden smiled a little. "You have no idea." He slipped his hand into mine to give it a squeeze before drawing it away.

I knew the quickest way out of the fair, and this time he was the one following me.

13

We didn't speak as Camden drove Max's car out of the fairgrounds parking lot.

In the strange and also strangely intimate minutes that followed, I stared out the window and thought about how getting to know someone is all about learning and unlearning at the same time. For every piece of new information you gain about that person, you might have to let go of something you thought was true.

Finally he asked, "So, that guy from your school we ran into. He was someone, right?"

"Ex-boyfriend," I said.

Camden nodded. "You don't have to tell me the story. Unless

it'll make me feel better."

"I was the one who ended it."

A pause. "That makes me feel better."

We were silent the rest of the drive. Camden seemed lost inside himself, sloshing around in places I had no access to.

When we got to the Barn, I followed Camden to the porch, where he stooped to fish a house key out from under the cushion of the wicker sofa. His Azor uniform was long gone. Now he wore only his white T-shirt and black pants and boots, and I couldn't help thinking that half of him had been stripped away.

The house was eerily quiet without the voices and the music, the *whirr* of Eliza's sewing machine. Once inside, I closed the door behind us. The sound of it seemed to startle him. I thought maybe he'd forgotten I was there, too. But he turned and looked at me, then held out both hands.

I took them.

"You've never seen my room," he said, his voice rough like he was struggling to retrieve it.

My stomach lurched. "No."

He tugged me toward the staircase, walking backward.

"Is it okay if I show you my room?" he asked.

"Yes," I squeaked.

I'd been in this situation before. Knowing you're there for the wrong reason. So aware that the way you want something is completely screwed up, but not caring. Sometimes wanting is a *buy now, pay later* deal.

I knew I should tell him to stop, that we needed to talk

about the whats and the whys.

I could not.

When we got to the stairs, he let go of one hand to walk forward, but kept the other. We walked like that to the top, past the big picture window, across the landing. Through the door Camden opened for me.

He stood aside so I could look around. The room was small, with a slanted ceiling and a skylight. Each wall was painted a different color: forest green, teal blue, burgundy, and white. The combination felt random, yet harmonious. In one corner was his bed, which I only glanced at quickly before feeling my skin flush. It was just a tiny twin, but it may as well have been a king-size water bed with velvet pillows and fur throws, under a banner that said *SEX!* in fifty-point font.

An overpacked bookcase filled the opposite wall. A beanbag chair sat in the corner, his laptop sunk into it. He had no posters or pictures up. Only a huge map of the world, dotted with plastic thumbtacks. Next to each thumbtack was a tiny slip of paper with writing that I couldn't read from a distance.

"Nice skylight," I finally said, leaning against the doorframe. I hadn't come all the way inside the room. I wasn't committing to anything. Right?

"Thanks," he said, staring up at the skylight. "My mom put it in for me when she bought the house." He paused, maybe snagged by a memory. "We'd been moving around so much, and now we were going to stay still. She wanted me to have a spot to watch the stars change position and remind us that at least the planet was still moving."

"How old were you? When you finally stopped moving around?" I asked, glad to be talking and sharing again, hungry for more pieces of him.

"Thirteen," said Camden. "And tired. Happy to be on solid ground."

I looked at Camden's face, which was still raised upward.

"Leave all the time-and-space traveling to the *Arrow One*," I said.

"Exactly." He smiled knowingly. "That's probably why I got so into the series, when I met Eliza and she showed me the reboot." He lowered his gaze to me now. Back in the present, returned to the here.

He went to the door and closed it slowly, then pushed me against it even more slowly. We kissed like that for a while, and I kept my eyes open, reminding myself this was Camden and not Azor. This Summer Camden and not Last Summer Camden. I realized I'd been shivering, then realized I'd stopped. Since that first true, unbound kiss at the Ferris wheel, we'd somehow already developed our own language of kisses. A knowable rhythm of soft, hard, here, there. Everywhere, anywhere.

Lost, and found.

Finally, Camden tugged me over to the bed. A little voice locked behind a miniature steel door in my brain started whimpering *No wait but.* I could barely hear it as I lay down on the black sheets.

Camden stretched his body on top of mine and leaned on his elbows, then paused for a moment to look at me. I took that moment to feel the excruciating safety of his weight, the warmth of his limbs mixing with the slightly different warmth of mine.

"I didn't expect this," he said, and I didn't know what he was referring to. Being here like this? Us in general? Me?

"I didn't either," I said, which was the truth any way you sliced it.

Camden kissed my neck, then my collarbone. He moved farther down, touching me through the plaid shirt, finally unbuttoning it, tugging it off my shoulders. It felt strange to shed that layer, even though I still had the purple tunic and white top underneath.

The voice in my head was trying harder to be heard now, and I started to see flashes of Lukas. The old couch with the rip up one side. The empty wine cooler bottles standing in clusters on the coffee table, like spectators. Ditching myself for a little while in the dim claustrophobia of Lukas's basement.

If I kept my eyes open, wide open, these flashes went away. I was here with Camden. There was only the Possible, surrounding us with hue and light.

I was waiting for Camden to lift up my shirt or slide his hand under the waistband of my leggings. But he just laid his head sideways on my belly, as if listening for something.

"Can I help you?" I joked.

"I'm a little overwhelmed."

Me, too. "Let's take a break."

He sat up at the end of the bed, then pulled me onto his lap so I was straddling him. Another combination of warmth, limbs, weight. He put his hands on either side of my ribs and with a bit of alarm, I could feel how aroused Camden was. It was scary yet amazing, knowing I could do that to him. That he belonged to me in this one way.

"God, Ari," he said, his eyes searching my face. "You make me feel . . . like I'm joining the human race."

"You've been with girls before," I said teasingly, stopping myself before adding *I've seen you with Eliza.*

"Not where I found myself doing this." He held out one hand in front of me. It was trembling.

I grabbed it, steadied it. We both stared at our hands as if we expected them to start acting on their own.

After a few moments, Camden said, "I'm sorry about tonight." He bit his lip. Pulled his hand out of my mine, which shrank back to my side. "It was so perfect. And then it was totally not."

"Even the imperfect part was perfect, to me. We all have a past, Camden. If we're going to be with each other, we can't ignore that."

As soon as I said it, Camden looked at my arm, then back up at me. When I didn't stop him, he turned back to my arm. He started to slowly push up my sleeve. It was tight at the wrist and wouldn't slide any farther.

"Can I?" he asked, and I knew what he meant. If he'd been

asking to take off my shirt, it could not have been more intimate than this.

"You've noticed the scars," I said, my voice catching.

"The first time we really spoke," he said. "That day with Dani and the diving."

He rolled up the sleeve until it hit my elbow, then turned my forearm so it was exposed. He took one finger and traced the scratches as if committing them to memory.

"They were shallow, and not anywhere near an artery," he said matter-of-factly.

"I wasn't trying to die," I said. "I was trying to feel better."

Now he just nodded. "Did you at least ice it down first?"

"With a bag of frozen peas."

He laughed nervously. "Did it work?"

"It was like someone else's skin I was cutting."

Camden lifted my arm. "I know this isn't going to make it all better," he said, "but . . ." Then he kissed my wrist a few inches from where the scars trailed off.

I inhaled sharply. "It might."

He looked up at me from under those giraffe eyelashes, my arm in his hand, and kissed it again. The voice behind the door stopped whimpering. He could have asked me to do anything. I would have taken on a thousand regrets just so I could have whatever he was giving.

"Ari," whispered Camden, placing my arm gently back down. "I need you to know something."

"Okay," I whispered back, not really ready for whatever he

was going to say but definitely ready to fake it.

"I want you here," he said. "I want to stay here in my bed with you all night but . . . I can't . . ." He made a waving motion with his hand. It took me a second to figure it out.

"Oh." Then a flooding rush of relief. "No. I wouldn't want to . . . I mean, it's too soon."

"Good." He sighed, then looked to the ceiling. "That's excellent." He put one hand to his forehead, like he was seeking shade from some blinding memory. "You have to understand the things I've grown up with. The stuff I've seen my mother do, and the guys who've come through our lives. And how she seems to lose a little piece of herself every time."

We were quiet for a few seconds, then I said, "So you've never . . ."

He looked straight at me again. "No."

I glanced away, partly because I didn't want him to see how glad I was to hear that. And how surprised. That any guy could date Eliza and not *go there*.

Because he was Camden, that was how.

"I haven't either," I finally said. It was technically true. Could it be that I was actually more "experienced" than he was? And how would that change things?

Camden exhaled and smiled a bit. He was glad. I was glad he was glad.

"You understand, then," he said, lacing his fingers through mine. "Why I can't seem to touch you enough but I can't . . .

I'm not going to do something just because some unwritten rule somewhere says we should."

I nodded, blocking out the memory of Lukas saying, *Come on, Ari. We've been going out for three months.*

"Should I leave?" I asked Camden.

His eyes widened. "No! I mean, I don't want you to. I'd like you to stay. Can you stay?"

I knew he was really saying, *I don't want to be alone.*

"I'm supposed to be sleeping at Kendall's, but she said she'd cover for me."

Camden nodded, suddenly businesslike, and patted the bed. We unfurled together, stretching out on the sheets, our heads touching on the pillow. I wrapped my feet around Camden's feet. He reached up and cupped my cheek.

"You told me about the scars. I want to tell you a secret about Gus. The one who died."

"Tell me," I said, staring up at the skylight.

Camden moved his arm so it was across my waist. Took a deep breath.

"He was an asshole."

I let out a nervous, surprised laugh, then quickly sucked it back in.

"I hated him," added Camden. "It feels really good to say that out loud to someone."

"What did you hate about him?" I asked, because I wanted him to continue the telling.

"When my mom wasn't around, he'd say nasty things about

her to me. Then he'd say nasty things about *me* to me. He took money from her purse and dared me to squeal on him. So a few times before the night he died, I wished he were dead. You know, the kind of wishing that comes out of you like you're swearing, you're just letting out your anger."

I nodded against his shoulder.

"Then, when he did actually die . . ." Camden's voice closed up, tied tight with a string.

"You thought you'd made that happen."

"I was twelve."

"You never told anyone?"

"God, no. I felt so guilty. Happy and relieved, but guilty."

"Traumatized."

"In a multilayered way."

"Wow," I said.

Camden sighed, and the movement of his body as it took on extra air, then released it; I could feel that movement in every part of me.

"I've never told anyone that," said Camden.

I put my hand on the hand that was on my waist. It felt like he'd gifted me more than I'd gifted him. We were pushing through each other and maybe if we stopped now, we might never make it to the other side. Then we kissed for a long time and I imagined that the stars floated down through the skylight to where we were. There was no floor or ceiling anymore, no ground or sky. There was only everything, mixed in together.

Finally, I bit his lip gently and pulled away, feeling raw.

There was something about him strong and solid against me, like a foundation. I decided to act on this tiny thread of courage before I lost it.

"I've got another secret for you," I said.

"Another one?" he asked, amused.

I shrugged.

"Don't feel obligated," he added. "This isn't like a Secret Smackdown."

"I know. I just want to tell you. Think of it as a bonus."

"Okay."

I took a deep breath, in my mind flying away from the person who was warm and breathing and next to me in his bed in his house where we were alone and the whole universe might as well have been ours. Away from me now, back to me then.

"When we first met, you said you remembered seeing me at the lake before."

"I did," he said.

"I remembered seeing you, too. Last summer." I paused. "Actually, I had a huge crush on you."

I closed my eyes and buried my face in his neck. I felt Camden take a deep breath.

"But you didn't know me. We never talked. Did we? Shit, if we did and I forgot . . ."

I forced myself up again, to look at his face. A small frown creased his forehead.

"No, we never talked. It was one of those from-afar things."

Camden lay there for a few more moments (that frown, ugh)

and then asked, "What was it about me that made you have a crush without actually meeting me?"

"I've thought about that a lot," I said. "It was only four months after that night with the Lady Bic. I was fighting to feel better. To feel like I had the strength. And I'd watch you—" Oops, I hadn't meant to tell him about the watching. Too late now. "You seemed so confident. Free. As if you had it all figured out and maybe you could show me." I pressed my lips closed tight to keep myself from saying any more.

After a few seconds, Camden shifted away from me, rolled over onto his side to face the wall. I couldn't see his face.

"You're weirded out, aren't you?" I joked.

Camden didn't answer right away, and with every second that passed without him saying *No, not weirded out at all!*, I died inside a little more.

"I'm glad you told me," he finally said. He didn't sound the least bit glad about anything.

"You okay?"

"Just really tired all of a sudden. I was super-wired earlier but now I think I might drift off."

"Let's drift," I said, lying down on my left side. I didn't dare get closer. I left a little cushion of space between us as we lay in identical positions on his bed. Air rushed into it from the open window above, making that distance feel wider.

I only half-slept that night, tense and angry in my dreams. I kept seeing Camden fighting with Lukas. Then Max yelling at Eliza, Kendall screaming at the guy who was overdosing in front of the gyro shack. One person would morph into another, and sometimes it would be a real person and sometimes it would be a character from *Silver Arrow*. Also, there were batter-dipped hamburgers everywhere.

I opened my eyes covered in sweat, sunlight coming in diagonally from somewhere. A green wall. A trapezoid of yellow. Wooden floors with the dust visible and fairly sparkling, like dew. I had no idea where I was.

Then I felt Camden next to me, a presence rising and falling with breath, and things made sense again. I stared at the outline of him, still turned away from me in the bed. The delicious curve of his shoulder blades against his T-shirt. The small patch of skin visible at the base of his neck. Most people look younger, more vulnerable when they're asleep. But Camden looked strong, as if his peace were power.

Last summer, the view of his back always hurt a little. It was a reminder that I saw him, but he didn't see me. Now I reached out and touched two fingers to it just because I could. What would it be like for us now that we'd shared all these secrets and I'd gone one truth too far? Would he still be acting strange? I didn't want to wake him and find out yet.

So I crawled out of bed and found the bathroom, feeling lighter in the places he had touched me, stripped to something essential. I looked in the mirror to see if that showed, but saw only a tired-looking girl in a rumpled Satina Galt uniform.

Back in Camden's room, I dared get closer to the world

map on the teal-blue wall, and the messages next to each thumbtack. Each slip of paper had a person's name and a few scribbled notes like "Ice-skating and tomato soup."

He'd been so many places, met so many people. Not all of them had been happy or good. They'd left marks deep inside. Yet I was the one with the visible scars. Me, with my stable home and the family who loved me, and a life where nothing truly bad had ever happened.

I went downstairs and filled a mug with water, then sat on the couch outside on the porch. The sun was squatting fat and obvious in the sky, and I couldn't help wondering if Mom had come home and gone to bed, if Dani was up. A horse in the field next door glanced at me in that sideways, knowing manner. He seemed to be asking, *So. What next?*

I had no idea. All I knew was now, with the mug heavy and solid in my hand, the fleeting comfort of a place that didn't belong to me.

"Hey," said Camden's voice behind me.

I turned around to see him leaning in the doorway. He'd changed into fresh clothes.

"Hey." I paused. He was staring off into the distance, not looking at me.

"I have to bring Max's car back to him. I can drop you at Kendall's on the way."

"Okay," I said. "But I have time. I don't need to be home for a while."

Camden gave me an awkward look.

"Are you all right?" I asked him.

"I'm fine." He smiled quickly, then let it drop quickly. "But we should go soon." He walked into the house and called behind him, "Max needs his car."

When he came back out, he had my boots in his hand.

"You didn't bring anything else inside, did you?" he asked.

"No. My backpack's in Kendall car. My wig's . . . oh, my wig's in there." I pointed to Max's car. "And Rasta Penguin, of course." I laughed. He didn't.

"Okay, good."

The cold, detached way he said this felt like a palm slapping my face. The sting of it shot through the rest of my body and rendered me silent.

Camden motioned for me to follow him to the car. It felt stupid to do it, but even stupider to sit there on the porch. I watched his slumping shoulders as we walked and wanted to grab them, shake them, demanding *Why are you doing this?* I swallowed hard. Holding it together, holding it back.

After we were both in the car, I turned to him. He was purposely not meeting my glance.

"Camden," I finally choked out.

"Hey," he said.

"Did I do something wrong?"

He looked at me quickly, then away.

"What do you mean?"

"Please don't pretend," was all I could say.

Camden exhaled sharply as he backed up the car, then

remained silent as he turned us around and headed down the driveway. I kept staring at his mouth, waiting for it to do something.

Finally, I looked at his eyes, and saw that they were shiny with tears.

"Camden?" I asked.

"I shouldn't have asked you to come home with me. I shouldn't have asked you to stay." There was something hollow about his voice now.

There were a million smart, witty, true things I could have countered with, but instead all I had was, "I wanted to stay."

"My problems shouldn't be your problems, Ari. At least not at this point, where we barely know each other. I'm sorry I brought you into them."

"You were happy to bring me into them," I said. I had to keep going. I had to say it, because he clearly wasn't going to. "Happy, that is, until I told you about last summer."

His knuckles on the steering wheel tightened, then relaxed. He took a long, slow, deep breath.

At last he said softly, "I'm not this perfect guy."

"I don't want you to be." Then I realized it was true. If I'd wanted him to be perfect, I would have kept him in the distance, framed as something I could admire from far away.

"I'm not even any of the things you thought I was. You're going to be disappointed."

"I won't . . ."

"Do you know how many times my mom thought she was

experiencing love at first sight and went chasing after some guy? And you know how often she was wrong about him? Always."

"You clearly have a low opinion of your mother," I said angrily. "And now, me."

Camden shook his head in that Camdenish way again.

"No, no, I didn't mean it like that. I'm just leery of this whole 'instant love' idea some people have. How much it can hurt, in the end." He glanced quickly at me. "And I guess it scares me, that you saw that stuff in me. Because I don't see it in myself."

He took one hand off the steering wheel long enough to wipe a tear, then put it back.

"You'll have to tell me how to get to Kendall's," he said.

"Camden . . ."

"I want to stop talking about this right now."

So it would be like that. I stared out the window, not able to look at him anymore.

"Make a right at the next intersection," I murmured.

That was the rest of the drive. Directions, turns, stops. Silence except the sounds of the car, the turn signal clicking and the squeak of the brakes. When we pulled into Kendall's driveway, I grabbed my wig and jumped out, slammed the door without saying good-bye. I left the penguin behind.

By the time Kendall opened the front door, I finally dared to turn around and see that Camden had actually, truly driven away.

And then I finally let myself cry.

14

"He's fucked up," said Kendall as she cleared a seat at the breakfast counter and pushed a glass of water toward me.

"I'm such an idiot," I said as I swallowed down my medication. "Why would I tell him about last summer?"

"Do not blame yourself here! I won't let you blame yourself."

I sighed. "Okay. Yeah. He's fucked up. So am I."

"So am I," said Kendall. "So are we all. But that is *not* how you handle it when you're weirded out or have low self-esteem or whatever. It's in the manual."

I couldn't help but smile. She was so good at doing that to me. "There's a manual?"

Kendall shrugged. "It just came out. I'll lend you my copy."

She paused. "So, what exactly happened? Did you . . . sleep with him?"

"No! I mean, well, yes. We *slept*. Nothing more. Nothing that would be on, like, a sex checklist." Kendall gave me an odd yet somehow relieved look. "That's in a different manual."

She laughed. "I'll trade you."

It lasted only another second, the feeling that everything would be okay. Then it was gone, and I dropped my head into my arms on the counter. The tears pressed forward. Stupid me, who thought honesty was an all-or-nothing proposition. That you can get to a place with someone where the known world drops away and you can hyperspace into the Possible. There are always baby steps, and backward steps, and sideways steps. It's the only way you ever get anywhere.

And now, maybe, we'd stopped dead.

I'd had that quick rush of feeling capable, and now I'd set us on a different trajectory. That hurt. An image flickered in my head. My arm. A razor blade drawing a line across it. Even the thought of this gave me some kind of relief, still. Even after all this time, that image always came to me when I called it. At least now, I understood why. At least now, I didn't take it seriously.

I blinked it away, then sat up and wiped my face with the kitchen towel. It smelled like cinnamon. "Tell me about Jamie. Tell me about your night."

Kendall described what sounded like an absolutely darling evening. She and James took photos of the 4-H kids holding their rabbits and chickens, grooming their goats. Kendall got some great shots of the lemurs in the traveling zoo. They bought milk shakes. They went on whatever rides they safely could, with their cameras in tow, and split a blooming onion. Later, they met up with Max and Eliza, who overshared that they'd messed around behind the horticultural pavilion.

"Do you like him?" I asked.

"A lot," she said. "*A lot* a lot."

"Should we ask Camden or Max to talk to him, find out whether he likes you back?"

"No way. Too embarrassing." Her features tightened up. "Besides, if it were meant to happen, it should just happen, right?"

"Who says?"

"I don't know. Maybe that's bullshit. But for once, it would be great if something came to me easy the way it comes to everyone else."

I knew she wasn't only talking about boys. For years, she'd watched me finish homework quickly and get As while barely studying. I thought the fact of my depression had canceled that out in her eyes—*see, not everything's easy for me*—but maybe not.

There was a knock at the front door, but before Kendall could even move toward it, the door opened. My mother poked her head in.

"Hello? Kendall? Ari?"

I froze and stared at my backpack on the hallway floor,

which Kendall must have brought in from the car when she got home. Which contained my regular clothes.

"Mrs. Logan!" said Kendall. "What are you doing here?"

I stepped into the shadows of the kitchen. There was no way I could get to my backpack without Mom seeing, but at least I could stall for a moment.

"I was out anyway, so I thought I'd pick up Ari and save you a trip."

"Ari?" Kendall called, turning around. Totally not getting why I was hiding near a coatrack.

I gave her a dirty look, indicated my Satina costume. Revelation lit up her face.

"Oh, shit," she whispered. "I'm sorry."

Now my mom walked into the house and closed the door. She saw my backpack and picked it up. "Ari?" she called again. "Ready to go? I'm bringing you straight to the store."

"What do I do?" I mouthed to Kendall. Kendall shrugged. I imitated her shrug. She looked annoyed.

"For God's sake, Ari," she said, forgetting to whisper, "it's not like you shaved your head or got a tattoo."

"Who got a tattoo?" my mom asked, rounding the corner into the kitchen.

She looked at me. I looked back.

She smiled impatiently, but then her eyes traveled down from my face. The tunic, the *Arrow One* pin. The leggings and, in new context, the purple boots.

I watched as Mom's glance swept back up my body, the

change in her expression happening slowly. It looked like it might be the beginning of a smile, maybe even a laugh.

"I don't . . . ," she started, then restarted. "What . . . why are you dressed like Satina Galt?"

I couldn't answer right away.

"You should see it with the wig," said Kendall, who was holding Satina's hair. This was not the response I would have gone with, personally.

Mom glanced at the wig, both confused and amused now.

"I went to the fair this way," I finally said. "Me and some other kids."

"To the *fair*?"

"It's called cosplay."

"We took photos of them re-creating some scenes from an episode," added Kendall.

"'Ferris Wheel,'" I said.

"Ari was amazing," said Kendall.

My mom shook her head, maybe trying to speed up the processing of all this information. "Which other kids?"

"Some new friends."

"Have I met them?"

"No, Mom. This is what you're going to focus on? They're just some kids we met at the lake. They're nice."

Mom stepped forward and took the wig from Kendall, who had been twirling a few strands around her finger.

"It's good, right?" I said. "Exactly like her."

Mom looked at the wig for a long time, her mouth twitching

further into a smile. "Yes, it's good," she finally said. Her expression flatlined. "But I need to meet these friends. Or at least, the boy. Because there's a boy, right?"

I sighed.

Mom scanned my costume again. "And you need to change before going to the store. It's weird enough to walk around the fair like that, but—"

"*Of course* I'll change. I was about to when you showed up."

I took the backpack from Mom and started to move down the hall toward Kendall's room.

"Wait a minute," said Mom. "Why are you still in the costume now if you wore it last night?"

I froze. Opened my mouth, but nothing came out.

"I dared her to sleep in it," said Kendall quickly. "She was complaining about how she didn't want to take it off."

I nodded. "I got kind of attached. I mean, look at this!" I motioned to the tunic with a flourish.

"Well, there's always Halloween," said Mom dismissively. "Go get dressed now, please. I told Richard you'd be there at ten."

"Yes, sir, Captain," I said.

On my way to Kendall's room, I stole a glance back at my mom. She was still holding Satina's hair, staring at it like she'd just run into an ex. Like she couldn't decide what to see, the everything between them or the nothing at all.

"Here," Mom said as she handed me the wig when I came

back, changed, a few minutes later. She paused. "Be careful with it. Satina was always so particular about her hair."

A few hours later, I was driving Richard's car on my way to pick up some paint at a warehouse in the next town over when my phone rang. It was sticking out of my bag so I only saw "CA" on the screen. But that was enough to make me pull over.

"Do you think I'm an asshole?" he said when I picked up.

"I don't know," I lied.

"*I* think I'm an asshole."

"Don't think that."

"Now you see I'm not that confident, carefree guy you thought I was."

I was about to say something along the lines of *And I like you even more for that,* but a gigantic truck thundered by.

"Where are you?" asked Camden.

"By the side of the road on Route 44-55."

"Well, crap. Call me back later."

"It's okay. This is actually the most privacy I'm going to get for a while." I rolled up the windows and leaned the seat back. "Let's talk."

I heard him take a long breath, and maybe heard it shake a bit.

"Last night was . . . amazing, really." His voice lower now. I closed my eyes and tried to pretend we were on his bed beneath the universe, and with that voice came hands and fingers that touched me.

"I thought you said it was a mistake."

"I guess it was both," he said after a pause, sounding pained. "I keep thinking of you next to me, letting me see your arm. I wish I could stay in that moment infinitely."

"*That's* the moment you wish you could stay in?"

Camden laughed nervously, then his voice got soft again. "There were a lot of moments, Ari. But I guess that one . . . that was where I felt the least freaked out. Knowing you'd been through stuff, too. Survived it. Can we get back to that part, where you were telling me about the scars?"

That was before I'd told him about last summer. I was more than happy to go back to that part.

"Where did I leave off?"

"You said you weren't trying to kill yourself. But what set it off?"

I closed my eyes to the aggressive, almost obnoxious sunlight streaming in through the windshield. Maybe it was trying to scorch away the memory of that cold, midwinter night over a year ago.

"That's the million-dollar question, isn't it?" I said. "Thing is, I'm still not sure. My mom was in the final months of nursing school and always gone. I'd had a big fight with Dani because I was trying to finish a science report and she wouldn't leave me alone. I knew Kendall was at a movie with some of her newspaper friends and didn't invite me. On the outside, there wasn't anything special about the day, except that it was one more in a long string of crappy days."

I paused, opened my eyes.

"But on the inside . . ." I couldn't articulate it to him. Didn't want to. "Let's just say, I had no control over it. It did what it wanted to. In a twisted way I was actually trying to manage it."

After a few moments, Camden said simply, "I get that." He was silent for another few moments, then added, "So what did you do with it? The blood, I mean."

This I had an easy answer for. Facts embedded in a clear memory. "I watched it for a little while. Then I blotted it with toilet paper, and I watched that."

A red-snake trickle down drip drip drip. The specific feeling of pleasure mixed with pain, gratitude mixed with guilt.

"What happened then?" he asked, almost whispering now. "Did someone find you?"

"No. I think that only happens in movies."

"Ah, right."

"I wasn't sure what to do after I got tired of watching the bleeding. I was just sort of sitting there. I was maybe even a little bored. I'd made a lot of cuts and they were starting to hurt, because the peas were wearing off. So I left all the . . . evidence . . . and went out."

I kept talking and telling. About my mother frantically calling my cell phone, then Kendall frantically calling my cell phone because my mother had frantically called her. I described myself driving north on Route 32 until an unexpected snow started falling, and I got nervous, then turned around and drove south until the car fishtailed at a stoplight.

That was when I knew it was time to go home and step into the situation I'd created.

We listened to each other breathe for a little while after I stopped talking.

"So how did you get here from there?" he finally asked. "How did you get better?"

"Therapy. Medication." Bad decisions. Better decisions. Him. "I started believing in something I call the Possible."

"Is that what you were doing last summer, at the lake? Believing in the Possible?"

"Yes."

He didn't respond, and I started to worry that we'd been disconnected. At last he said, "Keep believing in that, Ari."

"I will."

"Keep believing in me, too."

Tears welled up in my eyes. It was all I wanted. That, and being able to reach through the phone and bite his ear.

"Okay," I said. "But first, you're going to have to meet my mom."

"Arrowhead Mom?" he asked, sounding relieved, unburdened. "Uh, yes please."

"She's not really that cool anymore. Or ever."

"Pshaw."

"I'm talking about dinner with the family and everything."

"A normal family dinner? That's like a fantasy of mine."

"My family isn't normal."

"Normal is relative."

I sighed. "I guess you'll see where we fall on that spectrum."

"It'll be fine, Ari," he said, as if aware that he could make anything okay as long as he added my name at the end. *I'm going to chomp the heads off baby ducklings, Ari. Do you mind if I date two other girls while I'm dating you, Ari?*

We said good-bye and I held the phone in my hand for a while, feeling its warmth as a substitute for the warmth of Camden's skin.

"Okay," I said to myself, moving the seat back into position. I turned the ignition back on, felt the blast from the AC hit me square on the cheek. I wasn't sure what the conversation had accomplished, what we'd just agreed to. We were still nervous and uncertain, directionless and green. Maybe we'd simply agreed to be all these things together, and that was enough for now.

I pulled onto the road and drove toward the address Richard had given me, glad that at least in one respect, I knew exactly where I was going.

15

"Tonight, tonight, a boy is coming over tonight!" sang Dani to the tune of her favorite *West Side Story* song, squeezing in syllables where there should not have been syllables. This was cute the first three times. Coming up on the twentieth, not so much.

Mom was at the stove, cooking moussaka. She was starting her new job the next day, which meant she had a lot of nervous energy. She'd vacuumed *and* dusted *and* brought out the linen place mats. It was all a little horrifying.

What had Richard told her about Camden and his friends? And what had Dani told her about "the dude who Ari likes to swim with at the lake"? She wasn't letting on. What Mom definitely knew about Camden: that his mom was an artist, that he went to Dashwood, that he lived in a converted barn, that we'd met at the lake.

What Mom *didn't* know: everything else.

Since that morning at Kendall's, Mom and I hadn't spoken about the cosplay at all. I'd washed the Satina costume and hung it in my closet, the wig in a bag hidden on a shelf where Dani couldn't get to it. I'd almost put the boots in there, too, but after half a day in sandals I slipped them on again.

I brushed dirt off the left boot as I sat on the top step of our porch, waiting for Camden. Richard was mowing the lawn in the hazy early evening half-light. Crickets made a racket and I felt a very particular combination of anticipation and dread.

When Camden's car drove up, I met it in the driveway. He rolled down the window and there was his face, that face. I leaned in, wanting desperately to kiss him. But I didn't know if that was okay, with Richard there. If it was okay, after what happened at the Barn.

"Hey," I said.

"Hey," he said back, smiling like I'd said infinitely more than that. He looked way too excited, and way too handsome, to be here.

"They don't know about your mom being away this summer."

"Oh, I'm getting a debriefing?"

"Be quiet, I only have a few seconds. They also don't know I stayed over on fair night."

Danielle ran out of the house just then. "Camden!" she

yelled, her face lit up. Camden got out of the car and Dani threw herself into his arms for a hug. Mom stepped onto the porch in time to see this. Richard, who had stopped mowing, finally turned off the mower and walked over to the car.

"Camden, this is my mom, Kate," I said.

They shook hands and I could see it on Mom's face. That she thought he was attractive. She smiled.

"It's a pleasure," said Camden. *It's a pleasure.* It was such a grown-up thing to say. I got the sense Camden had been saying *It's a pleasure* to adults since he was three years old.

Mom smiled. "Same here," she said. "So tell me, who are *you?*"

"Pardon?"

"In the *Silver Arrow* cosplay game."

"Good God, Mom. It's not a *game.*"

"It sort of is," said Camden. "Well, I used to cosplay Atticus Marr. But now I'm Azor."

Something softened around my mother's eyes. "Azor," she whispered, nodding.

"I hear you're a fan, too," said Camden.

My mom twitched. I may have been the only one who saw it. Or maybe I imagined it.

"Yes," was all she said.

Camden reached into his car and pulled out a brown paper bag. "I brought some raspberries. We grow them on our property."

Danielle grabbed the bag and opened it. "Yum!"

"Come inside," said Mom.

She and Richard led the way, Dani following with her hand already full of berries.

I turned to Camden. "You're good."

He shrugged. "I've been around more adults than kids in my life," he said. "I know how to work the system." Then he leaned in close and whispered warm in my ear. "Do I get to see your room?"

I felt a chill go down my neck. Why was he able to make these innocuous questions sound so sexy?

"Sure," I whispered back, casually, even though I'd spent the day cleaning it up.

We stepped inside the house and Camden took a deep breath. "Mmmm. Smells fantastic!" He said it loudly so my mom could hear from the kitchen.

I motioned for him to follow me down the hall. On the way, he examined the photos on the wall. Baby pictures of Dani, a wedding photo of Mom and Richard with me standing between them in a lavender dress. Camden paused and touched the me in the photo briefly with his fingertip.

When we moved into Richard's house after their wedding, Mom had gone to work hanging photographs, like she needed these reminders that her life was full of people, that she had proof it had all happened.

"Don't look at that," I said as Camden examined a frame designed to showcase every one of my school pictures since kindergarten. Only the last opening was blank now.

Camden looked anyway. Hard. Grinning. "Why? Because it's the most awesome thing ever?" He pointed to my picture from second grade. "Two front teeth missing. That's a great look. I wish you'd kept it."

I swatted him playfully and scanned the photos, trying to see them through his eyes. But from any angle, they were undeniably ordinary.

"We don't have actual art on the walls like you guys do," I said.

"Who says this isn't art?" he replied, pointing to the particularly mortifying picture from fifth grade, in which I looked like someone just off camera was poking me with a pencil.

I tugged his hand. "Can we move on?"

We went into the kitchen where Mom was putting the raspberries in a bowl and Dani was setting the table in the way I'd taught her, making the napkins into little beds for the silverware.

"Anything I can do to help?" asked Camden.

"Thank you," said Mom, "but we're almost done."

"We'll be down here . . ." I pointed toward my room.

Dani started to follow us, but Mom grabbed her shirt. "Nuh-uh," she said.

As I led the way, I kept trying to see my house as Camden might be seeing it. The low ceilings and the tiny windows. The beige carpeting that had so many stains, I'd come to think of them as a pattern. More pictures on the walls, including framed landscapes of places none of us had ever been: the

Grand Canyon, the Pacific Ocean, the Florida Keys.

When we stepped into my room, I turned to Camden. "We have to leave the door open."

He nodded like he already knew, and I wondered if he was thankful for it.

I sat on the floor with my back against the bed and let him take a self-guided tour. My desk, piled high with college brochures. The big chair covered with stuffed animals I couldn't bring myself to give to Dani no matter how hard she begged or how often she kidnapped them, because each of those animals had been a big deal to me, because I didn't have a thousand of them like she did.

"This reminds me," he said. "I have Rasta Penguin. He's safe and sound at the Barn."

"You can keep custody until next time I'm there."

Camden moved over to the *Silver Arrow* posters and pictures, things I'd cut out of old fan magazines or printed from online. He spent a long time at my bookcase, examining the shelf that was a rainbow of *Silver Arrow* novels, each one a different color.

"Oh, man," he said.

"Have you read any?"

"No."

"You can borrow whichever one you want."

He turned his head so he could read the titles on the spines, then drew out two books and sank down on the floor next to me.

Simply leaning against my bed made the memories of fair night tumble over me. If my parents weren't in the house, if we were somewhere else, would we have picked up right where we left off? Or had we gone a certain number of steps backward?

"Which do you recommend?" asked Camden, holding out the books, one flat on each palm like he was literally weighing them.

"Well, *Planet Jasmine* has the most Satina action. But the story is a little silly." I plucked the other book, *Time Enough*, from Camden's hand. "In this one, they're in 1940s Hollywood. Lots of old-time film references. You'd like it."

There was also less Azor in that one. I didn't want Camden to think I was lending him a book laced with hidden meaning.

"I love that you have these books," he said, taking *Time Enough* from me and clutching it to his chest. "I love your room. I love your whole house."

"You haven't seen my whole house."

"I'm extrapolating."

"But this is a cookie-cutter ranch house filled with stuff from chain stores. It's everything the Barn is not."

Camden continued to examine every inch of my room from his spot on the floor. Then he dropped his head back against my bed and closed his eyes.

"You know where I lived before the Barn?" he asked. "A yurt. You've heard of yurts?" I nodded. "Yeah, the yurt sucked. And the Airstream trailer. And the artists' co-op. The Barn was the result of years of me begging my mom for us to live in something halfway normal. Then my grandmother passed away and for the first time there was money, and we could do it."

Ah, okay. So Maeve was not the rich and successful artist I'd assumed she was. Everything I knew about Camden's life clicked into another fresh focus. *Learning and unlearning.*

Camden paused as Dani peered around the corner of my doorway, thinking we couldn't see her.

"Hi," he said. She popped out of sight. We smiled at each other, knowing she hadn't gone anywhere.

"I love the Barn, too," continued Camden, softer now that Dani was eavesdropping. "But sometimes it feels really empty. My mom is either gone or in her studio most of the time. Why do you think my friends practically live there?"

I wanted to say *Because you shine. You're the flame and they're the moths.*

Camden didn't wait for my answer. "Because I ask them to."

This sounded so strange to me, especially coming from him. When things got bad for me, when it felt like my life was all about my responsibilities to everyone else, the only thing I'd wanted was time alone. To press the Pause button on the world, to have a chance to catch my breath and then, actually listen to it. I couldn't imagine being lonely.

Camden ran his finger along my left side, then glanced furtively into the hallway.

"What happens if I kiss you?" he whispered.

"Don't," I said, so glad he wanted to. Almost happy to have a reason to deny him. "Dani," I mouthed.

"Hey, Dani," called Camden to the empty doorway. "I want to ask you something."

Slowly, the blond hair appeared, followed by the little pale face and the big hungry eyes.

"Yes?" she asked, gripping my doorframe.

"What happens if I kiss your sister?"

Dani looked at him, her eyes growing impossibly wider, then at me, then made her most grossed-out face ever.

"Yuuuuuuck! Please don't!"

She disappeared and we heard her run off down the hall.

"She's going to tell my mom," I said. "She has no filter."

"Who cares?" he said, then grabbed my face with both hands and kissed me quickly before drawing away. "I'm sorry. I've been thinking about doing that since five minutes after I dropped you off the other morning."

"*Shhhhhh.*"

Footsteps pounding down the hall again. Dani poked her head in. "Dinner's ready!"

Camden stood, then offered his hand and pulled me up, too. Dani watched with a smirk. I wasn't sure what she'd seen or heard. But then again, *Who cares?*

Mom served dinner on the dining room table that we never used, because it was always piled high with papers. Camden answered my parents' questions about his mom's art—what inspired it and how she made it and who bought it. When they asked him to, he talked about Dashwood. How it wasn't a place where kids ran around like *Lord of the Flies* as they'd heard, but rather an environment where you could study what you wanted and were encouraged to be responsible for your own education.

"It's not perfect and it's not for everyone," he said. "But I like it."

Camden sat straight with those square, confident shoulders, breezily brushing his hair out of his face, making pictures with his hands. His voice steady and musical, eyes reflecting the light. It was easy to see him the way my family was likely seeing him, the way I'd seen him at first. Knowing even a few of the truths behind all this made me feel powerful and privileged.

My mother told him her real name was Katia, which was Greek, because she was Greek and yes, she'd heard all the goddess jokes. She told him about the kinds of crazy things that happened during the night shift, and what her new job was going to be like. Richard told his best "wacky art supply store customer" stories.

Dani kept poking Camden with the trunk of her stuffed elephant, Ivory. Which meant she loved him, of course, but didn't know it yet.

After dinner, Camden and I did all the dishes. It was a strange kind of heaven, to be doing this boring task together. As if we were real people, simply living our lives. Mom and Richard were watching TV with Dani and I couldn't remember the last time that had taken place, whether or not it was all an act for Camden. And if it was, was that because Mom knew he was special? They'd certainly never done that for Lukas.

When the kitchen was clean—it still felt absurdly cool, knowing he and I had made it that way as a team—I walked Camden downstairs so he could say good-bye. More handshakes, more use of the word *pleasure*, along with *lovely* and *delicious*.

"How was I?" he asked as he leaned against his car, once again clutching the copy of *Time Enough* he was borrowing.

"Let me get this straight," I said. "You got freaked out when I stayed over, when I told you about last summer. But you're not freaked out about meeting my family."

He shrugged. "I never said it made sense."

"So. What happens now?"

"Well, there's the SuperCon. Eliza has plans for that. I hope your mom will let you go, since she's met me and I've hopefully impressed the bejesus out of her."

"That's what happens next week. What happens *now*?"

Camden seemed stumped, then searched my face, maybe looking for an answer he could borrow. He glanced toward the house and reached out, pulled me close so we were pressed up against each other. His heart drumming against my chest. I still didn't know what truly kept it beating. The secrets of him lay just under his skin but I could not reach them.

"This," was all he said. "*This* is what happens."

The front door creaked open and I jumped away.

"Camden!" called Dani as she ran out. "Wait! I want to watch you leave!"

"She likes to watch people leave," I said, feeling the heat drain from my cheeks. "It's her thing."

Camden smiled. "We all have a thing."

We watched him together, sitting on the porch, until his car was out of sight.

Five minutes later, Mom stepped outside and put her hands on Dani's shoulders.

"Pajama time," she said, and steered Dani toward the door like she was a puppet. "Daddy's waiting to help you. I'll be there in a few minutes."

Dani resisted at first, planting her feet far apart, her hands on her hips. "Hmph."

"I'm serious, Danielle," said Mom in a different voice now, a layer of softness stripped off. "We've had a nice day. Don't ruin it."

Dani gave me an imploring glance, but I nodded at the door. "Go." And she did.

After the door closed behind her, Mom stared out at the street. The sun had finally set, the light scattering quickly. Our neighbors were visible in their living room window.

"The Gustafsons are playing after-dinner poker again," said Mom. "I often notice them when I leave for work."

She sat down on the top step next to me. It felt awkward, creaky. Had my mother and I forgotten how to quietly coexist in the same space?

Please, I thought. *Don't talk about Camden*. Then another thought: *Please talk to me about Camden*.

"He's great," she said.

I flicked a look at her, trying to hide my surprise, then glanced away. "I think so, too."

Mom let out a small laugh, like tiny bubbles. "I can see why he'd make a good Azor."

Warmth and relief flushed down the back of my neck and made the hairs stand on end. Something about her even saying the name *Azor*.

"Here," I said, sliding my phone out of my pocket before I could think of all the reasons not to. Kendall had emailed me about a dozen of the best fair photos from her camera. I pulled them up and handed Mom the phone, which she took hesitantly.

I couldn't read her expression as she browsed through the images. It was like she wasn't sure whether to smile or cry. She seemed on the verge of either, the lines on her face capable of going both ways. I didn't know what I expected or wanted here, only that this was something I had to give at the moment. When it came to my mother, there had been so little I had to give, above and beyond what I was expected to . . . or what she took from me, depending on how I wanted to see it.

When she finally handed me back the phone—I think she must have looped through the photos at least twice—all she said was, "Looks like fun."

"It was. Much more than I thought it would be."

"Nobody gave you a hard time for being dressed like that?"

"We got some stares. But, you know. It was the fair. People probably thought we were part of a stage show or something."

"It's funny, how you've stayed a fan of the show. I always thought it was something you put up with because of me."

"No. I loved it, too. Really, I did."

Mom nodded and smiled distractedly, then looked at the Gustafsons' window again, tilting her head to get a better look at what they were doing.

"The other kids in the pictures . . . ," she asked.

"Eliza and Max. They go to school with Camden. And there's a guy named James who doesn't cosplay but he takes photos." I almost said, *Kendall is totally hot for him*, but caught myself.

"They're good kids?" She turned to me. "I trust your judgment here, Ari."

"They are," I said. "You can."

I didn't ask what her definition of "good" really was. I'd never thought about what *my* definition was, either.

"I remember what it was like to discover new people," said Mom. "After growing up with the same crowd." She paused, seemed suddenly stricken. "It's easy to make bad decisions, when you're distracted by what's different and exciting."

"I'm not making any bad decisions." Secretly staying over at Camden's: admittedly bad. Not having sex with him: good enough to cancel that out. Right?

"Okay," Mom said. "But I need to mention it. Trust me when I say, I've been there."

I waited for her to elaborate, but her mouth stayed closed and I could see the muscles in her jaw tightening.

"It's clean fun, Mom," I said. "And they're all as mature and responsible as Camden, I swear." I almost added *They'd love to meet you*, but I didn't want them to meet her. Giving up Camden had been hard enough.

"And now with my new job, you're losing your free afternoons to hang out with them," she said. "I'm sorry about that."

I wasn't sure which was worse: the fact itself, or that she knew it and didn't feel compelled to change it.

"Too late now," I said.

Mom swallowed hard.

"I get nights, right?" I pressed. "I can still go out at night?"

"You still have a curfew, but yes, of course you can go out at night. I want you to. Really, not that much will change, except now you don't have to tiptoe around the house during the day because I'm trying to sleep."

She saw it in such simple terms. The numbers on the clock, the puzzle pieces of child-care coverage and household tasks that fit together. What she didn't see was this:

That Danielle would get even more high maintenance. The less she saw of Mom, the more she'd teeter precariously between Normal Child and Melting Child. She'd need me more, and not in ways you could measure in hours. Yes, I would be free to go out as soon as Richard came home, but I would not be free to leave without Dani making a huge ridiculous deal out of it, crying and begging me to stay.

Another thing Mom didn't see: how it looked from my end. That my freedom, my chances to see Camden and my new friends, not to mention spend time with Kendall before she left—that was all at the mercy of her work schedule.

I couldn't see what it might look like from Richard's end, but I could imagine. Mom pressing silently against his guilt about the store not being enough to provide for us. Her wrapping everything into the prospect of them being able to sleep in the same bed at the same time again, as if something that happened while they were unconscious could solve all of their problems.

"It's going to be fine," Mom said in response to nothing.

"If you say so." It came out more sarcastic than I'd meant it.

She shot me a look that made me think of old books when they described someone as *cross*. It was a great word. I wished people used it more.

I didn't want to leave it at that; I didn't want her to zip up the way she often did at the first sign of discord. And I wanted to know what I wanted to know, this likely being my only chance to know it. I looked at the phone in my hand and asked, "You haven't told me what you think about this *Silver Arrow* thing."

Mom stared off at the Gustafsons again. It looked like Mr. Gustafson was working a corkscrew on a bottle of something.

"I'll be honest. I think it's really weird."

"Well, of course it's weird. That's the point."

She sighed. "It's so different, being a fan of anything now."

"It's better . . ."

"Maybe," she said.

What I was really asking was, *Mom, do you think I make a good Satina* the same way I used to ask *Mom, do you think my drawing is good? Mom, look how high I climbed! Did you see I got a 100 on my spelling test?*

I hated that I had to ask. I hated that the answer she would have given, regardless of what she thought, would have been the *Yes* she always gave. But maybe that would have been enough, because I suddenly realized that I needed her approval on Satina even more than I needed her approval on Camden.

Finally, I decided to make the most of my window. "There's a convention next week in Connecticut called the SuperCon," I said. "It's a pretty big gathering of fans, anyone who's into comics, science fiction, video games. We want to go as our cosplay group. It'll be on a Saturday when you're off, and it's only a day trip."

"Cosplay group," Mom repeated, arching one eyebrow.

"This is where most people are in costume, so we won't look like freaks. Plus, Eliza thinks by then that so many people will have seen the fair photos, we'll practically be celebrities."

Mom's eyes swiveled to my phone, which I was still holding in one hand. "Why will so many people have seen these photos?"

Oh. Maybe I shouldn't have mentioned that.

"Because they're posted on Eliza's page in an online community where a lot of cosplayers hang out, called AlternateArt," I said as casually as I could. "The whole point is to take the photos and then share them."

Her frown line deepened. "Pictures of you dressed like Satina Galt are all over the web?" She sounded so horrified, so embarrassed.

"Not all over," I said, feeling anger form into an actual shape in my throat. "Just on this one page."

Mom shook her head. "This sounds dangerous to me. Is your name associated with the photos?"

"No!" I felt my voice getting louder and higher. "Eliza uses an alias on her page. I'm sure she gave us aliases, too." Then, because that anger was getting big and there was no way I was going to swallow it down now, I added, "But way to take all the awesomeness out of it, Mom."

She looked at me like I'd kicked her.

"I'm sorry, but it's my job to keep you safe. Especially after everything you've been through. Especially now that things are going so well."

I laughed. "Going so well? For you, maybe! Have you looked around at the rest of us?"

Mom stood up. "Ari. We've had such a nice day. Don't ruin it." The same tone she used with Danielle, but stripped of at least three more layers of softness.

I laughed again. It may have sounded a little maniacal.

"You're using that line on me now?"

She held up her hands. "I'm not continuing with this conversation. I'm done."

"Okay," I said, standing up, too, and climbing a step so I was taller than her. "Are we also done with our little show for Camden's sake? We can take off all the makeup now. We can stop pretending we're a family that actually cares about one another."

Mom stared hard at me, scanned me head to toe in much the same way Eliza once had. It was possibly the most she'd looked at me in a long time. Then she flung open the door and disappeared inside the house, slamming it behind her. There was something profoundly satisfying about the sound of that slam. *Boom.*

I waited a few minutes, staring out at the street, watching the top of Mr. Gustafson's head bob up and down. Finally, I went inside.

It was dead quiet.

I paused in the hallway to look at that fifth grade picture again. The girl in the photo looked different to me now. Camden had seen her. She stared back at me with a knowing expression, like she'd seen him back.

As I moved down the hall toward the bedrooms, I started to hear some noises. I lingered between the closed door to Dani's room and the closed door to Mom and Richard's room.

Behind the door to Dani's room, I heard the sound of Richard's voice, rising and falling in a lilt from Narnia.

Behind the other door was the sound of something high-pitched yet soft, jagged but shapeless. It was something I used to hear a lot.

My mother, crying.

I went into my room and picked up the copy of *Planet Jasmine* that Camden and I had left on the floor. Then I started to read.

16

Vera the dog had been found.

She and her owner stopped in to the store the next day to give us the good news and remove the flyer from the bulletin board.

"Where did she turn up?" I asked the guy after he crumpled the flyer with great ceremony.

"In the parking lot of the nature preserve," he said. "About two miles from our house. She climbed into the bed of a truck that looks like mine, and some dude drove around for half a day before he noticed her in there."

I crouched down to pet Vera. "She looks happy to be home."

The dog's ears stood up at the word and she gave me an

expression like, *You have no idea.*

On their way out, they held the door for someone coming in, who turned out to be Camden. Followed by Max and Eliza.

"Hey," said Camden, leaning across the counter to kiss me. I assumed it was going to be a quickie and drew away after a moment, but he reached out and pulled me back toward him for another, longer one. He tasted like grapes. When we finally managed to separate, I turned to face Eliza.

"Sweet," she said. "You guys are sweet together."

The proclamation felt important somehow.

"Although," Eliza continued, a wicked smile spreading across her face, "the words people are using most often include *hot, crazy sexy, OMFG,* and my personal favorite, *Satinazor.*"

"People," I said.

"The AlternateArt people," said Camden. "Apparently, my Azor and your Satina are the couple of the moment. Among the geeks and freaks, that is."

Eliza fiddled with her phone and hoisted herself onto the counter so she could lean in next to me. "See," she said, and showed me a phone-sized view of all the comments.

"I really don't need to read them," I said, waving the phone away.

"You really don't," added Camden, giving me a meaningful look before turning to Eliza. "Who cares what other people think of the photos? We did it for fun. For ourselves."

"Maybe *you* did that," said Eliza.

"I'm not sure Eliza is capable of doing anything that's not

for the benefit of others to enjoy," said Max, who was wandering down the greeting card aisle.

"*Excuse* me?" she snapped at him.

"What? You live to entertain. You know that already."

"Why would you say it like that?"

"Like how?"

"Like a dickhead?"

"I was *kidding*," said Max. "Christ. What happened to your sense of humor?"

Eliza gave him what I would classify as the most withering look I've ever seen, then hopped off the counter and put away her phone.

Camden motioned for me to lean in close to him. I did. His breath was warm as he whispered, "We're here to steal you."

"What?"

"To the lake. It's a gorgeous day."

I drew back. "You can't steal me."

"Uh, stealing doesn't really operate that way. You don't need the stealee's permission. You simply do it."

"I'm at *work*."

"Can't you ask Richard for the rest of the day off?"

"I'm not really supposed to . . ."

"He's your stepdad, for God's sake," said Eliza. "He's not going to fire you. The worst that'll happen is that he says no."

"My mom will kill me." As soon as I said it, I wasn't really sure it was true. Would she? Would she care that I wavered from the schedule, on her first day at her new job to boot? And would I care that she cared?

"Nobody will kill you, Ari," said Camden calmly.

My eyes found his and I felt something that might have been a hunger pang, if I hadn't just eaten breakfast.

"You are absolutely right."

I went to the back room, where Richard was standing on the stepladder, reaching to put something on a shelf. His shirt hiked up and I could see how white the skin on his back was. Poor guy. Had he been outside in the sunlight at all this summer?

"Hi," I said softly, worried that if I startled him, he'd fall.

"What's up?" he asked, distracted. He hadn't been his usual Mr. Sunny Sunshine all morning. Starting when, you know, my mom left the house at 7:00 a.m. in a supernova of jitters, snapping at each of us and cursing her way out the door.

"Camden's here. He wants to say hello." That was good.

"Oh, okay. I'll be out in a bit."

"His friends Eliza and Max are here, too. You can meet them."

Richard nodded. I turned away and started back into the store, my courage deflating now. It really was a bad day to do this. Even if there wasn't a single customer in the next few hours, he seemed so down and . . . lonely.

But there was Camden, leaning against the counter with his hair falling across his face, and I didn't know which I wanted to touch more—the hair or the face. We hadn't been truly alone since the morning after the fair, and my fingers itched for him.

There, too, was the blue sky through the store window, and the promise of cool water and the sand between my toes and basically everything else in the world.

"Actually," I said slowly, as if this were a brainstorm coming to me now. "I'm wondering if you need me here today. They're all going to the lake and I really want to go with them. I'd leave in time to get Dani from camp."

Now Richard turned all the way around and sat down on the top of the ladder.

"You're wondering if I need you here today . . . ," he repeated.

"Well, maybe I'm a little more than wondering."

Richard sighed. "No," he said with a shrug. "I don't need you here."

"Sorry it's so slow."

He sighed again. "Me, too. But Ari, your mother . . ." He raised his eyes to me now and really looked at me, then out the door toward where all my temptations lay. Temptations he seemed jealous of. "You know something?" he said, his tone changing suddenly. "To hell with your mother. You're seventeen and it's summer and you have a boyfriend. Go to the goddamn lake."

"Really?"

"Seriously."

"I owe you one," I said, when I really meant to say "thank you." Because the truth was, I didn't owe him one. I owed him zero.

"Don't forget about Dani," Richard said, trying to keep a

stern voice, but he was already beaming. Probably because I was beaming.

I stepped out of the back room to find Camden waiting just outside. When I flashed him a thumbs-up, he threw his head back and laughed in that Peter Pan way of his. He wrapped his arms around me and lifted me off the ground.

I know he put me back a second later, but I never felt it.

I had to make a quick stop at my house so I could change into my bathing suit and grab a towel. Camden came with me, and Max left with Eliza. James was picking up Kendall, I'd been informed. It was all planned out, they said.

As I drove with Camden away from the store and Main Street, into the infinity of the day, Camden put his hand on my knee. I rolled down my window and let my left hand greet the rushing air, ribboning through my spread fingers. In this way, it was almost as if he was holding me down so I didn't fly out of the car like a balloon. Because I felt that light, that capable of being carried away.

Camden waited in the car while I ran into my house, then back out again five minutes later. When we got to the lake, the early birds had just arrived to stake out their spots. Mabel was writing the day's ice cream offerings on her whiteboard. The place had that Heart of Summer feel, another day where all kinds of life would happen here and it seemed impossible that in six months' time, the lake would be frozen and abandoned, the beach lost in a foot of snow.

Kendall and James were already there when we arrived. In our old spot. I looked at it and Kendall saw me look at it, then smiled at me.

"Brings back memories," she said.

"Shhh," I whispered as I leaned in to hug her. "Thou shalt not talk about last summer."

Kendall nodded and I spread my blanket out next to her. She watched James rather suspiciously as he went over to talk to Eliza and Max.

"What's the matter?" I asked.

"I'm befuddled."

"How was it when he picked you up?"

"Really boring," she sighed. "He came in. He met my mom. We drove away."

"Did he open the car door for you first, or did he get in on his side, then do a lean-and-unlock?"

Kendall's shoulders slumped. "He leaned and unlocked."

"I wish you'd relax and stop trying to figure him out. You like him, you're spending time with him. At the lake, no less! That should be enough for now. That's plenty."

"That's easy for you to say, newly crowned Queen of the Fangirls. You've got your king."

"Jamie told you about AlternateArt?"

"Yes." She snaked the *sss*.

I opened my mouth to say what was destined to be another platitude, something from the repertoire of supportive-sounding but clinically empty best-friend-isms. But then

Camden sat down next to me and wriggled out of his shirt. It was almost alarming to see him in a bathing suit now, his chest with the beads of sweat trailing down, his waist with the hint of fuzz in the middle. He hadn't been shirtless that whole night at the Barn, yet here he was in all his uncharted territory. There went my kneecaps again.

Then James and Eliza and Max joined us. A cooler bag was opened, tortilla chips and iced tea passed around. We talked about plans for the SuperCon: what costume tweaks had to happen, what panels we should attend, who was going to drive. Eliza told a hilarious story about a cat she'd been pet-sitting for.

"I thought he had a piece of pink ribbon stuck to his back legs. So I tried to pick it off, but then realized the ribbon was not stuck to his back legs. It was *coming out of his butt*."

We offered a collective *ew*.

"Did you pull it out?" asked Camden.

"Uh-uh. You're not supposed to ever do that. In case you pull its intestines out or something. No, I watched that litter box like a hawk for two days. Then . . . voilà. It was enough ribbon to wrap a present!"

We all cracked up.

"Please don't ever give me that present," said Max.

Eliza laughed, then eyed him sharply. "See, Max. I laughed. Evidence of a sense of humor."

Max opened his mouth to say something, but it seemed like he couldn't decide what it was going to be. On instinct,

I jumped in and told a similar story about Danielle eating a penny when she was four years old.

All of us here at the lake, being and sharing and enjoying. It was worth it, whatever consequences might happen as a result of me taking this day. I'd crossed over to something I didn't know was there until it manifested.

After the snacks were gone and the good stories told, we quieted down. It felt natural, part of the expected lazy rhythm of summer. In this lull, I stood up and took a step down the beach, then turned back to Camden and motioned toward the water. Suddenly I was traveling across the sand, not even feeling the jagged pebbles that I usually stepped over, knowing Camden was following me. I did a running dive and heard him do the same. The water. Finally warm, finally that ideal temperature that almost feels bittersweet on your skin because it lasts such a short time. When I came up for air, I scanned the beach, then realized I was looking for Danielle. I couldn't remember the last time I'd been here without her, where I didn't have to worry about her safety. To set a good example.

Now I swiveled around, looking for Camden. He was treading water a dozen feet away, waiting for me to notice him. He jerked his head toward the raft and I nodded back, then we started swimming.

I thought fleetingly of that day when he taught Dani how to dive, when I'd watched Eliza and Max doing exactly what I was doing now. It felt like eons ago.

Camden reached the raft first and when I climbed up, he

was already sitting there casually, his knees drawn to his chest. I crawled to a spot across from him and folded my legs to my side. The sun was beginning to get intense and I could already feel the heat grow on my back.

"Alone at last," he said, searching my face. Maybe he'd had those hunger pangs, too.

"Not really."

"Close enough."

He leaned in now and kissed me. Not quickly, not slowly. Just perfectly. I almost cried from the relief of it. We stayed connected for as long as we could, knowing there were surely people watching us.

When Camden pulled away, he sighed, then stretched out on his stomach. His elbows bent, his head sideways on his hands facing me. I lay down on my left side using my arm as a pillow and we stared at each other.

"Is this what you thought it would be?" he asked.

"Yes," I said simply.

He closed his eyes and nodded, and that was all. I searched for the sound of his breathing amidst the splashes and voices and birds overhead, and when I found it, I had everything I needed in that moment.

Take it, Ari. You deserve it.

I took it. I tried to soak it into my pores, the perfection of right-this-second. But when Camden still didn't speak after a few minutes, I poked his shoulder.

"Are you asleep?" I asked.

He smiled without opening his eyes. "Very much the opposite."

But he said no more, and after a few moments, all the uncertainties of my life—and his—started wandering in. I kept pushing them roughly away and they'd stagger right back.

Finally I asked, "Have you talked to your mom lately?"

"I talk to her every day," he said flatly, then propped himself up on one elbow. "Ari, you are here without your sister. You have several hours without any obligations or responsibilities. Can't you just *be*?"

It stung for a moment, what he said, but when I looked at him I realized he didn't mean it to. He was saying it because he cared. Because he wanted something for me.

"I can *be*," I said. "Hell, I can *be* the ass off anyone."

"Great," said Camden, lying back down. He slithered his feet around my ankles and kept them there.

Maybe it could be done. Maybe I could live both my lives. Or they could become one. I closed my eyes and felt the pressure of Camden's feet against mine, matched my breathing to his. In the middle of this *just being*, the thought came and I couldn't push this one away either.

I'm in love with you.

It was as easy and obvious as air. I let it fill me.

I'm not sure how much time passed. It felt like a month, but was probably more along the lines of five minutes. Then I heard splashing and raised my head to see Kendall swimming toward the raft.

"Hey," I said.

"You should come back to the beach." There was something heavy and dark in her eyes.

"Why? What's wrong?"

"Just come back," she said, and swam away. Camden and I looked at each other, then at the beach. I couldn't see anything except Eliza, Max, and James standing in a cluster.

"Come on," he said, clearly worried.

We dove into the water and swam.

I could hear Max's raised voice as soon as my feet found the lake bottom. Kendall stood nearby, holding out my towel, which I grabbed and wrapped around me.

"What's going on?" I asked.

"Talk to Max," she said, frowning.

Max heard us and turned around. Then he came toward me holding up an object. When he was two steps away, I realized what it was: a set of acrylic paints in a fancy wooden box. We sold the same set in Millie's. It was the highest quality paint we carried, with a big price tag to match.

Oh.

"I'm sorry," said Max. "I found this in Eliza's bag."

He offered the box and I responded on instinct, holding out my hand. He laid it on my palm, then we all looked at it, me and Max and James and Camden, like we expected it to do something.

"She stole this from the store?" I asked.

"She's saying she meant to pay for it when you came out of

the back room, but then forgot." He turned toward Eliza and didn't bother to lower his voice. "Which, based on some things that have gone down in the past, I don't believe."

I peered around Max to where Eliza sat on her blanket, her elbows resting on her knees, staring out at the lake.

"That's why she's banned from the knitting store," I said.

"And a few others," added Camden. "If it helps, it was always in the name of cosplay."

I looked at the box and wondered what Eliza had planned to do with it. "That doesn't really help."

I walked past the boys to Eliza, unsure of what to say or do when I got there.

"Hey," I said.

Now she finally looked up at me, right in the eye. Eliza never looked anywhere but right in someone's eye, and I realized how much I respected her for that.

"I really did mean to pay for it," she said. "We were so excited that you could come with us, we were amped to get on our way and I totally spaced."

"I'm sure," I said. What I didn't say was, *Then why was it already in your bag?*

What she didn't say was, *I'm sorry.*

"I'll bring it back to the store, then you can come in and buy it later."

Eliza frowned. "Can't I just give you money the next time I come in?"

"We don't really let people do that." It was simply a fact I was stating, but I knew to her it meant much more. I was lumping her in with the general, ordinary public.

She sighed and waved her hand. "Keep it, then. Take it back. I don't need the paints right away, or I can get them somewhere else."

Why did it feel like I was letting her down? That I hadn't fulfilled some kind of obligation?

I turned away and put the box in my own bag, then casually zipped it shut. Kendall and James met my glance, and it was clear they weren't buying Eliza's story, either.

What had happened here? Five minutes ago the day had been storybook. Movie montage. I'd rejected my own tendencies and embraced it. But things had exploded anyway.

"Be right back," I said, swallowing something that was rising in my throat, then walked toward the restroom building. *Privacy dark alone quiet.* I'd just grabbed the handle of the women's room when I felt a hand on my shoulder.

"You sure you've got the right door?" asked Camden.

I let out a laugh, realizing I hadn't been breathing properly since coming out of the water. The end of it shook down into a sob. I leaned into him and put my head on his chest, and he put one hand tentatively on my back.

"This is where we first met," he said softly after a few seconds. "I'll always associate the smell of toilet cleaner with that."

I laughed again, wiped my eyes. Leaned in harder.

"That was a really crappy thing for her to do," I said. "I'm not sure how to feel about it."

His chest inflated, then deflated, in a long sigh. It was like riding a wave.

"Eliza has her own stuff," murmured Camden. "She hasn't had it easy, either. I don't think she meant to hurt you or make you feel taken advantage of. She just gets tunnel vision sometimes."

I drew back to examine his face. "Are you defending her?"

"No. I'm giving you context."

"Because she's your ex-girlfriend. This could be seen as dangerous territory."

"Thanks for the map." He dropped his hand off me.

I stepped away from him. "I'm going to pee now."

As I moved toward the door, he grabbed my wrist. "Ari," he said.

"What?"

"Don't be mad."

"I'm not. But I need to know you're on my side. If, you know, this ends up being a thing with sides."

Camden looked uncomfortable, like he'd never been asked to make this kind of choice for anyone.

"Always," he said, swallowing hard.

I nodded. I tugged my wrist free. He let it go. I wasn't sure which happened first.

From the moment I came out of the restroom, it was like we were three pairs of strangers at the lake who just happened to put their blankets near one another.

Kendall and James went swimming together, and I watched them sit on the edge of the dock. Their heads close, their mouths moving. From that distance, it looked like James could have been desperately in love with Kendall or completely ambivalent toward her. But Kendall's body language was large enough to be read from where I sat. She wanted everything he had to offer, and probably a lot of things he didn't.

Eliza and Max went for a walk to the creek. I didn't know who had suggested it, only that they were gone when I returned, and that I was glad they were gone. Also, that I felt sad to be glad.

Camden and I lay on our backs, our heads touching, him reading my borrowed copy of *Time Enough* and me reading *Planet Jasmine*. Every once in a while, one of us made a joke about what was happening in our story.

"Uh-oh, Marr," I'd say. "Keep it in your pants."

In this way, the reality we shared right then was the one that mattered, the *Silver Arrow* reality we knew would have a happy ending even if it took us a while to get there.

Eventually, it was time for me to leave so I could pick up Danielle.

Kendall was out on the raft with James, so Camden walked me to my car, hobbling in his bare feet over the hot pavement of the parking lot. We kissed good-bye briefly, only halfway on the lips.

"Do you regret letting us steal you?" he asked as he opened my door for me.

"Never," I said.

But it wasn't until I was driving away from the lake that I realized I'd actually meant it.

17

"Why are we going to Millie's?" asked Dani from the backseat, twirling a pink-and-yellow lanyard she'd made that day.

"Don't you want to see Daddy? He'll let you pick out some stickers."

We rarely brought Dani to the store. All she wanted was to take stuff home. But I needed to get the paint set back on the shelf before closing time.

"Hey!" said Richard when we walked in. "What a surprise!"

He came around the counter and scooped up Dani. I looked at the pile of receipts and noticed there were more than usual. It must have gotten busy after I left.

"She wanted to come see you," I said.

"No, I didn't," said Dani.

"Well, it seemed like she did. And I think I left my book here."

Richard nodded, more preoccupied with the lanyard Dani was shoving in his face.

"I made it all by myself!" she said. "With my counselor! And a C.I.T.! It's for Mommy on her first day of work."

"She'll love it," said Richard. "Want some stickers? I got new ones."

He put her down in front of the sticker rolls and put his head close to hers, showing her the options.

I took this moment to step into the paint aisle and dig the set out of my bag, stick it back into the empty space on the shelf like it was the final piece of a puzzle. I wished I wasn't so good at arranging the displays. Richard would have noticed it was missing when he was doing his end-of-the-day rounds.

I took a deep breath and turned away from the paints. Dani was watching me over her shoulder as Richard was putting some sticker sheets into a paper bag for her.

Here I was, right back on the track of the day. Back in the store, tasked with a few hours to keep Dani entertained. It was easy to feel like the hours at the lake, the messy intensity of it, had all been a dream I'd come up with while stuck at the counter, waiting for the front door to ding open.

Mom had said she'd be home at six thirty but it was past seven with no sign of her. Richard and I sat at the table, watching our tortellini get cold. Dani had already eaten and retreated to her room.

"This isn't going to work," I said. He knew I meant trying to eat together as a family.

"Traffic," was all he could respond, then took a forkful of pasta. "It's ridiculous for us to wait. I'm digging in."

"Maybe from now on Dani and I should eat together, then you can wait and eat with Mom."

Richard raised his eyebrows. "*I* can eat with Mom?"

"Why, don't you want to eat dinner with your wife?"

He speared another tortellini, not meeting my glance. "Of course I do. I don't know what I meant by that."

I started eating, too. After a minute or two of silence, I finally paused and said, "Thanks for today."

Richard smiled. "I'd say *anytime*, but I can't, really."

"I know."

"I'm glad you had fun."

I hadn't said I'd had fun. But why wouldn't he assume that? Who wouldn't have fun on a perfect summer day with a boy she's just realized she's in love with? That would be me.

"I know the store got busy," I said. "I hope you were okay."

He shrugged. "It's good that it got busy."

We finished our pasta and I stood up, took Richard's bowl to the sink for him.

"Let me know when it's time to kiss Dani good night," I said, then went to my room. That was when I heard Mom's car drive up. I shut the door and put on earphones so I could listen to music instead of what happened next.

Later, there was a knock, and Mom poked her head in.

"Hi," she said.

I took the earphones out. "How was your first day?"

She came all the way into the room and leaned against my doorframe.

"Hard. But good. Really good. I'm going to like it there."

"Are you mad about dinner?"

She sighed. "No. I just didn't expect that particular plan to fall apart so quickly."

"Did you still get a chance to read to Dani?"

Mom nodded. "She wants you to go in and kiss her good night."

I started to get up, but then Mom held up her hand. "Wait a minute. Richard's in there with her now, and I need to talk to you about something."

She closed the door, and I burned with a feeling of betrayal. Richard had told her. Richard had told her!

"What is it?" I asked casually, all my defense mechanisms kicking into gear.

"Dani says she saw you take something from your bag and put it on a shelf at the store."

I froze. Dani? It was unlike Dani to be confused by some-thing and not instantly ask me about it. Maybe it hadn't struck her as strange until after the fact.

I forced a laugh. "Oh. Yeah." I waved my hand and rolled my eyes.

"What's the story there?"

I was about to make something up, like I was going to buy it for myself but changed my mind, but then remembered something my teacher told us in journalism class. *All facts are friendly.* Eliza had told me a story, and I would stick to that story.

"This girl Eliza stopped by the store today. She's a friend of Camden's. And mine, too, now. She's Atticus Marr in the cosplay photos . . . Anyway, she told me she took this paint set off the shelf to buy, but then forgot to pay for it. So she gave it to me to put back until she can come in again."

So okay, all facts may be friendly, but sometimes they sound too stupid to believe.

Mom put her thumb and forefinger on either side of her nose and squeezed. "Ari, I've had a long, stressful day and three hours in the car. Tell me your new friends are not stealing from the store."

"They're not stealing from the store."

"But they tried."

I burst into tears. It all came now, how angry I was at Eliza, how betrayed I felt. How Richard had given me this gift of a day and this was the thanks he got. "Just one. One of them tried."

"This is the girl who's arranging the trip to the convention? That MegaCon?"

"SuperCon. Yes, but . . ."

"You can see why I'm not comfortable with you going."

I stood up. "You're going to punish me for something *she* did?"

Mom looked stricken for a moment, then shook her head. "I'm not punishing you. But you want me to let you go on a road trip out of state to some convention with people like this?"

"Not people. Person! One person! Not Camden, not his friends Max or James. Kendall will be there. And Eliza may have her issues but she's responsible. You've never even met her. Why don't you meet her first?"

My mother sighed. "I would like to meet her. But this is all a moot point. The thing is, Ari, I found out that I have a required training session at work that Saturday. We need you to be with Danielle."

It was as if this information was something she'd thrown into the air between us and lit on fire. We stood there for a speechless few seconds, watching it burn.

"You *just* found this out."

"Well, I found out on Friday. But I hadn't been able to bring myself to tell you yet. I knew how much you were looking forward to the convention."

"It's more than a 'looking forward to' thing, Mom. They're depending on me for the group cosplay. . . ."

"Sweetie," she said in a decidedly unsweetened tone. It was a tone that welcomed no more comments. "We'll talk about this tomorrow, okay? I need to eat and your sister is waiting for you."

She turned to leave, then stopped halfway out the door, turned back around.

"You had Dani with you when you put the paint set back. Exactly when did this girl give it to you?"

For the record, I didn't want to lie. I'd gotten this far without it. But when you're in a corner, you're in a corner.

"She knew I picked up Dani at camp," I said after a second, "so she found me there to give it back."

Mom looked at me for a long time, then slowly closed her eyes. She took a deep breath.

"God, I'm tired."

And then she left the room.

At first I thought Dani was asleep when I stepped through her doorway, and I thought, *lucky break*. But I must have put my weight on the One Creaky Floorboard and her eyes fluttered opened.

"Ari?" she asked.

"It's me." I sat on her bed. "Did you give Mom the lanyard?"

Her mouth curved down. "No. I left it at the store."

I got it, then. Without this offering to the mother she hadn't seen in twenty-four hours, something that would capture her attention and get a reaction, Dani had reached for a replacement. Perhaps that's why she'd held on to what she saw me do at the store, knowing instinctively that it might have value. I'd done the same when I was her age. A hundred times over. A thousand.

But I'd never done it at the expense of someone else I loved. At least, I didn't think so.

"Will you sing me a song?" she asked, her voice high and squeaky in the semidarkness.

"I thought you only wanted a kiss good night."

"A kiss *and* a song. Two songs."

She'd had Mom read to her, and Richard come in to chuck her on the chin and tell her she was beautiful. Why couldn't these things give her what she needed? Why was it always my closing act that finally filled up her void to the brim?

"Not tonight," I said, leaning down to kiss her on the curved part of her nose, the part that felt like it was on a doll's face. "My throat hurts."

I'll admit it. It felt good to deny her, to withhold what she took for granted.

"But Ari . . ."

"I said no." More firmly now. I'd committed. I couldn't waffle.

"But . . ."

"No."

Suddenly, it was her perfect little mouth expecting, her eyes wanting, her hands grabbing, that embodied everything I resented about my family.

Yes, the normal rules of give-and-take back-and-forth don't apply to a seven-year-old child. Yes, she didn't understand how it wasn't simply a song but so much she had no control over. I knew that intellectually. But this one time, because she was here in front of me and because I could, I needed to spread out my empty palms and say, *Sorry, kid, I'm all out.*

It was what filled *my* void right then.

"Good night," I said. "See you in the morning."

Then I walked out before she could say anything back.

"Shit," said Camden on the phone when I told him.

I was in bed with the covers over my head. Here, I could make the world consist only of me and the voice of a boy I loved.

"This is what my life is like." I tried to keep from sounding completely beaten down. I didn't want his sympathy; I just wanted someone to bear witness. "I mean, really. Am I their daughter or their au pair?"

"Don't blame your sister. She's a little kid."

"That's precisely *why* it's easier to blame her."

"Maybe you can find her a babysitter for the day."

"Who would I call? We've never needed a babysitter because, you know, *me*."

"We'll figure something out," he said confidently. "You *are* going to the SuperCon. You are."

We were quiet for a moment. I heard him breathe, then crunch on something.

"What are you eating?"

"White cheddar cheese crackers."

"Great. As if it wasn't already hard enough, that I'm not there with you."

He laughed, then there was more silence as Camden crunched. This seemed absurdly sexy. I pictured him at his kitchen counter, so sure everything was going to be fine, able to eat cheese crackers or drink wine or do whatever the hell he wanted without needing it to be preauthorized.

"You're lucky you don't have family bullshit to deal with," I said with a sigh.

The crunching stopped. After a pause, Camden said earnestly, "You're lucky you have a family to have bullshit with."

I felt my ears turn red, glad he was not there to see it. I swallowed hard. "Point taken."

"Sorry. My mom called a little while ago. It was a weird one. She's feeling lonely."

"What did she say?"

"She said, 'I'm feeling lonely.' She also said, 'Come stay with me for the rest of the summer.'"

I wasn't moving, but I froze anyway.

"What did *you* say?"

"I said no." He paused, and I heard him take a shuddering breath. "I guess there's a first time for everything. But I don't want to quit the hotline; they need me. I have responsibilities and plans. And you. She understood. Or at least, she did a good job of faking it."

There was victory in his tone, like he'd struggled and won.

"Who's there with you tonight?" I asked.

"Just Jamie. Eliza's mad at me for not believing her about the paints, and Max didn't want to get in the middle."

I didn't want to talk about Eliza. Hearing her name made all the Bad Things about the day come creeping into my little bed fort. By way of diversion I said, "You know, Kendall's crushing hard on Jamie. She has no idea if the feeling is mutual."

Camden started crunching again. "Jamie's a hard one to read. He got his heart stomped on pretty hard last year. Do you want me to do some reconnaissance?"

"Sure," I said. "No, wait. Don't." Then I thought of Kendall's slumping shoulders at the beach, the way she'd said *You've got your king*. "Then again, yes. If you could casually mention something . . ."

"Done," said Camden. "Kendall's great. He shouldn't leave her confused."

"Thanks." I didn't want to hang up. It was snug and perfect under the covers, and Camden's voice against my ear felt so very much mine. "What part of *Time Enough* did you get up to today?"

"Bram and Azor just got cast as extras in a gangster movie."

"Oh, that's a great scene. Will you read it to me?"

I could almost hear him smile on his end of the phone.

"Our phone calls keep getting weirder," he said.

"Not weirder," I said. "*Better.*"

He began to read.

I woke up late the next morning, after Mom had already left for work. On the kitchen counter was a shopping list for later, and instructions that I'd find Dani's camp lunch and snacks in the fridge. I could hear Dani's cartoons on the TV in the family room. Richard sat at the table, reading the paper with his coffee cup pressed to his chest like something precious.

He looked up at me with red eyes rimmed with dark circles. He wasn't sleeping again. There was probably a blanket and pillow on the couch. So much for Mom's bed-sharing promises.

"She told you about Eliza," I said. Richard nodded. "I'm sorry."

"You have nothing to be sorry about. You did the right thing, by getting it back on the shelf. I get why you didn't want me to know."

"Thanks," I said.

"But I told your mother about letting you go to the lake."

"What? Why?"

"I had to. She guessed it and asked me point-blank. She's my wife, Ari, I'm not going to lie to her. Especially not these days, when everything's already so . . . difficult."

I sank down onto a chair.

"I put it all on myself," said Richard. "I explained how I urged you to go. So she's mad at both of us, if that's any consolation. But it means I can't fight for you on this convention thing."

I stared at him. He couldn't look me in the eye.

"It's a moot point anyway, with her training session—" he began.

"Yes," I cut him off. "Mom gave me the same official line.

You don't need to repeat it."

I never acted this way toward Richard. I never huffed or hissed or pouted. He looked genuinely hurt.

"Ari, this stuff is not easy for me," he said, rubbing his eyebrow. "I try not to get between you and your mother. I don't have a right. But I see things that should have been dealt with a long time ago, before your depression, and they're still not dealt with, and it scares me."

It scares me, too, I wanted to say. And also, *What things?*

"Thanks for sharing," was all I did say, avoiding his glance. This was too much, too much when I was already running so late I didn't have time to eat breakfast and I was wearing the same clothes as yesterday and Camden's voice reading *Time Enough* still echoed in my ear. I grabbed the car keys and shouted down to Dani. "We're leaving in two minutes! Your shoes had better be on!"

"Ari?" asked Richard, turning my name into an open-ended question.

I grabbed Dani's lunch and snack from the fridge, stuffed them in Dani's backpack and zipped it up, then grabbed my bag.

"See you at the store," I snapped, rushing to the foyer to find Dani struggling with her shoes. I bent down and shoved one on, then the other, then opened the door for her. All without looking her in the eye. Miraculously, she followed.

We were both quiet in the car on the way to camp. Now that I'd given myself permission to resent my sister, she seemed suddenly much older, more restrained. I kept waiting for her to ask about what she saw at the store, or to tell me I'd been a big fat meanie last night. I wanted her to. I wasn't sure what it would mean if she didn't.

She didn't.

When we arrived at the rec center and got out of the car, I slowed my pace out of habit so Dani could grab my hand. She didn't grab it right away, but waited a few more steps than usual. Because I couldn't help it, I gave her fingers a squeeze.

Before Dani could squeeze back, she saw her counselor and let go, running to her. She wrapped her arms around the girl's waist. I'd never seen her so happy to be at camp.

"Mikayla!" Dani shouted.

"Hey, pixie," said Mikayla, who seemed genuinely glad to see her. She looked up and smiled at me.

That was when an idea dawned.

"Mikayla," I said. "Are you by any chance free next Saturday?"

18

There was an episode of *Silver Arrow* where Atticus Marr got a severe case of hypersickness. The crew had to tie him to a chair on the bridge because he was speaking in nonsense words. As Azor took over the captain's seat, leading Satina and Bram as they steered through an asteroid field, Marr kept yelling things like "Shrimp!" and "Toaster in the horse manure!" It was one of my favorite episodes when I was a kid, because it made my mom laugh.

This reminded me of that. Minus, of course, my mother laughing.

Instead of Marr, it was Eliza dressed as Marr, riding in the middle row of James's parents' minivan. She did not look happy, being relegated to second tier. The Tri-State SuperCon was her idea, her plan, her expected triumph. But Max knew how to get there, Max had the good GPS on his phone, so Max rode in the shotgun navigation position next to James. It was something he decided and directed, and he seemed to enjoy the look on Eliza's face when he told her to get in the back.

To be honest, I enjoyed it, too.

Kendall sat in the other middle row seat. Camden and I sat in the way back with our hands interlaced, our feet entwined. Basically every part of us touching, as far as the seat belts would allow. I needed this contact as a constant reminder of why I'd done what I'd done, and why I shouldn't feel guilty.

I'd sent one text message to my mother and Richard telling them these facts and these facts only: where I'd gone, when I'd be back, the name and number of Mikayla, who was at the house with Dani and would be there until Mom came home. I typed out the word *Sorry*, but then slowly backspaced over it.

After I sent the message, I turned off my phone. My hand shook as I held down the button.

If this day was going to cost me, I was going to make it worth every penny.

Now the phone was tucked away in my Satina satchel. We were already in our costumes, except for the wigs, and except of course for Kendall and James.

This seemed to irk Eliza. As James pulled us onto the highway, she scanned Kendall head to toe and said, "You should have let me put together a Victoria Ransom outfit for you. It would have been so easy."

Kendall shot a puzzled glance over her shoulder at me.

"She was a teen who stowed away on the *Arrow One*'s maiden voyage and got stuck on the ship," I told her.

Kendall turned back to Eliza. "Up until five seconds ago, I had no idea who that person is. You want me to spend the day dressed up as her?"

Eliza shrugged. "You'd rather spend the day wearing an X-Men T-shirt?"

"What's wrong with my X-Men T-shirt?"

"You may as well be wearing a plain black T-shirt. Because it doesn't say anything! X-Men is a given."

"It's better that I cosplay a character I've never heard of, from a show I've never watched?"

Max turned around from the front seat now. "Eliza. You know that's not how fandom works."

Eliza snapped her head away from him and stared out the window. "She might feel out of place, is all I'm saying. Frankly, I'm surprised she came, even if it does mean spending the day with Jamie."

Kendall turned red and glanced quickly at James, who raised his eyes to the rearview mirror for only a second.

"Enough," said Camden, leaning forward and putting his hand on Eliza's shoulder. "It's going to be an amazing day."

He leaned back and his fingers found my fingers again. He didn't look like he truly believed what he was saying.

Azor, I told myself. *I'm here again with Azor.* I hadn't come for Eliza, to honor all her plans. I could barely look at her or talk to her. I'd come for me and for him.

The memories of those few magical hours at the fair were so vivid and tangible, I thought for sure I could step right back into them. But the truth was this: Camden was different now, because I knew him better now. And that meant his Azor was different, too. Maybe this is what it would have been like, had Satina and Azor actually hooked up. It would not have been simple.

Then again, neither of them would have wanted it to be.

We pulled into the parking lot of the Hilton Garden Inn shortly after 10:00 a.m. It clearly pleased Eliza that so far we'd stayed on schedule. We got out of the van and instantly, I could tell this was not going to be like the county fair. Because right over there was Iron Man, locking his car and slinging a backpack over one shoulder. A few cars away, two girls dressed as the tenth and eleventh Doctors from *Doctor Who* adjusted each other's jacket lapels. A couple with a baby walked past, dressed as Na'vi from *Avatar* (even the baby was blue).

I turned to Camden, who had already slid his wig into place, his eyes sharp with excitement.

"This is it," he said. "These are our people."

He took the wig from my hand and slowly lowered it onto my head, glancing back and forth between the hair and my face, trying to get the position just right.

"There," he finally said. "You're Satina again. Hi, Satina."

He leaned in to kiss me but Eliza stepped between us. She inspected me, then Camden, then gave a nod of approval.

Max, Kendall, and James had already started toward the hotel entrance, so we rushed to catch up. I watched as Kendall took pains to fall into step behind James, not next to him.

Inside the lobby, a huge sign on an easel said WELCOME TO THE TRI-STATE SUPERCON. Arrows pointed us to a registration table down the hall.

"Look," said Camden. "The arrows are silver. That's a good omen."

"Watch what happens when they recognize us," whispered Eliza.

After we signed in and got our badges, we crossed the threshold into the heart of the SuperCon, aka a hotel ballroom filled with booths selling comics, books, figurines, T-shirts, costumes, and accessories. Most of the people browsing the booths were dressed as something. There was a lot of hugging and picture-taking going on.

Eliza grabbed my arm briefly, indicating that I shouldn't move on yet. She wanted us to linger. To wait and see if anyone noticed us.

Her plan was this: we'd spend the morning on the exhibit floor, then there were a couple of panels to check out. Somewhere in there, we'd have lunch. At four, there was a costume contest—the highlight and whole point, really, of the day. At six, the dinner and dance party began. We'd be on the road by ten and home at eleven.

Eliza scanned the crowd and said, "I saw on the message boards that there's a group here cosplaying the *Silver Arrow* Reboot. We have to find them."

"Then we rumble," said Max.

Kendall snorted but Eliza gave him a dirty look. "If you're not going to take this seriously . . ."

"I'm here, aren't I?" He spread out his hands and waved them all around himself. "I'm dressed as a silver-haired alien and trying as hard as I can not to feel like a douche bag! How much more serious do you want me to get?"

Something in Eliza's face softened. "No more serious, babe." She took his hand. "You look great."

Max drew a deep breath and let her keep hold of his hand, but he didn't relax into it the way he usually did.

"Why don't we split up for a bit, meet back here in an hour?" I suggested.

"No!" said Eliza. "We have to stay together. Well, *those guys* can take off." She indicated James and Kendall with a dismissive wave. "But we are a cosplay *group*. We are basically one costume."

I nodded. It was a nice try, I guess.

It's going to be an awesome day, Camden had said, and I said it again to myself now. It would be awesome because I would make it awesome. The fact that everyone seemed on the verge of slapping one another had nothing to do with it.

Kendall turned to James. "Do you want to go off on our own, since we're not part of 'the costume'?"

"Yeah," he said, looking relieved. "Let's go. We'll meet you guys at the cosplay panel later."

As they walked away, Kendall gave me a quick, hopeful glance over her shoulder. I nodded. *Go have fun.*

Two girls came up to Camden and me. "It's you guys! Satina and Azor!" squealed one.

"We loved your pictures," chirped the other, who then ran her eyes slowly up and down Camden's entire body. I found myself reaching out to grab his hand.

"Can we take pictures with you?" asked the first, and we nodded. She turned and handed her phone to the closest nearby person. Who was Eliza.

Eliza not looking happy.

"Can you . . . oh, it's you!" the girl said. "I love your Atticus Marr! Really brilliant!"

Eliza smiled, but the girl still had her phone out, expecting Eliza to take it. She did, and after the girls posed with Camden and me, she dutifully took a couple of shots.

Then Camden said, "Here, let's get Marr and Bram in here, too," and beckoned Eliza and Max to join us. All of us huddled close with these two people we'd never met. We found a passing Bender from *Futurama* to snap the photo.

After the girls left, Eliza led us forward through the exhibit floor. The booths were supposed to be the whole point of the place, but clearly, the real action was in checking out everyone else's costumes. Calling out a person's character, stopping to compliment him or her. I thought of the way it felt that day in the parking lot at the lake, when we all found ourselves talking Arrowhead language. The sensation of being seen, of being welcomed back to a tribe you didn't know you'd lost.

This was that, times a thousand.

At one point, Eliza was out of earshot and I turned to Max and Camden.

"Why is she being such a dictator?"

"She's planned this day for six months," said Max. "You know how important this stuff is to her. Although I know that doesn't help when she's making it so much less fun for the rest of us."

Camden added, "Cosplay is the thing that helps her keep it all together."

Max and Camden exchanged a glance. I couldn't decipher its meaning.

"What does she need to keep together?" I asked.

Camden and Max answered simultaneously, speaking over each other.

"Stuff," said Max. "We all have stuff."

"Maybe she'll tell you another time," said Camden.

They wanted me to try and understand her. For them, maybe I would.

As we wandered through the floor, at least a dozen other people recognized us from the "Ferris Wheel" shoot, asking for a photo. Camden and I would lean in close to each other while Eliza crouched in front and Max stood behind. Smiling blindly, as if friendship and fun and fandom were all bound up in one simple story we had to tell.

At Merlin's Sci-Fi and Fantasy Bookstore booth, Camden tugged me toward the bins of vintage books. "Are there any you're missing?" he asked.

"A few."

"Let's see if we can find them."

We sifted through two boxes labeled "Sci-Fi TV" and there, under the layers of tattered paperbacks, was a book called *When the Stars Spun* that I'd been looking for online for at least two years. It was a gap in my bookshelf that always bothered me, the numbers on the spines jumping from eleven to thirteen. This was number twelve. I fanned through the pages to make sure the book was in good shape.

"You know what that is, don't you?" asked Camden.

"The universe wanting me to have something?"

"Bingo."

Then Camden went to pay for the book.

I bought a stuffed animal for Danielle that I knew was some kind of character from some kind of anime series, but I just thought it was cute.

At a booth that sold replications, I found an Original *Silver Arrow* flight pin. I showed it to Camden.

"This is nicer than the ones Eliza found online," I said, holding it up to the pin on my tunic. The metal was heavier, more expensive.

"Why don't you get it for your mom?" he suggested.

I shook my head, but didn't put the pin back. "It would seem like I was trying to buy her forgiveness. If she even wanted it. I don't think she'd even want it."

"It doesn't matter if she'd want it. What matters is whether or not you want to give it to her."

I looked him in the eye and he looked right back at me. God, how I loved him.

I bought the pin and tucked it into my Satina satchel. As we were walking away from the booth, Camden said, "Your mom must have started watching *Arrow* in 1988, when it first aired."

"I guess," I said, not wanting to admit I had no idea when she first started watching it. To me, she had always been watching it. "She would have been in college then," I added, mostly to myself as I did the math.

"How terrific it must have been to watch when it was new." He paused. "And how horrible to have to wait a week in between each episode!"

Huh. I'd never thought about my mom's *Silver Arrow* life before me; but she'd had one, of course. And despite everything that had happened between her and me, I was still so grateful for all those afternoons in front of the TV together. We'd both gotten something we'd needed at the time.

Now I had my own life with *Silver Arrow*. Maybe I could live it for both of us.

An hour later, Kendall and James found us on our way into the "Cosplay Tips and Tricks" panel.

"Hey," I said. "Having fun?"

Kendall had a light in her eyes. She bit back a smile and nodded. Then she saw Eliza, who was settling into a front-row seat by herself, and leaned in to whisper, "Wait, are you sure I'm allowed to be in here? Isn't this just for cosplayers?"

I laughed. It felt good to do it at Eliza's expense.

A girl stepped around us but stopped when she saw my costume. I looked up at her.

Reboot Satina. She was with a Reboot Marr and a Reboot Azor. Their costumes were good, but not great. Not as good as Eliza's had been at Camden's party, for sure. This must have been the group Eliza was on the alert for.

"Hi," I said. "Nice Satina."

The girl laughed and smiled warmly. "Thanks! You, too. I loved your 'Ferris Wheel' photos. I never got into the Original *Arrow* but I'm told they were very accurate."

"Thank you. That means a lot."

We stood there staring each other down, not sure what to do with this strange familiarity the costumes gave us. Then the flow of people entering the conference room pushed her forward, and the three of them moved on.

We found Camden and Max, who were saving some spots on the floor because all the seats were taken. Over the next hour, we learned about cosplay supply websites and catalogs, how to get coupons for craft and fabric stores, and why planning one's cosplay up to a year in advance can really save you money in the long run.

After the sci-fi/fantasy panel called "New Trends in Other

Worlds" and a session previewing the biggest upcoming movie releases, we headed outside to a landscaped courtyard to kill the hour before the costume contest started. Grass, a scattering of flowers, a single tree—all tokens to remind us of the boring and normal earthbound world we knew, so easy to forget about in the windowless hotel conference rooms. Nobody was what they wanted to be, anymore. They were back to being people trying to eat their sandwiches without spilling on their costumes, drink their lattes without ruining their makeup.

We found a patch of lawn we could claim as our own and James jingled his keys. "I'll make a run to the McDonald's down the road. Who wants what?"

After we gave him our orders, which he actually wrote down on a pad, he turned to Kendall. "I'll need some help. Want to come with me?"

"Yes, please," she said, and they left.

Eliza stretched out on the ground and put her head in Max's lap. I opened up my new book and Camden looked over my shoulder, and we began to read. We were too tired to speak, too busy processing the day. My phone sat like a dead weight in my bag.

When Kendall and James came back with the food, she looked stricken.

"What's the matter?" I asked her. James went straight to sit with Max and Eliza.

"Bathroom," she whispered as she leaned down to hand Camden and me our bags.

"You feeling sick?"

"Meet me in the bathroom!" she whispered louder.

Camden and I exchanged a look, then I followed her inside. The hotel hallway was crowded and I almost lost her a few times, but eventually, somehow, we ended up locked in a handicapped stall together. She crumpled against the wall, put her face in her hands.

"That was *so* horrifying," said Kendall.

"Jamie?"

She only nodded.

"Tell me," I said.

"'Kendall,'" said Kendall, in a weird dumb-guy voice. "'You know I like you as a friend, right? You know I'm not looking for anything romantic, right?'"

I stepped forward and put my hand on her head. "Because you're supposed to magically know."

"He'd be such a jerk, if he weren't so *great*."

I paused. "I'm sorry, Ken. Maybe it's for the best, with you leaving and all."

She gave me a dirty look. "Don't try to help. I just want to be sad and pissed for a while. And the worst part is, I'm stuck at this stupid SuperCon with him until tonight."

"You're not with him. You're with me. And Camden and Max."

"And she who shall not be named." Kendall laughed a bit, but the weight of her emotions pulled down the corners of her mouth again. "Why doesn't he like me?" she asked.

"Camden told me James had a bad breakup last year. Maybe he does, but he's afraid."

I'd never been here before, giving relationship advice to Kendall. I felt like a fraud. Who was I to pretend I had any wisdom?

"None of that helps me." Kendall looked up at me. "Why is it so easy for everyone else? Last year you wanted a boyfriend and boom, there was Lukas as your boyfriend. Then you wanted Camden and boom, there was Camden as your . . . Camden. What is wrong with me that I can't make it happen?"

I was quiet. I didn't want to echo the default answer— *there's nothing wrong with you.*

"The *boom* may be easy, but everything else that comes after it is totally not."

"I would welcome the everything else," said Kendall. "If someone would only go there with me."

Kendall and I ate our Happy Meals in the hotel lobby. We were silent, chewing and drinking and people-watching. It felt a little like being in the cafeteria at school with her. We didn't need to talk; simply being present for her heartbreak was enough. Then she left to go for a walk while I met the others for the costume contest.

The room was filling up fast and I searched the crowd for Camden. I thought I saw him by the water fountain, but when I got closer, I realized it was the other Azor. The reboot version. Which would have been horrifying on multiple levels.

"Hey," said the right Azor with a hand on my shoulder. "We

were starting to worry you wouldn't make it. Is Kendall okay?"

"Not really," I said.

"Do you want to leave?" he asked, but I could tell he didn't want me to say yes.

"No."

"Don't stay for Eliza."

"This is for me. A hundred percent." *And for you*, I wanted to add.

"Good." He smiled. "But I'm sorry about Kendall. I talked to Jamie about her, like you asked. I didn't think he was going to—"

"Azor! Satina!" barked Eliza from nearby. "We're saving you seats!"

We followed the sound of her voice until we found her and Max. They were sitting right in front of the reboot group.

"Hi again," I said to Reboot Satina, who waved back at me.

Eliza pulled me down into my chair. "What are you doing? You're fraternizing with the competition."

"I'm celebrating the Satina sisterhood."

"Not when there's a group cosplay title on the line, you don't."

I laughed, thinking she was joking, but she glared at me. Okay, then. I scanned the room and spotted James over near the stage, fiddling with his camera. Was I supposed to hate him now? I didn't want to hate him. He didn't feel hateable.

Camden sat down beside me and put his arm around me, then a few seconds later, he took it away. I looked at him and he whispered, "We shouldn't block anyone's view."

The host of the contest was a local cosplay celebrity known as RedSmoke. (The term *local cosplay celebrity* came from Eliza.) She stood tall on the stage in black high heels, silver lamé minidress, and a completely shaved head.

"Hello, all you fabulous freaks!" she called. The room erupted in cheers. "Are you ready to blow us away?"

More whoops and hoots and hollers. A chill pushed through me. I hadn't planned on getting excited about this, but the excitement got *me*.

RedSmoke called up the contestants in the Individual category. They paraded one by one across the stage. There were superheroes and warriors, creatures and characters. Time periods and competing realities intersected and exploded. The crowd went nuts for each one.

It was the closest thing to pure shared joy I'd ever experienced.

By the time RedSmoke announced the Group category, I'd almost forgotten that I had to go up there, too.

"Ready?" asked Camden close in my ear.

I mentally reviewed everything Eliza had laid out for us. She had a whole Atticus Marr pantomime planned. She was supposed to run up, pretend she saw some huge threatening creature, draw her weapon, then beckon to the rest of us. We'd rush into formation behind her, staring out at the crowd with approximations of the expressions our characters were best known for.

After a group dressed as gaming characters left the stage, RedSmoke said, "Next up in the Groups, we have Temporal Anomaly!"

Which was us. Eliza led the way up the steps to the stage and started to do her bit. When it was time to fall into position, I paused. The reality of being on stage in my Satina costume felt suddenly huge, insurmountable. Camden stepped away from me, then glanced back and saw my hesitation.

"Come on," he said, with that mischievous smile, offering his hand. I took it.

As soon as I did, the applause from the crowd swelled louder.

"Azor! Kiss Satina!" someone shouted.

Camden stared out at the audience for a second, then gave me a questioning look. I nodded imperceptibly, on impulse. He pulled me to him and we kissed. For the first time ever, it didn't feel right. Who was I even kissing? The applause rained down around us.

When we pulled apart, the first thing I saw was Eliza glaring at me.

I didn't look at her again until later, after the reboot group and several others went up, already acting defeated, their efforts halfhearted in our wake.

It was only when RedSmoke announced Temporal Anomaly as the first prize group cosplay winners that I dared to glance at Eliza again.

"Wow," I said to Max as we let Eliza lead the way to the

stage to retrieve our trophy. "Is that what she looks like when she's truly happy?"

"I wouldn't know for sure," he said. "Take a picture before it goes away."

Camden reached out for my hand and I took it, but I let it go as soon as we were on our way to our seats.

19

I'll admit this: when we walked into the Tri-State SuperCon Dinner and Dance with our trophy, it felt like the whole party was for us. It was almost a wedding reception receiving line, the gauntlet of people we had to move through. There were claps and cheers and unexpected, slightly creepy pats on the back. I smiled and said *Hey, thanks* all the way down.

At some point, Camden took my hand again, but I didn't notice right away. It felt like part of our costumes now, that we had to be connected. We were no longer us but rather, the Azor and Satina who'd finally hooked up and defied every rule of the *Silver Arrow* universe.

I couldn't wait to get out of my Satina costume. The fabric on my skin felt heavy and old; the weight of the wig pulled me unnaturally to one side.

What had changed? Maybe there was a border between doing the cosplay for myself and doing it for someone else. Or in this case, a lot of someone elses. I'd crossed it.

Once we got through the cluster of people at the entrance to the party, I took a deep breath and let go of Camden's hand. He took a step away from me, as if he'd been wanting the break, too, and in seconds he was gone from sight.

And it was okay.

I felt a tap on my shoulder and turned to see Kendall, her eyes red, eyelashes crooked with dried tears.

"Where did you go?" I asked.

"I bought a book," she said, holding up a tattered paperback. "I found a table in some unused conference room and sat there and read."

"God, Kendall. You win for having the crappiest time here," I said.

"It was peaceful, actually. And I overheard some fascinating conversations through the doorway."

My best friend. She was an expert at making awful situations into something not-so-awful. I guess she had no choice.

Eliza appeared and pushed plastic cups into our hands. "Someone bought us a bottle of sparkling cider!" she exclaimed, then started to pour from a bottle. We let her, nobody speaking a word, and then she moved away.

I stared at the popping bubbles in my cup, the mist of fizz they created, until Kendall knocked her cup against mine.

"To surviving the Tri-State SuperCon," she said.

"In more ways than one," I said, and we both drank.

"I'm starving," she said. "Should we go find the hors d'oeuvres?"

"You lead, I'll follow," I said. We started to make our way through the crowd, which had gotten denser and louder.

"Satina Galt!" said a guy stepping in front of me. His T-shirt said GOT GEEK? "It makes me so happy to see young people who know the Original *Silver Arrow*."

"Thanks," I said, smiling yet also trying to keep a visual lock on Kendall.

"Have to say, I got a little emotional, seeing you guys up there at the contest. That show got me through some hardcore personal shit." His voice cracked. Maybe he'd been drinking, maybe he was just a weirdo. Either way, he was clearly sincere, and that cut through all the unease.

"It got my mom through her depression," I said suddenly, and realized I'd never said that out loud.

I took a step backward and found myself against a wall. The guy smiled, bowed his head to me, then moved away. I'd lost Kendall in the crowd.

I was sort of trapped there. Which actually felt good and safe, and made me think of Maeve Armstrong watching her own party while also being apart from it. Maybe it was okay to want all this, to love it even, but just need a break.

"Hey," said someone close to me, and it took me a second to realize it was Camden. He held out a soda.

"My savior," I said.

The crowd pushed us, pressed Camden into my body.

"Sorry," he said, looking uncomfortable.

I reached up and put my hand on his cheek. It was Camden right there, I knew that for sure. I felt balanced.

"Woot woot!" some girl shrieked. "Satina and Azor getting busy!"

I yanked my hand back and looked down into my drink.

"Ignore them," said Camden.

"Uh, impossible," I replied. "Besides, didn't we ask for it?"

"I guess we did," he said, searching my face. "I wouldn't ask for it back."

Camden touched my hair and then drew away, realizing it wasn't really my hair.

"I wish I could kiss you right now without it feeling . . ."

"I know." This party would end, and we would leave, and go back to real life, and maybe even the weirdness of this whole day would end up being a good part of the memory.

"Should we find the others?" asked Camden.

I nodded, then scanned the crowd and saw Max's head towering over it. Thank God for Max's head.

"Come on, I see Max." I took Camden's hand and we pushed into the crowd. People gave us high fives and smiles and nods along the way.

When we found Max, he was leaning against the bar, sweat

dripping down his face. He looked terrible.

"Are you okay?" I asked.

"I'm just . . . really, really hot. This jumpsuit material does not breathe."

"Take off your wig for a few minutes, that'll help," I suggested.

He pulled off the wig and grabbed a cocktail napkin, wiped his drenched hair with it.

"That's pretty gross," said Camden.

"I don't care. It feels amazing. How are you guys holding up? It's like you're the prom couple."

Camden just made a face, which made Max and me laugh.

Eliza appeared. I wasn't even sure where she'd come from or how she'd broken into our little triangle.

"Where's your wig?" she asked Max. Not asked, really. Yipped, like a terrier. She had a neon orange frozen drink in her hand.

"It's right here," he replied, indicating the wig, which looked like an alien pet, sitting by itself on the bar.

"Put it back on," she said, and took a sip of her drink.

"I'm dying of heat. I'll put it back on when I've cooled down."

"It's embarrassing if you're not wearing it," said Eliza, glancing around. "Everyone's hot, but nobody else is stripping off their costumes. It looks lame."

"Why the fuck should I care how it looks?" said Max with a frown. I'd never heard him swear before. He was always so good-natured. If Eliza was the terrier, Max was the golden retriever. But now he was baring his fangs.

"Because *I* care," said Eliza slowly. "Isn't that enough?"

Eliza picked up the wig and tried to put it back on Max, but she couldn't reach. Max snatched it out of her hand.

"Back off, Eliza," he said.

Camden and I exchanged an awkward glance.

"Please, please, *please*," she said in a tone that totally did not match the word *please*. "Don't do this to me. Keep it on so everyone can see it."

Max stared at her. "I am so sick of everything being about you. It was funny for a while, this vision you had. But now it's irritating as hell and actually, kind of sad. I'm sorry all the attention is on Ari and Camden. That was your idea, remember?"

Eliza was silent for a moment, then calmly took another sip of her drink. "I thought it was *our* vision. We did this together."

"I'm tired of being bossed around. The same way Camden got tired of it."

Eliza looked at Camden with utter surprise. Camden drew in a quick breath as if he was going to say something in protest, but then froze.

Eliza narrowed her eyes, then turned back to Max.

"I wouldn't boss you around so much if you didn't enjoy it so much."

Max stared at her, his eyes scanning her face for something. I wondered what it was.

"Fuck this," he said. He tossed the wig into the crowd. Someone must have caught it because we heard an *oooooooh*.

Then Max pushed his way past us. The crowd opened to let him in, then closed around him, and after a few seconds I couldn't even see his head.

Eliza sighed and slammed her drink onto the bar. "Drama queen," she said with a laugh. Camden and I did not laugh. "Oh, come on," she added. "Don't you think that was over the top?"

I thought of everything I'd seen of them since we'd all met. How I knew next to nothing about relationships, but I did know, with every fiber of my being, that theirs was not healthy.

Someone came up to Eliza and asked her to dance, and after a quick glance at us, she nodded yes. We watched her move off toward the dance floor.

"Do you want to?" asked Camden.

I shook my head. "I don't really want to be on display anymore."

So we did the next logical thing. We found the food table and stuffed our faces.

A little while later, James appeared. "*There* you guys are."

"Have you seen Kendall?" I asked, then wished I hadn't.

He looked pained. "No," he said. "I'm sorry about what happened. She was pretty upset, wasn't she?"

"What do you think?"

"I figured it was better not to lead her on. I wasn't sure she liked me until today."

I paused, looked hard at him. "I have a tough time believing that."

He glanced away and squeezed his cup until it dented. "I didn't want to deal with it until I had to. It was like, I knew what I had to do, but couldn't do it."

I thought of Lukas's face, asking me what was wrong. Asking me to tell him the truth. *Do you want to be with me or not, Ari?* How it was so much easier to keep saying one thing but then doing another.

"The timing could have been better," said Camden.

"I know," said James, wincing. "It's not like I planned that. We were on our way to get the food and she kept looking at me like she expected something and I just—"

"She'll be fine," I said, cutting him off. He seemed relieved. "Thank you for being honest."

"There's more to it than what I told her," he said.

"I don't need to know that." I scanned the room again. "Right now I only need to know where she is."

"Maybe she texted you."

Maybe. Probably. Which meant I needed to turn on my phone.

I took it out, ran my finger over the dark screen. Admired the beautiful blankness of it.

Camden put his hand on my shoulder.

A deep breath, then I was pressing down on the power button. As the phone woke up, it vibrated and dinged and danced. I unfocused my eyes and let the text messages come as a series of blurs. The screen was full of them, but I only looked at the ones from Kendall.

I couldn't take it in there anymore, sorry. Jamie left the
van unlocked so I'm hanging out here.

It was from a half hour ago.

"She's outside in the van," I said. "I'm going to go see if she's
okay."

"Do you want me to come with you?"

"No, I'm good." The thought of a few minutes alone seemed
suddenly marvelous.

I wound my way out of the crowd and into the hallway,
then the hotel lobby. I pulled my wig off as the lobby doors
slid open, and even the humid night air felt fresh against my
skin and head.

"Wait up!" someone yelled from behind me. It was Eliza
again. She ran to me, stopped, saw my wiglessness and shook
her head. "Et tu, Brute?"

"I'll put it back," I said, then felt mad at myself.

"Where are you going?" she asked.

"I'm checking on Kendall."

"Have you seen Max? I don't think he came back to the
party."

I shook my head and kept walking into the parking lot
toward the van. Eliza kept pace beside me.

"That was great, don't you think?" she said in a cheerful, un-
Eliza tone. "I didn't get a chance to tell you how fantastic you
did at the contest. And all day, really."

I was about to say thanks when we reached the van and
Eliza stopped abruptly. She stared into the front window.

"What's the matter?" I asked.

I moved closer to see what she was looking at.

Which was Kendall and Max in the front seat. Kissing.

All was quiet for a moment. Not just Eliza. The whole world, it seemed, was frozen on the edge of something. Then Eliza exploded.

"Are you fucking kidding me?" she yelled, then started banging on the windshield.

Max and Kendall broke apart, startled. Their oh-my-God expressions identical.

"Get out of the van!" shouted Eliza.

Max shook his head. And who could blame him, really?

"Goddammit," said Eliza, and threw herself at the driver's side door, flinging it open.

Kendall scrambled out the other side of the car. I scrambled to meet her.

"Kendall," I whispered.

"I'm sorry," she said, her hand still gripping the car door. "I was here and Max showed up and we started talking, and I started crying, and then . . ."

But Eliza was walking toward us now. I turned and tried to stand as strong as I could next to my friend.

Quickly, so quickly nobody really had any time to react or guess what was about to happen, Eliza stepped up close to Kendall. Her arm went out and for a flicker of a moment, I thought she was going to slap Kendall. Or worse.

Her hand reached for the collar of Kendall's X-Men T-shirt.

And she pulled. Hard. Harder than I thought someone as small as Eliza could.

The collar started to rip before Kendall smacked Eliza's hand away. It made a loud *thwack*, comics-style, as their skin made contact.

"Stop!" yelled Max, crawling out of the van now.

"You," said Eliza, holding out one finger and jabbing the air with it. "You do not get to do this. Not to me. Not with my boyfriend."

Kendall whimpered, clutching the collar of her shirt. Eliza put her hands on her hips in a gesture of victory.

Because girls like Eliza always won. They always owned and they always received. They never expected anything less.

A second later, I was shoving Eliza up against the side of the van.

"*You* do not get to treat people like that!" I yelled. "You can't bark orders and try to control everything!"

Eliza's face. Not angry, but shocked. Her eyes and mouth all perfect *O*'s.

"Ari!" someone shouted from somewhere, but I didn't turn to look.

My hands gripped her shoulders and held her there, and I was surprised how easy it was. She wasn't even fighting back.

"Ari, stop!" someone shouted again.

"You also do not get to steal things from people and expect them to let you!" I hissed. "You do not get to take advantage of people who thought you were their friend!"

I let Eliza go for a fraction of an instant, then pushed her again. The tinny noise of her body against the metal of the car. It was suddenly the *best noise ever*. Who was doing this? Ari wouldn't do this. Satina? Maybe.

Or maybe Ari was always doing this, somewhere deep down. Not to Eliza, but to everyone and everything I wanted to push back against.

I wasn't thinking about that. I was only thinking about the satisfying sensation of Eliza's body on the other side of my hands. How the way she was looking at me made me feel so present.

Then, tears pooled in her eyes and she started to sob.

Arms wrapped around me, pulling me back. Max grabbed Eliza and walked her down the aisle of cars until they were a good distance away from us.

I turned to see that it was Camden who'd yanked me away. He kept his arms tight around me and I could feel his breath panting against my ear. I realized I was panting, too.

Kendall opened her mouth to speak, but nothing came out. The three of us stood in suspended animation.

"Hey," said James, ambling across the parking lot toward the van. I could tell he hadn't seen or heard a thing. "Is it time to go?"

Stating the obvious: the drive home sucked.

Eliza sat up front with James, while Kendall and I were in the middle. Camden sat with Max in the way back.

I would never have believed that six people could be that silent for that long.

To pass the time and to avoid looking at Camden behind me, I read my new *Silver Arrow* book. When I felt carsick and could read no longer, I spread my hands in front of me, examining my palms whenever something outside would flicker light into the interior of the van. I moved my fingers, twirled my wrists. Were these really my hands that had pushed and held Eliza against the side of a car? And my brain had told them to do that?

It didn't make sense. One of the things I knew for sure about myself was this: when I got angry, it stayed indoors. I never let it out to roam and roar and scratch. It hid in a corner or burrowed inside a couch, easy to ignore. A thousand silent times, I'd raged against my mother or Dani or the thought of my father. But it had screeched out now, and who knew what the consequences would be.

Somehow the hour passed and we were back in town.

James dropped Eliza off first, of course. No discussion necessary. I'd never seen Eliza's house and she never talked about it—she never talked about her family at all—so I wasn't sure what I expected. Certainly not a McMansion in a subdivision called Morningside Meadows. She climbed out of the van and didn't look at any of us. James followed, walking her past a Mercedes parked in the driveway and around to the back of the house. He returned a minute later.

"Dude," said James to Max when he slid behind the wheel

again. "Why was it me who just did that?"

Max gave him a dirty look and pulled out his earphones. "Can we get everyone else home now, please?" He leaned his forehead against the window. Kendall stared straight ahead.

When we pulled into Kendall's driveway, she gave an unashamed sigh of relief. I found myself hopping out of the van with her.

"I'm sorry," I said softly so nobody would hear.

"What do you have to be sorry about? I'm the one who kissed another girl's boyfriend and caused some kind of nuclear reaction. By the way, that was both amazing and scary as hell, what you did."

I couldn't help but laugh a little. "Way to make your first kiss extra memorable."

"I'm glad you can joke about it. Guess who has to deal with the fallout while I skip town?"

Oof. This reminder hit me square in the chest.

"You leave in what, two weeks?"

"Eleven days."

"At least you're not counting or anything . . ."

Kendall gave me a bittersweet smile. "We'll hang out between now and then. A lot."

"Do you want me to come in with you?" I asked. "I could stay over."

Kendall's smile disappeared. "You can't avoid going home, Ari."

"I know that. But I don't want you to be alone."

Kendall searched my face and then glanced quickly at the

van. "But actually *I* do. Want to be alone. We'll talk tomorrow, okay?"

"If my parents haven't killed me or taken away my phone."

I hugged her tighter than she hugged me back, then watched her hurry into the house. When I turned back to the van, I saw that James had been watching her, too. There was an expression on his face that I could only describe as *suffering*, and I instantly knew there was more to this story.

"Where to, lady?" James asked me after I got back in the van. He'd regained his composure.

I finally forced myself to glance back at Camden and Max. Max was staring at Kendall's house, where her bedroom light had just turned on. Camden was staring at me, a thousand questions in his eyes.

"I'd like to go to the Barn," I said.

Camden nodded, and James made the van move again.

In my message to my parents, I said I'd be home by eleven. We'd left the SuperCon two hours early, and now it was only a little past nine. That gave me almost two hours before I had to face their music.

But first, I had to face Camden.

The front steps felt rigid, unwelcoming as I climbed them. The porch light was off and there were many more shadows than usual.

I followed Camden inside. "Be right back," he mumbled, then went straight upstairs.

I went into the bathroom, pulled a T-shirt and jeans out of my backpack. Taking off Satina's uniform in the same place I had first put it on, that felt important. I knew I'd never wear it again.

When I came out, everything was still dark and too quiet. What was the Barn without Eliza in her captain's chair at the big table, Max's oversize figure filling up all this empty space? The banter and the chatter of a very different, truly wonderful kind of family: one that had chosen itself.

I opened the sliding glass door to the patio and stepped out into the night. So strange, that it had been right here, not long ago—that moment at his party with all of us dancing and the air thick with unfiltered Possible.

"Hey," said Camden behind me. His voice was strained, tired. He'd changed, too, into shorts and a T-shirt. He looked wrong and it took me a few seconds to figure out why.

"You're not wearing a button-down," I said.

He surveyed himself. "They were an experiment."

"I thought they were your thing."

"Really?" He seemed genuinely surprised, but not flattered. "I didn't feel that. I tried them because I thought somehow they'd make me feel more normal. Mainstream. But that was really a form of cosplay, too."

I stepped close to him. Every time he opened up a secret like this, it drew me that much nearer.

"I liked the button-downs," I said, and touched his arm where the sleeve of the T-shirt stopped at the curve of his bicep. "But I like this just as much."

His skin tensed where I touched it. I looked up to see his jaw tightening.

"Tell me," he said. "Tell me why you did that to Eliza."

"Did you see what she did to Kendall?"

"Yes."

"Kendall was scared. I reacted."

"No kidding." His voice was icy now.

"That's not me. You know that's not me."

"Do I?" He searched my face. "Based on that, I'm not sure *who* you are. Not the person I thought, for sure."

I felt a burst of heat on my neck, the back of my ears. "Well, then. That makes us even, doesn't it?"

He considered that, and his shoulders slumped. Everything about him softened. He sank down onto the patio sofa.

"Yes, it does," he said.

"You know why Eliza did what she did, right?"

Camden nodded. "I heard what she said to Kendall."

"So is *Max* still the person you thought he was? Aren't you mad at *him*?"

"A little, but he made a mistake. Aren't you mad at Kendall?"

"What you just said." I moved to stand facing him, my knees touching his bent ones. "I made a mistake, too. Look, I've never touched anyone like that in my life. If I could undo it, I would." I would, wouldn't I? "Camden, I don't know what else to say. It happened. But everyone's okay and it won't ever happen again."

Camden grabbed his forehead with both hands.

"Everyone is not okay," he said. "Eliza's been through a lot. I'm not making excuses for the way she treats people, but what you did . . . to someone else it might be no big deal. To her . . . it might be."

"I'm sorry," I whispered. "You know I had no idea."

He gazed at the sky and took a deep breath. "We all survive things, but what she's survived is a little more intense than the rest of us. Also, she means a lot to me. She helped me put together a group of friends when I first got to school. She gave me the closest thing to the life I wanted, and she also gave me *Silver Arrow*. Then when I met you and we were all spending time together . . . that got me even closer to that life. But now it's ruined."

We were silent for a moment while I worked out what that meant.

"Oh," I said. "She won't want you to see me anymore."

Camden sighed. "It would be like, me choosing between you and my family, if that makes sense."

My throat closed up. I was going to ask the question before I chickened out.

"Are you still in love with Eliza?"

"What? No! God, no." He looked straight at me now, caught his breath. What if he said *I love YOU*?

Then again, what if it didn't matter whether he said it or not? I'd already done one brave thing. I was on a roll.

"Good," I said. "Because I'm in love with *you*."

He continued to stare at me while I continued to not breathe. Then he reached out and yanked me onto his lap, where the pressure of our bodies together took on a new shape and sensation.

I laughed nervously, until he kissed me hard. I kissed hard back, for a long time, and during that time it was easy to believe everything I'd ever wanted from him, his strength and confidence and devotion, was not misguided.

Somewhere in there, along that line between pleasure and pain, I began to cry. The sobs started deep within me, muffled by the kisses, but then they began to escape. It took Camden a few moments before he noticed and pulled away, putting both hands on my face.

"What? What is it?"

"What you said about the life you wanted. I wanted that, too. You gave me those things, too. And now it's all turned to crap. In addition to the other stuff that was already crap."

I sobbed again. Camden reached out and tentatively stroked my hair.

"I'm sorry about Eliza," I said with a sniffle. "I'm sorry that's a side of me, and I'm sorry it showed itself. I'm sorry I've never found a way to deal with it except to, you know, cut myself open."

Camden watched me for a few moments, like we'd just peeled another layer from between us and he was seeing things raw again. "Ari, you're making it hard for me to be angry with you."

"Go ahead, be angry with me. Please. But forgive me a little, too, okay?"

He bit his lip and nodded quickly, then kissed me. I pulled him down onto the couch. Or he pushed me. Maybe both at the same time. Now we were lying next to each other with the blanket of night above us.

Camden turned onto his side. He propped his head up with his elbow and began to trace the skin of my collarbone along the top of my T-shirt, back and forth in delicate, devastating U's. Then he ran his finger down the middle of my chest like he was marking an equator. The border between the half of me who wanted to believe we never had to leave this place, and the half of me who knew the world beyond it was not going to make being together easy.

His hand was under my shirt now, pressing a sweaty palm on my stomach. He took a deep breath and pushed it farther up, touching the center of my bra. I slapped my hand over his and met his eyes. Then I moved that hand to one of my breasts.

"We can do this, right?" I whispered.

Camden bit his lip and nodded, his focus intense. I let go of his hand so it could move on its own.

"Tell me when you want to stop," I said.

He didn't answer. He only touched me, and I felt like I could get swallowed whole in the quicksand of it. After a few moments he whispered, "What if I don't want to stop? . . . And *you* don't want me to stop?"

I wasn't sure what he was asking. I didn't care. All I knew

was that it meant we could keep touching each other, existing only in the moment of what happens now.

I answered by kissing him lightly, holding his bottom lip between my teeth. It must have tickled because he laughed. Maybe this was how people did it. With every moment of skin plus skin, you were pressing the reset button on your past experiences. You could close your eyes and pretend you were coming to this person with your hope for love still arranged in clean, unbroken lines.

I reached up with my left hand and started to slide it under the waistband of his shorts, then dared to check his expression. It was something halfway between wonder and fear, which was excellent because that was exactly what I felt, too.

It was impossible not to think about Lukas but it was okay, like the memory of him was there to help me understand myself. Lukas had guided my hand that night of his party. Grabbed it, desperately, and placed it where he wanted it. It was not where I wanted it but I couldn't make my hand do anything differently. But here, with Camden, I was in charge of my own actions.

Camden sighed so hard he started coughing. Then we both cracked up.

"To hell with all of it," he muttered, pressing his body into mine.

I wasn't sure what *it* was but yeah, send it to hell. Let it stay there a good long time.

Because I understood, now, why this might be worth risking

everything. I knew I had another person all to myself. That there was only one thing in the world we both wanted at that moment, and we were giving it to ourselves and each other.

We were kissing and moving to a kind of rhythm now. The beat of it got faster, more urgent. All it would take now was a few pieces of clothing not being where they were. Camden had his eyes closed, biting down hard on his bottom lip.

"Camden," I whispered, wanting to make sure he was with me, that we were making this decision together.

He didn't open his eyes. He just kept kissing me, gripping me tighter.

"Camden!" I said more loudly. "Stop! Look at me!"

His eyes popped open and it was like a spell had been broken. "What?" he said, his voice scratchy.

"Look at me, please."

He did. And I knew.

"We can't do this," I said. "Not like this."

Camden sighed and slowly pushed himself up, off, away from me. He knelt at my feet at the other end of the couch and I scrambled to sitting.

He clutched his chest. "You kill me."

"Sorry." God, that sounded so stupid. But what else could I say? "You stopped us the last time. We're tied one-one."

He huffed a half laugh, then fell serious again. "I don't know how to do this."

"This?"

"Be with someone, that is. Not sex. I could wing that part

based on what I've seen and heard . . ."

"Right," I said, holding up my hand for him to *halt*.

"The problem is, I have no examples to go by. How are we supposed to figure it out if we have nothing real to base it on?"

I shook my head. "No idea."

I pulled my shirt down, and something in that made Camden look pained. Had I done the right thing, stopping him? Was I going to regret this?

"Please stay," he said. "You can sleep in my mom's room."

I leaned forward and rested my forehead against his for a second. That was all I dared. Ninety-nine parts of me wanted to say yes and wrap my arms around him so hard they'd have to be pried away, eventually. But that one last, hundredth part. It had learned some things.

"It'll be infinitely less awful for me if I go home now," I said. "I'll call Richard."

Camden nodded, traced a circle on the back of my hand.

"I'm going to go into the house but I don't want you to come with me," I continued. "I want to think of you as being right here."

He nodded again, closed his eyes.

I went inside and didn't look back. I found my backpack, turned on my phone. There were no more new messages and that felt ominous.

I called Richard's cell phone. He picked up instantly.

"Ari?" he asked.

"Hi."

"Are you on your way home?"

"I'm actually at Camden's. Can you come pick me up?"

He paused. "Yes, of course. I just need the address."

It was the *of course* that got me. I found myself tearing up.

"I'm so sorry, Richard."

"Save it for later," he said, but kindly.

I went out onto the porch and waited for the next act to start.

20

Richard pulled into our driveway and put the car in park, but didn't shut it off. We hadn't said a word to each other since leaving the Barn. He turned to me now, and I got the sense he'd been so quiet on the drive because he'd been preparing for this moment.

"Ari," he said, finally looking at me, and it was a damn good thing he hadn't until now, because that was all it took for the tears.

"Richard . . . ," I said, my voice shaking, with no idea of how I planned to finish that sentence.

"The only thing I'm going to tell you that's not obvious, that you don't already know, is that Dani had a great time with Mikayla."

I smiled and let out a breath I didn't realize I was holding. "I'm glad."

"Hold that thought," said Richard, and turned the car off.

Danielle came running out the front door, her hair wet from a bath. I could feel my heart curl toward her.

"Hey, kiddo," I said when I got out of the car. "What are you still doing up?"

She hugged me, her arms tight and desperate around my waist, then drew back and gave me a dirty look.

"Waiting for *you*. Duh."

"I'm back now."

Richard brushed past us and into the house. After the front door shut behind him, I leaned down close to her and said, "Me going away with my friends, and Mom and Dad getting mad. You know that had nothing to do with you, right?"

"*Yes*," she said. Danielle stared hard at the ground, frowning. "I made Mom a card when she was crying. She said it was the best one she's ever gotten."

"She was crying?"

"Well, first she and Daddy got into a fight. Biggest one ever. Then she went into her bathroom and locked the door and I listened through the wall. She doesn't know I did that."

"Come inside," I said and started walking, taking her hand. I thought of Camden's question: *How are we supposed to figure it out if we have nothing real to base it on?* But the way Danielle's hand felt warm and perfect in mine—that was real.

The thought of my mother crying in the bathroom. That was real, too.

When I came into the kitchen, Mom was sitting at the table, facing the other way, and didn't turn around. I stood watching the back of her head for a few moments as she carefully flipped the page of the newspaper she was reading.

Then Dani said, "Mommy! Didn't you see that Ari's home?"

My mother dropped both hands to her side and sat quietly for a moment, then slowly swiveled in my direction.

It wasn't like I hadn't prepared for this. I'd played the scene over and over in my head for days now, letting it go one way, then another. Trying out different things to say and a range of reactions to feel. In this little mental theater of mine, Mom was always the same: Angry. Indignant. Unreasonable. (Also, Wrong. Eternally Wrong.)

Problem was, right now she was not any of these things. All I could see in her face was pain, unfiltered and stripped of pretense.

Her pain triggered *my* pain. There and then and always, for as long as I could remember.

It was different now because I knew I was the cause of it. None of my rehearsed imaginary reactions applied here.

I ran down the hall to my room and slammed the door.

Ten minutes later, Richard rapped softly on my door. I knew he'd just come out of Danielle's room after reading to her. "She wants you," he said.

Danielle was already tangled up in her covers, like she'd

purposely thrashed around to create the effect. Her still-damp hair spread out on the pillow and I winced to think of how badly it would be knotted in the morning, and how much she'd scream when we tried to brush it.

"Hi, kiddo," I said, sinking onto the bed next to her.

Dani was staring out the window. "I wrote a note to Jasmine the other day. She took it but she hasn't answered me yet. Do you think I should write another?"

In my resentment, I'd stopped checking the windowsill for fairy mail every night. Maybe my mother had collected the note, or maybe it had simply fallen between the wall and the bed. I'd have to check in the morning when Dani wasn't around.

"I guess it depends," I said. "What did your letter say?"

"I know it's silly," whispered Dani, her eyes following something on the ceiling. "But I asked her how to tell when people have stopped being in love with each other."

The Biggest Fight Ever must have been exactly that.

"What were Mom and Richard fighting about?"

Dani looked at me guiltily.

"I need to know so I can apologize to them," I lied.

Danielle grabbed two items from her windowsill: a figurine of a fantasy wolf-creature with wings, and some miniature creepy Barbie that had come from a Happy Meal.

She made the wolf speak in a low, deep voice that actually sounded nothing like her father's: "'Kate, what's the big deal? She got a babysitter and prepaid her, for chrissake.'"

"'But honey,'" said Dani as my mom in a dead-on imitation, "'she's never gone against the rules before and it scares me.'"

"'You can't control everything.'"

"'But I'm so busy with my great new job and I have to support us now and I'm so great and me me me! *Memememememe!*'"

Danielle looked up at me. "Okay, she didn't say that last part." She put her toys down. "They *have* stopped loving each other, haven't they?"

Who knew. Not us. Probably not them, either.

"I'll be interested to see what Jasmine has to say on the topic," I said by way of an answer. "Will you show me her letter, when it comes?"

Danielle smiled. "Sure," she said. "Are you confused about that stuff, too? Like with Camden?"

I lay my head down on the pillow next to hers and looked into her clear, clear eyes.

"Everyone's confused about that stuff. Always."

"Except the fairies."

"Well, obviously."

Dani's hand found my left wrist and she tried to circle it with her small fingers.

"Will you stay until I fall asleep?"

"Sure," I said, "but you know my rule. No talking."

She nodded, and we lay like that for a while, staring at each other until her eyelids or my eyelids shut first. It was probably a draw.

When I woke up a little while later, the light had gone

completely from the room. All I could see above me was the cracked ceiling of my sister's room. If I unfocused my eyes, I could pretend it was the sky above Camden's patio. But that exact sky during our exact moment would never happen again.

Without it, it was easy to feel like the Possible had closed itself off to me. I hadn't known what to do with it. I'd mishandled it somehow and lost my privileges.

I sneaked out of Dani's room and once I was back in my own room, I did the only thing that seemed like a solution anymore. I called the boy I loved. Who now knew I loved him but hadn't said it back.

It rang and rang and rang, until his voice mail picked up.

I didn't leave a message.

When I walked into the family room the next morning, Mom was pulling a blanket off the couch. There were folded sheets and a pillow on an ottoman nearby.

"Did Richard sleep in here?" I asked.

"No," she said, shaking out the blanket so it made a curt snapping noise. "I did." She checked her watch. "Richard's leaving for the store in about fifteen minutes, so you should get ready. With the Ribfest out at the fairgrounds, it could get busy today."

"Okay," I said, then leaned against the wall. She was speaking to me. That was something. "And then what?"

"Dinner at Moose's," she said. "Like always."

Except now with more awkward shittiness than ever.

"I meant, like, punishment."

Mom dropped the folded blanket on top of the sheet. She didn't scoop them up; I guessed she was going to leave them there for another night.

"Oh, yes," she said.

"Grounded?"

Now she looked at me and grabbed the pillow. "What do *you* think?"

"Cool. I've never been grounded before. And it always felt like something was missing."

She threw the pillow onto the floor and put her hands on her hips.

"This is no joke, Ari. What you did—"

"Hurt *nobody*. I heard Dani had a super-fun day with her babysitter."

"Hurt nobody?" She took a step toward me, and I pressed myself against the wall. "What about me? You don't think it hurt me that you lied and completely disregarded my judgment? That I feel like I can't trust you anymore?"

Her voice broke down at those last few words. She shrank back and sat on the arm of the couch. It made her seem less steady, not more.

"When I said you couldn't go . . . ," she continued after taking a deep breath, "that wasn't me being cruel for no reason. When I heard about the shoplifting and how they cajoled you into ditching your job for the day, I had a gut feeling. That feeling said, *These aren't people who are going to be good for you.*

Definitely not people you should go on a road trip to another state with." She paused. "And do *Silver Arrow* dress-up with."

I suddenly remembered the pin I'd bought her. I'd never give it to her now, even if Camden was right that it didn't matter if she wanted it or not. It would remain, forlorn and unappreciated, in its little box. Maybe I could sell it online.

Mom must have mistaken my silence for me actually processing what she'd said, as if it were something that made sense.

"Look," she said, lifting herself off the arm of the couch now. "Camden seems nice. . . ."

"Please don't talk about Camden," I said. "Don't even say his name."

"Honey . . . I've been where you are. There are some things I'd undo from that time, if I could." She paused, a shadow of something flickering across her face. "And I was older than you are now. Please trust me that I know what's best."

"Okay," I said. "Let me see if I understand how this works. You want to be gone fifty-five hours a week. You trust me enough to work in the store and take care of Danielle because . . . well, you have to. But you don't trust me to take care of myself."

I stopped, not sure how to continue. Mom was silent, probably unsure how to respond. Strangely, I liked it that way. But then there it was again: that expression on her face. That naked pain.

She dabbed something from her eye with the back of one wrist and, after a moment, yelled to the ceiling, "Dani! Get your shoes on! We're going to Target!" Then she leveled her glance at me. "I'm not talking about this anymore right now."

She marched down the hall and I heard her wrangling Dani out the door. After they left, I stood at the window and gave the car the finger.

I turned to see Richard, seeing me.

"Oh, come on," I said, slipping on my boots. "You know you've done it, too."

As Richard drove us to the store, I called Camden again. This time, his voice mail picked up instantly, a sign that he didn't have his phone turned on. I sent a text message.

Call me when you can. xo Ari.

Then I deleted the *xo Ari*. When did I start scattering *xo*'s in front of my name?

When we got to Millie's, Richard asked me to go into the back room and open some packages that had been delivered the day before. When I heard a customer come in, someone Richard knew, I retreated to the farthest corner of the room and called Kendall.

"Hey," she said stiffly.

"What's wrong?"

"Nothing's wrong. I'm at work. What's up?"

"I just wanted to see how you are."

"How I am."

"You know what I mean."

"I'm embarrassed," she said, her voice low and breathy now. I wondered if she had wedged herself into a similar corner at Scoop-N-Putt. "Also, horrified," she continued.

"Oh, good. That makes two of us."

"I've never had anything with anyone and then, bam. Two weird experiences with guys in one day. I must be on some accelerated catch-up program."

"And I've never . . . you know . . ."

"Been on the verge of beating someone up?"

"That," I said, laughing, hoping she would, too. She didn't.

"Ah, so we're both on this accelerated plan."

Another thought popped into my head. "I'm still confused. Did you ever get the sense Max was into you?"

"Ari, I can't talk about this while I'm consumed with regret. The specifics of what happened are still too weird."

We were quiet for a moment. I could still hear Richard talking to the customer, but I knew we didn't have much time. I wanted to tell her about the way James had looked when he watched her last night, what happened at the Barn with Camden. Where would I even start?

Suddenly, Kendall said, "Hey, I have to go, a van just parked and a ton of people are climbing out. It's like a clown car."

We hung up, then I started unloading the packages and breaking down the boxes. There was something really satisfying in making them flat again, removing a whole dimension.

I poked my head out into the store. "I'm taking some boxes to the dumpster," I said.

Richard flashed me a thumbs-up. Was there something different about his thumbs-up now? Less affectionate, more formal? Could be. Dammit.

I grabbed the stack of boxes and opened the door to the alley. Somehow I made my way through, my cheek against this wall of cardboard that blocked half my field of vision.

"Hey," said a voice that made me jump. I lowered the boxes and there was Camden's face.

"Are you lurking?" I asked.

"I knew you were at the store. I figured you'd come out eventually."

"How long were you prepared to wait?"

Camden leaned his forearms on the cardboard, each hand touching one of my elbows.

"A while," he said, with an intensity I'd never seen in him before.

I stared at him, drinking him in. I felt an ache.

"I'm grounded," I said. "I'm not supposed to see any of you until further notice. Or forever. Whichever comes first, I guess."

"I'm sorry."

I found myself tearing up. "Things are really messed up right now, at home. But we'll have to find a way to see each other, until the dust settles."

He stared at me, then said, "Let me help you with these," taking the boxes and walking over to the dumpster.

"I leave them leaning against the inside wall, so people can take them. People always take them."

Camden nodded. After he put the boxes away, more slowly and delicately than seemed necessary, he walked back to me. I noticed he was not meeting my glance.

"What's wrong?" I asked, swallowing hard.

Now he looked at me. "I'm going up to my mom's."

"Your mom's."

"In Vermont."

"Vermont? The Vermont that's like, four hours away?"

"Yes."

"Is she okay?"

"She's fine. But, like I told you. Lonely. I don't want her to be lonely."

Okay. Maybe a few days apart would be a good thing. A breather.

"How long are you staying?"

Camden simply shrugged. It was the most horrible shrug I'd ever seen.

"What does that mean?" I asked.

"Eliza came to see me this morning," he said, as if that was remotely close to an answer. "She's really upset. As bad as I've ever seen her. She wants me to break up with you."

"I see."

"Everything's messed up. Who am I supposed to be loyal to here?" Camden drew in a sharp breath. "I'm terrified, Ari. I haven't seen this kind of thing ever work out."

He didn't have to explain further. *This kind of thing.* It didn't need a name, but it had one anyway: love.

"So you're just going to run away?"

"Why not? I've seen my mother do this over and over again.

When a relationship gets tough, she takes off." He paused. "Well, first she makes a tapestry about it. *Then* she takes off."

We were quiet and the reality of what he was saying hit me.

"Look," he said after a few moments. "I'm coming back. At some point. But I need time to figure stuff out."

"Everything's messed up for me, too, Camden. Here. I can't face it without you."

He drew in a quick breath.

"Sure you can. You don't need some fuck-up like me. You're stronger than you think you are."

"Okay, maybe I can. But I'd rather not. Camden . . . I love you."

Another sharp intake of breath, like I kept jabbing him.

"Don't," was all he said.

"Too late."

"I'm not the guy from last summer. I'm not Azor Ray. Hell, I'm not even a youth hotline volunteer anymore. I quit that because clearly I can't handle a real crisis. I'm not any of these people you think I am."

"I only see who you are. Not who you're *not*."

He was quiet. "I see that, too. In you, I mean."

Say you love me. Say you love me, and it'll all be okay. You'll see.

Instead, he said: "Maybe things will be different in a few weeks."

No. No, no, no. "Summer will be over by then. And then, with school . . ."

Even saying the word *school*, even thinking about it, made me feel cold. Was he even going to come back to Dashwood?

I felt anger rise up in my chest. "I don't understand you. All summer you've talked about breaking away from your mother's way of life, and now you're jumping into it when you don't even have to."

Camden's eyes met mine. "But it feels like I have to."

"Then fight that feeling! And while you're at it, grow up. If you want to belong to something, you have to commit to it. You have to let it belong to you, too."

He stood there, completely still, and there it was again: the anger. *My* anger, I should call it, because I was ready to own it then. But I had to keep it tamed this time.

"I'm sorry, Ari," he said, moving forward and reaching out. I stepped away from him.

The alley door to Millie's opened. "Ari?" called Richard. When he saw the two of us, he looked alarmed, but I couldn't worry about his worry.

I turned back to Camden.

This boy. This boy who had been everything in one way last summer, then everything in another way this summer. Who had shown me so many foreign things that had been right there, knowable all along.

This boy was shaking his head again. "Don't hate me," he gasped.

Then he turned and ran.

21

Over the next three days, I did the chores and errands my family asked of me. I didn't complain or cry or pout. I did them while smiling, talking, and joking.

Every minute of it was a big, fat fake.

If I faltered for a moment, Mom would see the signs. I knew she was watching for them. I couldn't let her know that underneath the pulse of these days I was back in the place of *everything hurts*. Perhaps I'd always been. Maybe this was where I lived for good, and all that appeared to be normal life and happiness was only a fleeting illusion, a mirage when you're desperate in the desert.

Richard was watching, too. I could tell he wanted to ask

about what he'd seen in the alley but also respected my privacy. It was such a fine line, being concerned without being invasive. It bought me some time.

The thing that hurt the most was this: I didn't know who to be more angry at. Camden, for not being the person I thought he was? Or me, for not protecting myself?

My therapist, Cynthia, had often urged me not to push away memories of what the depression itself felt like but rather, get inside them. That way, she said, I could begin to understand and, eventually, begin to win.

I knew I should call her now. But she'd want my doctor to increase my dosage or switch drugs completely, and that would mean I'd lost again. I wasn't ready to concede, so in the solitary safety underneath my bedcovers early each morning and late each night, I answered the question she'd asked so many times.

What does it feel like, Ari?

Well, it felt like this:

Like there was always something incredibly awful that I needed to try and forget about.

Like some of my cells were somehow dead, injected with a serum that made them heavy and numb.

Like I had no idea what I wanted to do when I wasn't being told what to do or following the paved paths of my day. Work at the store, go somewhere with Dani, come home, help with dinner. Work, go, come, help. Those were the only things that made my body move.

On the morning of the fourth day after Camden left, the

images returned. They popped like flashbulbs behind my eyes and I let them come, fast and forceful. They were the images of my bare arms, a razor opening the skin and relieving some of the pressure. Letting it out. Letting it hurt. Letting it bleed.

Then, images of the contents of the shoe box in my closet: a three-pack of cheap razors with two razors left, a bottle of rubbing alcohol, and a pack of cotton balls.

I started running the logistics through my mind. I couldn't get any ice or frozen peas this time, not with Richard and Dani eating breakfast out there. But it would just be a small cut. Tiny, up high, so nobody would know. And I would still feel the release of it.

It wouldn't count, not really, but it would help.

I went into my closet, then poked around in the back until I felt the corner of a shoe box lid sharp against my fingers. The comforting whisper-rustle as I pulled it out through my hanging clothes. I sat on the floor of my room and drew the box into my lap. Broke the tape on either side of the lid and popped it open, my hands shaking.

But the razors and alcohol and cotton balls were gone. In their place was a white envelope that simply said *Arianna* on the front.

I stared at it for a few moments, trying to process what it meant.

Then I tore the seal on the envelope.

The letter was handwritten on yellow legal paper, cursive swirls in blue ink.

Dear Arianna,

When I found this box, my first thought was to confront you. (I wasn't snooping, I swear. I was looking for outgrown stuff to donate to the domestic violence shelter.)

But then I knew you had to be ready to hear what I have to say. If you're reading this it's probably because you're feeling the urge to harm yourself again. Which means you're ready now. Does that make sense? God, I hope so.

Ari, I need to say this: I have been there. I never got as far as you did. But I can say with certainty that I have felt what you've felt. I know you know this in a general way, and I'm sorry we never talked about the details. Maybe they would have helped you. Your therapist wanted me to, but I just couldn't. I realize now that I was struggling more than I thought I was, and in denial about that.

It has been so painful to know that you inherited this burden from me.

But I have to say, seeing you dressed as Satina Galt did something to me. It reminded me that I gave you good things, too, like this role model. The way you (and Satina, and yes, sometimes me, too) want so badly to do your best, to make everything okay for everyone, that you're not sure how to fit your own needs in there, too. The way you value strength and self-confidence—that was my wish for you. But I also know it's hard to actually achieve.

I think you're amazing. Maybe someday I'll be able to show you.

If you are in pain, let me see it. If you found this letter because you were thinking of using the things in the box, call me. Wherever you are or wherever I am, I will come.

Love,
Mom

I read the letter twice. Then I wept. Then I read it again.

My mother.

Dabbing alcohol on the cuts on my arms, then wrapping them gently with bandages and gauze. Not saying a word. Sitting with her knees at perfect right angles beneath the Disney Princesses poster in the waiting room of my pediatrician's office. Putting her arm around me as I stepped out, taking the prescription note from my hand. Filling it and leaving it on my bed.

It was the only version of her I wanted to think about. It was the only one that existed, right then.

I knew I should do what she requested, but I couldn't call her. Not yet. In the meantime, I took the box and walked it outside and stuffed the whole thing in the trash.

❊ ❊ ❊

"Sorry I've had them so long," I said to Kendall the next day, handing over a pair of black jeans with patches on the knees. I'd borrowed them months ago and forgotten until she asked for them back so she could take them on her trip. We were standing in my driveway while Kendall's mom waited in the car. They had a day's worth of errands and I was first on the list.

"No worries. I have stuff of yours, too." She produced a plastic grocery bag tied at the handles.

I took it, and burst into tears. I'd been on a bit of a hair trigger since I'd found the letter.

"It's not like I'm going away forever!" said Kendall. "I didn't want you to want any of this while I was gone and then be mad at me!"

I moved toward our front porch so Kendall's mom couldn't hear me.

"It's not that." I paused, wiped my nose. "Camden broke up with me."

Kendall came closer. "What? When?"

"A few days ago. He ran away to his mom's in Vermont."

"And you're just telling me this now?"

"I feel ashamed. I didn't want to talk about it because that made it real."

Kendall made a frustrated noise. "Ari. You have to talk about these things. And you have to talk to me about them. If we're going to stay friends and you're going to stay healthy, that has to happen. Understand?"

I nodded, almost crying again simply from the relief of being told what to do.

Kendall glanced back at her mom, who was drumming her fingers impatiently on the steering wheel.

"We'll continue this," said Kendall.

I hugged the plastic bag of whatever-I'd-left-at-Kendall's and nodded again.

Max came into the store the next day, when Richard was out.

"Hey," he said as the door swung shut, then came over to hug me across the counter. When we drew apart, he asked, "How are you?"

"Terrible."

"Let's come back to that. How's Kendall?"

"She's busy getting ready for her trip," I said, knowing that didn't really answer what he was asking.

He shook his head and sighed. "That whole thing was my fault. I was so mad and not in control of . . . you know, whatever those things are that keep you from doing stupid shit."

"She wouldn't tell me the details. So it was you who kissed her first?"

Max blinked. "Yeah. What happened with you and Eliza . . . that's on me."

"It's totally not." I shook my head hard. "If it hadn't been you and Kendall, there would have been some face-to-face drama between us eventually."

"I suppose you're right," he said sadly.

"My question about Kendall is, was that something you'd thought about doing before?"

"No. I've asked myself the same thing, and no." A memory seemed to overtake him. "But there was something about that time we spent in the van. What we talked about. The place we were both in, mentally. I can't explain it. Believe me, I wish I could. It would make my life so much easier right now—"

"You mean, with Eliza."

"As we work things out." He went over to the paint aisle, plucked the infamous paint set off the shelf. I couldn't be sure if it was the exact same one or not. "I came in to buy this. For her. Maybe it's a way to make things right for you, too. To show your parents we're not all bad news."

I took the box from him and started ringing it up. Then I found myself having to sniffle back tears.

"What's wrong?" asked Max.

"I didn't expect you guys to be the ones who stayed together."

He laughed sadly. "You and me both."

"But all those things you said to her that night were true."

Max sat on the counter. I didn't tell him not to. "Sometimes you feel like you can change someone," he said half-dreamily. "You want to be the one who does it. You figure it's worth trying."

Yes. Now that I knew Eliza better, I could see why it would be worth trying.

"And sometimes," I said, "you want a person to be the one to change *you*."

Max sighed. I didn't have to elaborate. I put the paint set in a gift bag and chose a silver ribbon to tie into a bow on the handles. Eliza would get the silver reference; it was the closest thing to communication that I could manage with her now, and possibly forever.

"The truth is," said Max as he watched me tie, "we all change each other. Maybe not in huge ways. Maybe not always for the better and how we expected or wanted. But it happens."

I nodded, my eyes tearing up again, and handed him the bag. We stared at each other, a comfortable stare like the kind I had with Kendall at our best moments. Regardless of everything, I was glad to have gotten to know this boy.

"Camden will come back," said Max.

"The issue is that he left in the first place. Just when I needed him most."

Max shrugged. "So he's not perfect. He's still learning."

"Where is the line between that and the deal-breaking stuff? The stuff that's not going to get learned. The stuff that makes someone wrong for you."

Max considered this, staring at the bag in his hands. "Ari, my dear," he said. "That is an excellent fucking question." He raised his head to meet my eyes, looking teary. "Let me know if you figure it out."

22

Another day. Another half-waking from half sleep, another push up from horizontal. Another putting down of your feet on the floor. Another set of motions to go through.

I was stepping out of the shower, wrapping a towel around myself, when the call came. The ringing startled me because I didn't even know my phone was there, hidden in the pocket of my shorts.

Then I saw the name on the screen, and I startled again.

"Hello?" I said in that voice you instinctively use when you want to pretend you don't know who's calling.

"Hey," said Camden.

The sound of it made my throat cinch tight. I swallowed

hard and sat down on the closed toilet seat. "What do you want?"

I'd thought it was possible I'd never hear from him again. So I should have been overjoyed. I was not overjoyed.

"Can you talk?" he asked.

Richard had taken Danielle to camp, and I was supposed to meet him at the store.

"For a few minutes, yes."

I heard Camden take a deep breath, but he didn't say anything. Was I supposed to do the talking?

"Camden? I'm here, you know."

"I know."

"Uh . . . how's Vermont?"

A pause. "It sucks," he said. "Without you, it sucks."

It's weird, when something flatters you at the same time that it makes you want to scream.

I tried to keep myself calm. "I'm sorry to hear that, but as you recall, nobody forced you to go."

"I did. *I* forced me. Too bad I gave in."

I swallowed again, as quietly as I could so he couldn't hear. "Then come back."

"I don't think I can."

"Okay, then." I let my voice sound sharp, annoyed. "So you're calling me because . . ."

"I want you to come here."

"Here," I said stupidly.

"To Vermont."

I had no response for that.

"You'd love it, Ari," added Camden. "There are hiking trails and lakes and a big hammock outside my mom's cabin. We could just be together, without the others. And without the bullshit."

I was so angry, still, but he spliced these images together like a trailer for an amazing-looking movie.

"Are you talking about a weekend?"

"You could stay longer than a weekend. You could stay . . . Hell, you could stay until school starts."

I shook the movie trailer out of my head. Why was he doing this to me? And why was I letting him? There was no way I'd be allowed to see that movie, much less live it.

"Camden, I'm grounded. And even if I weren't, my parents would never let me make a trip like that with you."

"Maybe they would if they knew how important it was to both of us."

"Right. Um, I don't think so."

"Then come anyway. You know that saying: 'Act now, beg forgiveness later.'"

"I'd like to know how often things worked out for whoever made that up," I said, trying to keep it together. "Besides, I have responsibilities here."

"Let them hire a babysitter. Let them hire someone else to sell craft supplies."

"Camden . . ."

"You don't have to keep giving them free labor. They'll be

okay without you." Camden paused and his tone got low. "But I may not be."

Ugh. I could even picture his expression when he said this, and how it would make me want to throw my arms around him and kiss hard and long until I'd given him everything I thought he needed. No fair.

"Camden," I whispered again, then asked the next question that came to mind: "Are you coming back?"

I listened to him slowly breathe in, then out. "I don't know. My mom's been invited to stay on through the fall."

"So . . . you'd stay with her?"

His voice broke apart now.

"Ari, 'with her' is one place I know I belong."

"You could belong to me, too," I said.

"Hence me inviting you up here."

I was back to being angry.

"Do you understand that you're asking me to choose between my family and you? The same way you felt like you were being forced to choose between *your* family and me?"

He was quiet a moment. "I guess you're right."

"You say you want to belong to something, but that means you have to follow some rules you may not like. It means you have to do some work."

"I'm not good with those two things."

"I've noticed."

"See, last summer you thought I was perfect. I'm not perfect."

No, he wasn't perfect. But through my anger right then, I

realized this: I loved him still. I loved him more, even. Because I loved what his imperfections were teaching me.

"Ari," said Camden into my silence. "You've saved me a little. Can you keep doing that, please?"

Maybe that was it. The thing. What he and I were all about.

I lowered my voice to match his and asked, "What do you need saving from, Camden?"

"Myself."

"Don't we all need that kind of saving?"

"Let's save each other, then."

"In Vermont."

"What better place?"

"You should start writing their travel brochures."

He laughed, then said, as casually as breath, "I love you."

I froze. I'd been hoping to hear that for so long. I thought it would bring all the answers, but it only created more questions.

There was suddenly another thing I knew for sure.

"I can't save you, Camden. Just like you can't save me. It's kind of something we have to do ourselves."

I heard him exhale. "We can help each other though, right? That's allowed?"

Arrrgh. He wasn't getting it. If we had this connection, why couldn't he see what I so clearly did? "And how are you going to help me, Camden? What are you going to give me?"

"What do you mean?"

"Look at our situations. Who has the freedom to go and be

wherever they choose at the moment?"

He was quiet.

"If you can't give that . . ." I felt my resolve weakening. "I can't be with someone who's only going to take. Who's not going to step up."

Camden was still quiet.

My thoughts were a tangled knot of sadness and frustration and anger and desire, but in the middle of that knot I could see a clean space. A little loop of understanding of what I needed to do next. I focused on that.

"Good-bye, Camden," I said into that loop, and hung up.

I put down the phone and crawled into the empty bathtub and cried for about a year, or maybe ten minutes.

Sometimes, there was no victory in figuring out something important about yourself. There was only reality and clarity, which were not much fun at all.

Then I got out of the bathtub and called someone.

"Hello, Mom?" I said when she picked up.

The menu at Moose McIntyre's was eighteen pages long. I'd never had the time to read the whole thing and appreciate how you could find falafel platters and chicken-and-waffle combos at the same restaurant.

Today, I had that time.

"Go there now and wait for me," Mom had said on the phone. "I don't want you home by yourself."

"Okay," I'd sobbed, so grateful for instructions. "Okay." I'd said it at least eight times.

Now I was sitting in a corner booth by the window, nursing a coffee and waiting. Every time the door opened, I looked up nervously like I was on a first date.

With my mother.

On the twelfth time the door opened, it was her. I watched her scan the restaurant for me. I could see the worry and urgency on her face, and that made me feel good. Was that bad that it made me feel good?

Then she found me and moved quickly to the table. I stood up, stepped out of the booth. When she reached me, I fell against her. The first thing I noticed when she put her arms around me was that she felt smaller than I remembered. Maybe I'd just gotten bigger. Maybe it had been that long since I'd truly hugged her.

"I got your note," I said into her shoulder. "You told me to call."

I felt her stiffen for a moment, then she tightened her embrace. "You went looking for the box."

I nodded, pinching my eyes shut.

"Come," she said. "Sit."

She shooed me back into the booth, then slid in beside me.

"What did you tell them at work?" I asked.

"Family emergency."

"I'm sorry you went all the way down there and all the way back. You didn't have to do that. It could have waited."

Mom looked at me full-on. Her hands flat and firm on the

table had moved the place mat so it was crooked. I wondered if she'd notice.

"Ari," she said evenly. "I had to do that."

I felt the tears come again but I bit down hard on my lip, willing them to stop.

"Do we have to call your doctor?"

"I don't know. Please don't be a nurse right now."

She looked taken aback for a moment, then softened. "This was about Camden, right?"

"It's kind of about everything."

"But you got hurt."

Before I could figure out a way to answer, a waitress came by with two glasses of water. Mom ordered a bowl of granola.

After the waitress left, Mom turned back to me and said, "Look, I know I can't always protect you. I can only hope you have the skills to do it yourself."

"Then why were you so against Camden's friends when you hadn't even met them?"

"I didn't understand at first, either. The thing about driving ninety minutes to work and back each day is that you have a lot of alone time to think about stuff." She paused. "Sometimes I think I took that job because of the alone time on the road."

Mom seemed to drift off for a few moments, then finally checked back in. "What did I tell you about how your father and I met?"

"That you went to high school together."

"That's right. Well, I'll tell you the rest of the story now. It's relevant." She wrapped one hand tight around her water glass, but didn't drink. "We'd never really known each other growing up. Until the summer after high school was done, when we worked as counselors at the same day camp. We had, you know. A summer fling."

The word *fling* felt creepy and wrong coming from my mother. I took a sip of my coffee and spent a long time gingerly placing the cup back in its saucer.

"Then summer ended," Mom continued. "We went off to start college in different states. But then the next summer we were both back at the camp. . . ." She looked at me and raised her eyebrows. "And the next—"

I held up my hand. "I get the picture." It was a gross picture.

Mom laughed a little, shook her head. "After we graduated, we both found ourselves back home. And back with each other. We started dating for real." Now she picked up the water glass and jiggled it so the ice clinked. "*For real* was different from a summer fling. We had our ups and downs but we stuck with it. Stayed on the track, you know? Moving in together, then marriage. Then we had you and I wanted so dearly to make it work."

"Why did you stop? Making it work, I mean."

"This stuff is really hard for me to talk about."

"You're doing great," I said.

Mom laughed. "Gee, thanks." Then she got serious. "Okay, it was this. I found out that he'd been having a relationship with another woman. For a long time. So I kicked him out."

"You always said he left."

"Well, the way I see it, he left the moment he cheated on me."

The waitress came back with a bowl of granola and a little metal container of milk. She hovered for a moment, but there must have been something about our energy that told her to get lost.

Mom didn't pour the milk. She picked up two pieces of granola in her fingers and popped them in her mouth.

"I know you weren't expecting to hear all this, but I do have a point and I'm getting to it."

"Take your time," I said. Who knew when this portal would be open again. It felt both natural and unnatural that we were here, having this very grown-up conversation. I liked that feeling.

Mom smiled at me, then her eyes traveled instinctively to the scars on my arm.

"When your father left," she continued, "I didn't expect him to go so far. Certainly not all the way across the country. But he had a friend there who offered him a job and he wanted to make a fresh start. I think he did truly plan on being in your life. He was just going to take some time to regroup."

"So much for that," I said.

Mom didn't seem to hear me. "Once he was gone and I was alone, a single parent of a two-year-old . . . I really thought I'd die." She swallowed hard. "I mean, I really thought I wanted to. For a long time. Three years, give or take. I don't remember much except thinking that maybe you'd be better off living with your grandmother."

I turned to look out the window, unable to meet her glance. "Then why are you here, alive, and I'm not sitting with Grandma watching soap operas right now?"

Mom laughed a bit. "A friend convinced me to get help. Then one day, my boss at the bank sent me to an electronics store to buy a DVD player for the conference room. They'd just released the first two seasons of *Silver Arrow*."

I turned to look at her now. She was shaking her head.

"Wait, wait. I need to backtrack," she added. "The *Silver Arrow* thing. One year in college, there was a guy in my dorm. He was socially, you know, awkward and wanted to be popular. So when the show went on the air, he'd buy beer and snacks for anyone who wanted to drop in and watch with him. At first, only a few people came but eventually, the whole hall-way would gather. I got addicted. It was so much fun to share something that way."

I wanted to jump in and say, *Yes! Duh! That is called fandom and that is why there is cosplay.* But my mother was now unreeling so much of herself, I didn't want to risk tangling her up.

"I could only watch it on and off after that year," Mom continued, "but I always loved it. So the day I went into the store and saw this big display with life-size cutouts of the crew, it was like bumping into long-lost friends. I bought the DVDs and a player to go with them. But watching it again, with you . . . reminded me of that time in my life when I had everything in front of me. It seemed so safe to dream big back then. I hadn't made any of my mistakes yet."

She picked up another piece of granola and held it between her fingers.

"It'll sound silly," she said, "but *Silver Arrow* and Satina and all the rest helped me rewind and find that hopeful person again. It helped me start fresh."

We were silent for a few moments as I processed all that. Mom took this opportunity to eat.

"So why don't you watch it anymore?" I asked. "Why do we never even talk about it?"

Mom shrugged sadly. "Those years were not a good time for me, Ari. It led me to a better time, yes, but it was so hard. Like I said in my letter, last year I was struggling, too, and couldn't admit it. Staying busy and focused on moving forward is one of the things that helps me manage my . . . feelings."

You mean, depression. Why did she have trouble saying that word?

"Why were you so against Camden?" I asked.

"Ah, right. I'm sorry, this all made so much more sense in my head when I was driving." She paused. "Those summers I spent with your father . . . I was too preoccupied with him. I missed out on other things."

I frowned. "You mean, other guys?"

"Well, certainly that," she said. "But also, opportunities. Even then I knew I wanted to work in medicine. Your grandmother begged me to apply for internships that would help me get into medical school, but I just wanted to work at the camp with this boy I loved."

Boy. It seemed absurd that my father had ever been some boy.

Mom finally mustered up some courage now, because she reached for and took my hand. It was harder than I thought it would be to let her.

"This is the thing, Ari. At exactly the moment where I've finally gotten back on the track I should have stayed on, I see you doing a little of what I did. At the exact moment in my own life where I felt I went astray. In light of your . . . that night . . . I was so scared of what would happen to you if things didn't work out."

She let go of my hand and drew her own close to her, tucked it into her lap. We sat there in silence for a while.

"And I didn't realize this until today," Mom continued, "but I think I was also a little jealous. Because, what I wouldn't give for a chance to be back there. In that place where love seems simple and fresh."

There were tears in her eyes now. I realized she wasn't talking about her past anymore.

"Are you and Richard going to break up?" I asked.

I expected her to say, *What? God, no!* Instead, she said softly, "I hope not."

"You're always mad at each other. You barely speak sometimes."

"We're not in a good place right now, that's for sure. But that doesn't mean we won't figure it out."

"But you love him," I prodded.

Mom took a deep breath. "I do. It's not the same kind of love it was before. It's more complicated. But maybe that's okay."

"Make it okay," I said. "Please make it okay."

She nodded and searched my face.

I reached into my bag and dug my hand into an inside pocket, where the box with the *Silver Arrow* pin was still tucked away.

"I got something for you at the SuperCon."

I pulled it out and spread open my palm, put the box on it. Mom took it and when she saw the pin, she smiled.

"This is fantastic," she said.

"You don't have to wear it. I just thought it would be fun for you to have."

Mom nodded, then started to break down. "I'm sorry for everything, Ari. Bear with me while I try to fit it all together. I want my life. I have good days and bad days."

"There are these things called therapy and medication that I highly recommend," I said.

She laughed. "Thank you. I'll look into it." Then she got serious. "Watching you slowly come back from that night you hurt yourself . . . it's made me so proud. Nervous and terrified, but proud."

"Thanks," I whispered, not sure if that was the right thing to say, and turned back to gaze out the window. This kind of intensity was blinding and it was hard to look straight at it for too long.

All this time with Camden, I thought I had no good examples of love, nothing to give me a road map or even a basic flow chart. But maybe I was wrong. Maybe love was not always going to be something I recognized when I saw it. Maybe it was not the reward you got for working through something, but the working through itself.

"Do you need to go back to the hospital?" I asked Mom.

"No, I took the day off. I think you should, too."

"Oh, yeah?"

Mom smiled. "I know the boss. I can pull some strings. We can do something fun."

"Don't tell me: you want to go to Target."

"Actually, I noticed there's a noon showing of some movie I've never heard of." She pointed out the window to the theater across the street.

I glanced at the marquee. "Oh, yeah. That's supposed to be really silly."

My mother heaved a bone-deep, tired sigh. "Silly sounds like heaven."

It really did. She paid for the tickets, but I bought the popcorn.

Late August.

Still summer, officially, but now there were tiny sadnesses everywhere.

The slightly stiff feeling of the weeds on the front steps under my bare feet, a sign they'd start dying soon. The night air stripped of a layer, revealing a new coolness that wasn't there before. Three annoyingly overachieving red leaves on the tree in our front yard.

Usually, this time of year was when I started savoring every morsel of summer. But now I wasn't sure I wanted to. Summer being over meant being able to seal the whole messy thing up and move on. Start school. Have a great senior year. Finish strong.

But first, I had to say good-bye to Kendall.

"Hey," said my best friend as she approached the Crapper at the lake, carrying the rolled-up towel I'd instructed her to bring.

We hugged, and maybe it was my imagination, but she already looked changed.

"Did you pay yet?" she asked.

I shook my head. "I thought we'd go this way first," I said, then pointed toward the entrance to the trail to the creek.

Kendall raised her eyebrows. I'd never told her what was back there.

"Where exactly does this trail go?" she asked. "I thought it just went a little into the woods."

"You'll see in a minute."

We walked the rest of the way in silence, and then she did see. The creek opened up before us and Kendall stopped dead in her tracks. I gave her some time to take it all in.

"How can this be here without us knowing?" she wondered aloud.

"I know, right? The nerve of it." We both laughed a little.

We went to the water's edge and found a wide, flat rock. I didn't want to go farther, out into the creek and possibly the rock where Max and Eliza had once ravished each other.

"Camden brought you here, didn't he?" said Kendall after we unrolled our towels and sat down.

"Yes. If you keep going along the creek, you can actually see part of the lake."

She nodded, staring at a spot where the water fell sharply, landing in a froth of bubbles before flattening out again.

After a minute Kendall said, "This summer has been . . . a summer."

"Did we have all the fun?"

She gave me a puzzled look.

"That night at the gas station," I added. "You said we'd have a lot of fun before you left. That we'd try to have no regrets."

Kendall sighed. "It's so easy to say that stuff at the beginning of something."

We were quiet. It would have been a creaky, awkward quiet anywhere else but here. Maybe that's why I'd chosen this spot, because I knew the scenery would fill in the blank spaces between us.

"But I did have fun," she continued. "What about you?"

"Oh, yes."

"And the regrets?"

I paused. "Only one, in the SuperCon parking lot."

"Me, too." After a moment she added, "I'm sorry I screwed

everything up for you."

"Eliza screwed everything up. Then I screwed it extra tight."

"But if I hadn't—"

"Please stop," I said. I didn't want to think about the what-ifs. "To be honest, part of me is glad I did what I did. Let that part of me come out. Because obviously, it needed to. Maybe I can really be okay now."

"Good. But I'm still worried about you, a little," said Kendall. "One of the things that made it easy for me to leave was knowing you'd made some new friends. Thinking you'd be with Camden and probably wouldn't be around much anyway."

"I'll be fine," I said, waving my hand, wishing I were really as certain as I sounded. "It's only a few months." I looked at her. "Although, you'll be different when you come back."

"God, let's hope so," she said, and I must have seemed surprised because she added, "But in a good way. Otherwise, what would be the point of going?"

"Or doing anything," I added.

"Exactly."

"I can't stay much longer," said Kendall. "My parents are driving me out to visit my grandmother at the nursing home. She doesn't know I'm leaving. I'm kind of dreading telling her."

"Okay. I'm just glad you were able to see this. And me."

Kendall nodded and bit her lip, and I saw suddenly that she was scared. It was a big thing, what she was doing. I felt an overwhelming urge to give her something that would bolster her.

Maybe I wanted to give her an extra reason to come back.

"I have to tell you," I heard myself saying. Kendall raised her eyebrows in curiosity and I continued. "When we dropped you off at your house that night of the SuperCon, you should have seen Jamie's face. It wasn't an I-feel-guilty face. It was more like an I-love-that-girl face. I think he really does have feelings for you."

Kendall sat completely still. She didn't react. For a moment, I thought perhaps she hadn't heard me.

"Don't," she said sharply.

"No, really. If you'd seen him, you'd believe me."

Now she doubled over as if I'd punched her in the solar plexus. "Why would you tell me this?" Her voice was high.

"I thought it would make you feel better about the whole summer."

"Well, it does *not.*"

She covered her head with her arms and took a deep breath.

"I'm sorry," I said. "But if it were you who had information like that, wouldn't you tell me?"

She took another deep breath inside her little self-huddle. "Yes."

"So . . . ?"

Kendall unrolled now and looked me straight in the eye. "A bad situation to cap off several other bad situations. On that note, I think I'd better go."

Crap, crap, crap she was angry. What had I done?

"I can't believe we're saying good-bye like this," I said.

"You mean like this?" she asked, then pulled me into the tightest hug I'd ever felt in my life. It actually hurt.

"See you at Christmas," I said.

"Check that blog link I sent you," she said. "I'll start posting stuff as soon as I can."

Kendall climbed off the rock and rolled up her towel.

"Are you walking back with me?" she asked.

"I'm going to stay for a bit."

She nodded and headed up the trail. She got a few feet away, then stopped to turn and wave. I waved back. We froze, neither of us wanting to be the one to lower our hand first. But then Kendall did. She started moving again and in seconds, she was around a curve and out of sight.

I lay back on the rock, my hands behind my head, and stared up at the sky.

In my mind, Camden came to lie on the rock next to me.

Holy cow, how I missed him. This ache. Like the ache I'd felt during the summer of watching and wanting, but in the core of me.

I started to cry again. The only thing I could make of this agony was the truth: Camden had given me what he could, but it was not enough. What I needed, I could only give myself. He had gifted me the ability to do that. By falling in love with Camden, I'd been able to fall in love with Ari, and for that reason, I wasn't lying to Kendall about having just one regret.

So which Camden was with me now? The first Camden, or the one who'd let me down so terribly? Maybe it was neither.

Maybe it was a parallel-universe Camden, a new Camden created by the things that could have happened but didn't.

Although, just because they could have happened didn't mean they should have.

I had to let that Camden next to me go.

I had to let them all go.

23

"Help me!" Danielle squealed from the top of the wooden tower.

I didn't budge. She was laughing now, as I knew she would be, and my spot on the playground bench was so comfy in the shade.

Labor Day.

It always felt melancholy, even with the weather perfect like this. I usually spent every possible hour of the holiday at the lake before it closed for the season at sundown. But this year, I couldn't bear to say an official farewell.

"You said half-and-half, right?" asked Mom as she plunked down a to-go tray from the café across the street.

"Thanks," I said, picking up my iced coffee. She sat down next to me, took hers out of the tray, and tore open a pack of artificial sweetener.

"Mom!"

"What?"

"You said that stuff is evil."

She shrugged. "I let myself have one a day at work. Sorry, it's my guilty pleasure."

"If *that's* your guilty pleasure, you have nothing to apologize for."

She laughed, and Dani raced past us, shrieking again. Then Richard came tearing after her. Roaring like a lion or a monster or some other terror she'd requested today.

"I remember Richard doing that with you, when I first met him," said Mom.

"Yup. It was love at first chase."

Mom smiled. "For me, too."

I watched her as she took a long sip of her iced coffee. "What time are you guys going out later?"

"The movie's at eight, but I'd like to leave at six so we have time for dinner at Lemongrass. Is that okay?"

"Of course." She'd never asked that before. She'd never needed to, or so we both thought. Maybe we were both wrong.

I thought of the World Wildlife Fund calendar hanging in the kitchen, now turned to the September page with the tiger cubs, already filled in with the details of our four different schedules. On the square of that coming Friday, there was only one thing scribbled in: that long-planned appointment with my therapist, Cynthia. Under my name, Mom had recently written Richard's and Dani's and her own.

Yes, we were all going to go, together. It would be something new and strange and probably cringeworthy. We might never do it again. But we were going at least once, and that counted.

Mom summoned Richard by holding up his coffee, jiggling it so the ice rattled loudly. He scooped up Dani and carried her over to us.

"Here, sweetie," said Mom to Dani after she handed Richard his drink. "I know you said you'd have a smoothie but I figured, it's the last day of summer. What the heck. I got you a chocolate milk shake."

Dani silently took her drink and sipped hard, closing her eyes. She seemed to be having a moment. Then her eyes popped open and she stared at Mom.

"Will you push me on the swings?" she asked, her voice shaky.

My mother sighed. I was prepared to step in with an excuse for her, but then Mom laughed and said, "Sure."

She got up and took Dani's hand.

"I want to go so high, my foot touches that tree branch. I just saw a kid do it. Can you push me that high?"

"I don't know," said Mom as they walked away from us. "But I'll try."

Richard followed them, ready to take pictures with his phone. I sank back on the bench and felt the warm-but-definitely-not-summer-anymore breeze on my neck.

Sometimes, all you can ask for is the try.

An hour at the playground, a chocolate milk shake. A movie and Thai food. Being able to sit and talk and listen and see what comes next.

Sometimes, it's all more than enough.

School. Senior year. Why wouldn't I be ready?

Kendall was gone, but there were new people, new possibilities, everywhere. The summer had taught me that much.

My first morning went fast. Precalculus, English, physics. It was going to be an interesting year, academically. These were classes I could lose myself in.

Step after step down a hallway, letter by letter scrawled as class notes on paper. That was how you did it.

You've never been stronger and more positive, I told myself, and believed.

But I'd forgotten about lunch.

Lunch, and its universal suckiness when you don't have a best friend or a to-hell-with-it attitude or even a plan.

When you have to stand there with a brown paper lunch bag and scan the room for a seat, but not so long that everyone sees how you're quietly dying inside.

The trick, I knew, was to keep moving. I circled the perimeter of the cafeteria, reaching into my pocket to feel the edges of a folded-up postcard I'd gotten from Kendall. *No regrets and all that*, she'd written on the back of a London aerial photo.

At one table, I spotted Lukas and Brady with a few of their friends. They were busy peering at someone's phone and didn't see me. There, too, were Kendall's newspaper pals, who suddenly looked so much nicer than I'd pegged them, but their table was full.

A dark, shaggy head flickered in my peripheral vision. I turned on instinct, saw only the crowd around the condiment station. Then I remembered that boy from last year who'd seemed so teasingly familiar. Great. Maybe I could pay him to cut his hair.

Finally, I zeroed in on a corner table that was only two-thirds full of juniors. I slid into a seat at the farthest possible end, not making eye contact. I heard them stop talking for a moment to establish that I was nobody worth acknowledging, then continue.

The meek crinkle of a paper bag. A bite of tuna sandwich. A drink of milk. *Come on, Ari. This is just lunchtime in your cafeteria in your school. It means nothing about anything.*

So why did I feel like crying?

Yeah, this was going to be bad.

Suddenly, someone threw themselves into the seat across from me, making the whole table shake.

I glanced up, annoyed.

The boy leveled his green eyes at me. Eyes the color of a diving board, on a dock at a lake that felt so far away, it would have taken the *Arrow One* a hundred light-years to get there.

I looked into those eyes and all I could say was, "Oh, crap."

Camden smiled, all his features bright and blinding.

"Hi, Ari."

I put down my sandwich and rested my palms on the table, needing to feel something solid beneath them.

"What . . . are you doing here?"

Camden searched my face, but I wasn't sure what he was looking for. "Fifth period lunch, just like you," he said, pulling a crumpled piece of paper out of his pocket—a class schedule—and consulting it. "Then, AP History."

"Oh. Me, too." I couldn't think of anything non-idiotic to say.

We stared at each other as I processed the fact of him existing in front of me, the class schedule with his name on it.

He swallowed, clearly nervous. "So. I was reading in the student manual that seniors can leave campus during their free periods. Is that right?"

"That's right," I said, glad to be asked a simple question with a simple answer.

Camden cleared his throat, stood up, and offered his hand. "Then, let's go."

The kids at the other end of the table turned to watch, suddenly alert to a happening.

"Go where?" I whispered. "We've only got, like, half an hour left of this period."

He moved closer, around the end of the table, his hand still outstretched. "Ari, this is me stepping up. Giving back. Following the rules and doing the work."

I started to draw a deep breath, but it fell apart into a sob.

"Don't do that," said Camden. "Or do that, but also take my goddamn hand."

I took his goddamn hand. Still warm, with suddenly lots to say to mine. I guess they had some catching up to do. He pulled me to standing and led me through the cafeteria, past all those eyes watching us. Out the doors to the parking lot. Toward his car.

"Where are we going?" I asked him.

"Wherever you want to go." He paused as he slowed his pace so we were walking side by side. "What's someplace we've never been together?"

As soon as he said that, I knew.

When we pulled up to Scoop-N-Putt, the first thing we saw was a big sign across the closed Order Here window. We both climbed out of the car to get a closer look.

Fall Hours: 5 P.M. TO 10 P.M.

"Great," I said. "I completely forgot about that."

"Eh, that's just a technicality," said Camden. He sat down on the hood of his car and patted the spot next to him. I crawled up, rested my feet on the front bumper. "Chocolate?" he asked, his eyes dancing, curling one hand to hold an imaginary ice cream cone, then the other. "Or vanilla?"

I laughed and pointed to the chocolate hand. He handed me my "cone."

We sat there, not knowing what to do next, watching the

traffic on 299 speed by. Where were all these people going in the middle of a Tuesday? I hoped it was someplace that made them happy.

Then, Camden reached down and laced his fingers through mine.

"What happened to your ice cream?" I teased.

He smiled and shrugged. "Nothing's better than the real stuff."

I felt the pressure of his palm against my palm, his forearm nudging my elbow, and realized he wasn't talking about soft serve.

All those fantasy nights I'd had that first summer, the dreams that made me sweat and ache. This right here, this was the moment. The point where I always woke up alone.

So now, a different kind of waking up, where you do it again and again, and feel the glory of it each time. Not a gift but rather, something you've earned.

"Hey," said Camden, leaning his head against mine and looking off toward the mini-golf course. "Is that gnome giving us the finger?"

With my free hand I turned his face toward mine and kissed him.

They say, be careful what you wish for.

But I say, how else does anything begin?

ACKNOWLEDGMENTS

Rosemary Brosnan, thank you for your faith in this story and also in me (as a writer and, you know, as a person). You guide a book into the world with such intelligence, affection, and grace.

My agent, Jamie Weiss Chilton, knows when to make her support gentle and positive, when to make it fierce, and when it's time to just chat about junk. She's terrific.

I'm grateful for the hard work of Jessica MacLeish, Kim VandeWater, Olivia Russo, the Epic Reads team, and the rest of the HarperCollins staff who do so much behind the scenes. Designer Heather Daugherty created a cover that's truly a thing of beauty in its own right, and I'm thrilled that anything that comes out of my brain could be associated with Thomas Doyle's stunning artwork.

I was lucky to have early readers in Stephanie Kuehn, Rachel Hartman, and especially Phoebe North, with whom a walk on the Rail Trail is often the cure for my angst of the moment. Kim Purcell, I love you for always being present and honest, and also for thinking Camden was so hot.

Bill Spring gave me everything I needed to get the work done, in whatever form and at whenever time, including a hand in the creation of the *Silver Arrow* universe. My daughters, Sadie and Clea, were endlessly understanding and excited and proud, even though they're not even allowed to read this yet.

I've run out of ways to articulate my gratitude to my parents, Jay and Sue Castle, for their wholehearted, multifaceted support. I'm reminded of Camden's question to Ari, when he asks how you figure out love without anything real to base it on. I'll just say, thanks to them—and the many treasured people in my life I don't have room to mention here—I've never had that problem. Every day they fill my heart with something-reals.